KATHIR'S REDEMPTION

Book Six of the Dragon Stone Saga

Kristian Alva

Eusebian Publishing

KRISTIAN ALVA

Other Books by Kristian Alva

Dragon Stone Saga
Book 1: Dragon Stones
Book 2: The Return of the Dragon Riders
Book 3: Vosper's Revenge
Book 4: The Balborite Curse
Book 5: Rise of the Blood Masters
Book 6: Kathir's Redemption
Book 7: The Shadow Grid Returns
Book 8: The Fall of Miklagard
Book 9: Sisren's Betrayal

Stand-Alone Novellas
Brinsop's Brood
Mugla's Magic

All books are available on Kindle Unlimited.

Dedicated to my children, the sweetest little dragons of all.

1. THE DUNGEONS OF BALBOR

T allin awoke in darkness, deep inside the dungeons of Balbor. Many days ago, their group had gone to Balbor to destroy the temple and had been captured. Tallin, his aunt Mugla, and two elf dragon riders, Amandila and Fëanor, had been dragged into the underground dungeons.

The Balborites abandoned them in a dark cell without food and then ignored them. Armed guards walked back and forth in front of their cell day and night, the sound of their boots striking the ground on the other side of the door. No one spoke to the prisoners or even acknowledged they were there.

Tallin glanced over at Mugla. She lay against the far wall, emaciated from hunger. Even Tallin, who was used to going without food for days at a time, could feel the lack of sustenance gnawing at him. Luckily, they had access to water, which was occasionally shoved through the door in a leather waterskin.

There were no windows in the cell—only a tiny slit in the door, which left the air inside stuffy and hot. They were all tied with enchanted ropes, except the elves, who were shackled against the wall.

Tallin felt his legs throbbing. He had been frozen

in the same position for hours. He tried to wiggle his feet to increase blood flow, but it didn't help much.

The Balborites had seized all their weapons, but Tallin had managed to conceal a small light crystal in his boot. Tallin kept the magical light deliberately dim when he used it. Any flicker of light was risky, but using the crystal was worth it to stave off despair. Sitting in the darkness made their situation feel a thousand times worse. The small spark of light that the crystal produced would have been barely noticeable to human eyes, but since Tallin was half-dwarf, it was bright enough to see everything around him.

While Tallin and Mugla sat on the floor, the elves were chained directly to the wall. They were in much poorer shape. Amandila and Fëanor's ears were pierced with iron wire, which was designed to disrupt their powerful magic, including their ability to shape-change.

Tallin had never thought he would feel any sympathy for elves, but it was impossible not to feel something for the two miserable-looking creatures who hung limply near his side.

The elves were both semi-conscious. With their ears pierced by iron wire, their carefully-maintained glamour was gone. Their eyes were slick and shiny, like glistening drops of oil. Bright purple bruises bloomed on their faces and arms.

Both had screamed in agony when their ears were pierced, but now they just groaned, twisting their bodies as the iron slowly worked its way through their bloodstream. The metal was poisoning them, weakening them by degrees. Though the elves hung near one another, neither seemed to realize that the other was even there. Or perhaps their pain was so great that they simply didn't care.

Tallin could reach out and touch them, and he had tried to remove the iron. But as soon as he had touched it, the wire only twisted tighter, causing Amandila to cry out in pain. He didn't try again after that.

Mugla raised her head weakly. "Do ye know what day it is, dear?"

Tallin shook his head. "I'm not sure. I think it's been five days, but I've lost track of time. I can't tell if it's day or night anymore." He kept his voice low.

Mugla sat up and propped herself up against the wall. She looked emaciated and had bleeding cracks at the corners of her mouth. But when she spoke, her voice was strong and level. "They're starvin' us, weakenin' us."

Tallin looked toward the elves. "What about them?" Their faces were almost unrecognizable—grossly swollen and puffy. "Will they survive?"

"The odds aren't in their favor, but at least they're still alive. Keepin' an elf in captivity is a risky business. Elves are powerful and vindictive if they escape. I'm surprised the Balborites haven't killed 'em yet."

"I don't understand why they haven't killed *all* of us," Tallin said.

"I'm sure they 'ave their reasons. The High Priest

probably wants to make an example out of us. As for the elves, they'll fare worse than us. We'll be hanged, but the elves will be tortured. The Balborites will kill them for sport."

Tallin raised his eyebrows. "What?"

A humorless smile lifted the corners of Mugla's lips. "An elf capture is a rare thing. The High Priest enjoys watchin' 'em tortured. Because elves are immortal, the show lasts a long time. They'll die eventually... but very, very slowly. Sometimes, they chain prisoners to a post and release dogs on them, to tear them apart. They kill rebellious slaves that way."

"That's barbaric," Tallin said.

A metal door clanged in the distance, followed by the sound of heavy footsteps approaching. Tallin extinguished his light crystal and tucked it carefully back into his boot.

They watched a square of light at the far side of the room grow as the door to their cell opened. Tallin blinked from the bright light that entered their cell.

Skera-Kina stood behind a single armed guard and one younger man, dressed in a simple cotton tunic. The younger man did not have any facial tattoos, but he was wearing leather wristbands with protective runes on them. Tallin guessed he was her apprentice.

She pointed at Tallin. "You there... *halfling*. Stand up. The High Priest demands your presence."

The guardsman covered his nose, but the sour

smell inside the cell didn't seem to bother Skera-Kina.

Tallin stood up and stepped outside, his hands still bound. The guard wrinkled his nose as he passed. The cell door was closed behind him, and the guard remained stationed outside while the two assassins escorted Tallin to a smaller cell at the end of the hallway.

The door opened to reveal a bucket of water in the center of the floor, and a clean pair of breeches and a tunic were folded neatly in the corner. Skera-Kina said a quick spell, and the enchanted ropes binding Tallin's hands fell away.

"Strip down and bathe yourself, dwarf," Skera-Kina said. "You must be clean if you are going to be in the presence of the High Priest."

"I wouldn't smell if you idiots had allowed us to use a proper toilet, or given us some clean water," Tallin retorted.

"Shut up, halfling filth!" the younger assassin growled.

"Be quiet, Gron," Skera-Kina warned. "Barking at prisoners does not impress me."

The young man scowled but said nothing more.

Tallin stripped down to his underwear and reached inside the bucket. The water was ice cold. There was a pebble of soap at the bottom, and he lathered his arms and face with it. He took a moment to scrub his hair before he poured the bucket over his head to rinse off. They didn't give him a towel, so he was still wet when he pulled on the clean clothing.

He smiled despite himself. After so many days inside a filthy cell, it felt good to be clean. He slipped his boots back on carefully, making sure that the hidden crystal didn't fall out.

"Turn around and put your hands behind your back," Skera-Kina ordered.

Tallin paused, biting back his desire to fight. He couldn't risk fighting both of them at close range, especially with Mugla and the elves still in their custody. He had no choice—he had to obey.

He turned around and put his hands behind his back. He felt new ropes being tightened around his wrists. His body tensed as they placed a cloth bag over his head and cinched it tight around his neck. Tallin stiffened.

"Where are you taking me?" he asked quietly.

"No questions," Skera-Kina said. "You'll see soon enough. Now move."

She grabbed his shoulder and pushed him down the hallway. Tallin winced as her silver-tipped nails dug into his flesh.

Tallin tried to focus on memorizing the space around him. He counted his steps as they walked and listened to the sounds. They paused a few times while more doors shut behind them. He couldn't see through the bag, but he felt the air go from sour to fresh and could tell when they walked from stone floors to carpeted ones.

Skera-Kina said nothing as they walked, but Tallin could hear her rasping breaths behind him.

Servants chattered idly, ignoring them as they passed. There was the sound of a mop slapping on the floor and the slosh of water in buckets.

They walked for a long time. When they finally stopped, the air smelled faintly of incense. Skera-Kina removed the covering on Tallin's head.

"We've arrived at the High Priest's chambers," said Skera-Kina.

They stood in front of a huge wooden door. Skera-Kina waved her hand in a slow arc. There was a spark, and the door swung open on its hinges. Then she removed the ropes that bound Tallin's wrists.

Tallin stepped back, rubbing his wrists and searching her face. "Why are you removing the ropes now?"

"Enchanted objects are dangerous in this area," she replied. "That includes your enchanted ropes. I'll explain why later. You must kneel in the presence of the High Priest, and do not speak unless he addresses you first."

"I'm not going to bow and scrape to one of your priests," he said.

She shrugged. "Have it your way. If you don't kneel voluntarily, they'll find a way to force you to your knees—and that won't be pleasant. Have no doubt about that. My responsibility is to deliver you to the High Priest's chambers for questioning. What happens to you afterward is not my concern."

Gron, her apprentice, shoved Tallin's shoulder roughly. "Get moving."

Tallin turned to face the young man. "Push me

like that again, and I'll break your arm."

Gron laughed, lifting his foot to kick the back of Tallin's knee. But the man was too slow. In an instant, Tallin spun around and grabbed his forearm. Tallin bore down hard, twisting the young man's wrist until his whole body turned. Tallin rammed his elbow down hard on the assassin's chest and heard a whoosh of air as Gron lost his breath.

Skera-Kina didn't intervene; she just stepped back with her arms folded across her chest and waited for the fight to be over.

They grappled, and both fell to the ground. Tallin rose to one knee and trapped the man's arm in a viselike grip. He brought his knee down onto the man's shoulder until the joint popped. Gron howled in pain.

"Stop. That's enough." Skera-Kina separated them calmly.

Tallin rose up and backed away.

Skera-Kina pulled the young man up by his collar. He cried out in pain. His right arm hung limply at his side, the shoulder swollen and jutting outward at an unnatural angle.

"I'm disappointed in you, apprentice. You've lost control and overstepped your boundaries again. Tell me, how will you train for the slave races next month with an injury like this?"

The apprentice hung his head. "M-mistress, forgive me, I only wanted to—"

"Be quiet, you hot-headed fool," she snapped. "Your temper has always been a problem. You must learn how to control it. Return to your chambers and await my displeasure there."

"May I request a healer for my injuries, Mistress?"

She flicked her chin at him. "No, you may not. I shall set the joint for you personally. But not yet. Now go." She dismissed him with a wave of her hand.

The apprentice's lower lip trembled, but he didn't argue. He turned around and left. Once he was gone, Skera-Kina turned back towards Tallin.

"I warned him not to touch me," Tallin said, matter-of-factly.

Skera-Kina merely shrugged. "Indeed, you did. Perhaps I should thank you. It'll be a good object lesson for him to live with the consequences of his actions for a few days."

"A few days?" asked Tallin. "He's your apprentice... and it's an excruciatingly painful injury. Would you really leave him that way for days?"

She stared at Tallin with an amused expression. "His injury isn't life-threatening. An apprentice must learn how to ignore pain, so this is a good lesson for him. Besides, it's only a temporary discomfort." She stepped aside for Tallin to pass. "Now, after you... *brother*...the High Priest awaits."

Tallin walked into a darkened hallway with Skera-Kina trailing behind him. Her steps were soundless on the thick carpet. Part of him wanted to dash for the nearest exit, but he couldn't attempt an escape while his aunt and the elves were still imprisoned in the dungeons below. His mind raced. He needed to come up with a plan that would allow all of them to escape.

The smell of incense grew stronger. Tallin reached out and brushed the embroidered tapestries lining the wall with his fingertips. The same gory scenes that he had seen in the temple also lined the walls here. But despite the gruesome subject matter, the fabric was thick and of excellent quality. A great deal of money had been spent decorating the High Priest's chambers.

They turned down another hallway and came to a stop before a locked metal door. There wasn't a single piece of furniture in the room. Another door on the far wall indicated more rooms beyond. Skera-Kina opened the first door with an oversized key that she drew from a pouch at her waist. The door swung open with a soft click.

"No magic this time?" Tallin asked.

"No spells can open this door. It is warded against magic, as is the High Priest's chamber. Anyone who attempts to open this door without the key will be killed instantly."

"By what?" Tallin looked around him. He saw nothing in the room except for a few wall hangings and some light crystals embedded into the walls.

Skera-Kina smiled, revealing her sharpened white teeth and tattooed gums. "Look under your feet."

Tallin looked down. The tiles below his feet had colorful spiral patterns on them. Observing them, he noticed that the designs seemed to move of their own volition, turning and churning slowly, menacingly. Tallin gasped. "Are those things..."

"Yes, those are spirit creatures," Skcra-Kina explained calmly, "trapped inside the floor tiles. They are stimulated by magic. Watch." Skera-Kina opened her palm and sent a single glowing spark toward the floor.

Tallin looked down and watched as the patterns swirled wildly beneath his feet. Ghostly, grotesque faces came into view, pressing against the tiles. They looked as if they were trapped behind a mirror.

The spirits screamed silently, pounding at the walls of their flat prisons. "You've trapped dozens of spirit creatures in here?" he asked incredulously.

"Many more than that. There are dozens in this room and even more in the chambers beyond. They are bound to defend the High Priest. That is the nature of the enchantment." Skera-Kina's voice was emotionless. "The spirits will kill anyone who attacks the High Priest with any spells. Between the spirits and his personal guard, he is well protected from both physical and magical attacks."

"It is evil," Tallin spat. "It's an abomination to trap spirits in this way."

"Evil? Is that what you call it?" Skera-Kina replied with a smile. "How can you be shocked by this? There are good reasons why Balbor has never been conquered. Our magic is not like yours. It is stronger. We are not afraid to use spirit magic to protect what is ours."

"Spirit magic is dark magic. It is the magic of death. Trapping a spirit is always risky, even for a mageborn as powerful as you. Plus, it's an evil thing to keep a spirit trapped in this way indefinitely."

Skera-Kina shook her head. "Only a weak-minded person would think that. Spirit magic is useful for many things."

She gestured for Tallin to step forward, and he went, stepping cautiously over the still-quivering tiles. "Now, the High Priest wishes to speak with you, and I shall not keep him waiting any longer." She pointed to a black spot before the door. "Kneel here in front of the door, with your eyes down."

Tallin shook his head. "No. As I told you before, I don't kneel to anyone."

"Don't be a fool," she said. "You know that we can force you to do anything we want, right?"

"You're certainly welcome to try."

Skera-Kina glared at him briefly, then buried a curse under her breath. They were interrupted by a clicking sound. Skera-Kina paused and looked expectantly at the door. After a few moments, a stick-thin old man appeared in the doorway, surrounded by armed guards.

Skera-Kina bowed deeply. "Your Grace."

The High Priest had been tall once, Tallin suspected, but now his back was bent with age. His face was gray and shrunken, and his dark robes hung loosely from his withered frame. The priest's eyes were still a piercing blue, glittering pinpoints buried in bony cavities.

At first, Tallin assumed that his skin was naturally dark, like a desert nomad's, but upon further inspection, he saw that it was the effect of his warding tattoos. They were extensive and were even darker than Skera-Kina's.

"Your prisoner isn't kneeling, Skera-Kina." Given his frail appearance, his voice sounded surprisingly strong. The rebuke reverberated in the open space.

"Begging your pardon, Your Grace," she said. "This prisoner is obstinate. He refuses to kneel and claims that he doesn't kneel to anyone—not even his *own* king."

The High Priest raised one eyebrow. "Is that so? Why is that? Are the Dragon Riders considered *gods* now?"

"No," replied Tallin. "The Dragon Riders do not purport to be gods or kings. We are independent of any political leadership."

The old man chuckled. He sounded amused rather than offended. "Heh, heh! You mainlanders and your silly ways."

Skera-Kina spread her hands. "I'm sorry, Your Grace. He is impertinent and bad-tempered, even more so than the other prisoners."

The High Priest looked thoughtful for a moment. "That reminds me—what about our other captives —the elves and the old dwarf woman? Have you questioned them yet?"

Skera-Kina shook her head. "We tried, Your Grace. The dwarf-woman is uncooperative, and the elves have been subdued through iron poisoning. They cannot speak. We could compel them to talk using... *other* means, but I am unsure whether they would survive the questioning."

The High Priest nodded. "Fine. I shall question them myself. Bring them to me. The rest of them, I don't want them dead. Not yet. You may leave this one here with me."

Skera-Kina glanced warily at Tallin, then back at the priest. "Are you sure, Your Grace? This prisoner is very powerful. I would advise you—"

"No one asked for your *advice*, Skera-Kina," the old man said. "I've considered the matter. I shall use our four prisoners as bait to lure other dragon riders to Balbor. When they arrive, their dragons will be captured and bred. We will finally have Balborite dragon riders again, as it was in the ancient days. This has always been my plan. It is time for Balbor to return to its former greatness."

"Your Grace," Skera-Kina implored again. "I understand your plans, but this prisoner..."

The High Priest's voice was cold when he spoke again. "Do not question me, Skera-Kina. Fetch the other prisoners. Leave this one here. My personal guards are with me. They can handle him."

Tallin felt Skera-Kina's hand tighten reflexively on his shoulder. He swiped an errant red lock behind his ear and lowered his head, suppressing a smile. This old fool was so used to everyone hanging on his every word that he ignored even sound advice!

"Please be careful with him, Your Grace," Skera-Kina warned one last time.

The priest looked Tallin up and down, and when their eyes met, Tallin could see boredom in the old man's eyes. "Somehow, I don't think he's going to be much of a threat. Now go. You risk my displeasure if I have to ask you again."

She bowed. "I hear and obey, Your Grace." Reluctantly, she exited the chamber. Once she left, the High Priest smiled and turned around. A casual flick of his hand indicated that Tallin should follow him. A guardsman sealed the door behind them.

Tallin followed the High Priest into a larger chamber lined with slender white columns, each lit with a giant red candle. Dozens of armed guards lined the walls. They stood and watched with tired expressions on their faces. One of them even yawned as Tallin passed by.

Tallin and the High Priest continued down an ivory-colored carpet and stopped in front of an elevated dais with a gilded chair. The same swirling tiles were underneath Tallin's feet. The tiles stretched far into the shadowed corners of the room.

The High Priest went up the steps and sat down in his chair. He saw Tallin staring down at the tiles. "Ah, so Skera-Kina told you about the spirit tiles, didn't she? It's quite a clever spell, isn't it?"

"No. Spirit-magic is evil and unnatural."

The High Priest chuckled. "You are too soft,

dwarf. The spirits serve an important purpose. They protect me as well as anyone else inside my chambers. Even the smallest spell upsets them, and any spell cast directly against me would mean instant death. I've seen them in action several times—it's really quite entertaining."

Tallin wondered what kind of man would find the sight of spirits devouring someone alive *entertaining*. But then, what kind of man was the High Priest of Balbor? He could sense that the High Priest was not mageborn. He had probably inherited his position from his father. He wouldn't even understand the consequences of such a dark spell.

"How long have spirits been trapped inside these floors?" Tallin asked.

The High Priest shrugged. "I cannot say. The tiles have been there for the entirety of my tenure, that of my father, and of his father before him.

Tallin's eyebrows shot up. "These souls have been trapped inside this floor for hundreds of years?"

"Yes...much longer than that, I suppose," he grunted. "Why does it matter?"

Tallin paused, forming a plan. It was a gamble, but he had to take it. "It matters, because spirit prisons become increasingly unstable over time. They eventually falter if the spirits aren't fed regularly or released."

The old man laughed and wagged a bony finger in Tallin's direction. "You're lying, trying to frighten me! It's not going to work, though."

Tallin shrugged. "I'm not lying, and today you're going to find out why this type of magic is so dangerous. These shadow-spirits are going to blot you out of existence."

The old man's eyes narrowed dangerously. "Your glib attitude is wearing thin, dwarf. I think it's time for you to kneel. Guards! Help this prisoner to his knees!"

The guards closed in on Tallin from all directions. He raised a glowing hand defensively.

The priest shook his head. "Don't even try it! Remember, to attack me with magic inside these chambers means instant death!"

Tallin looked down. The tiles were already swirling wildly at his feet, vibrating underneath him. Tallin lowered his hand and snuffed out his magical bolt. The tiles stopped moving. The priest wasn't lying about that—the spirits seemed to agitated by *any* type of spell, even a minor one.

Tallin lowered his body into a fighting stance. "I guess we'll do this the hard way, then."

The old man cackled. "Ready for violence, are you? Good, good! Because I needed to break you."

A single guard advanced toward him. The guard was younger than Tallin, but he had a protruding belly that suggested overindulgent drinking. "Show some respect, prisoner! Kneel before His Grace with your head bowed!"

The guard grabbed Tallin's arm roughly and tried to wrench him to the floor. Tallin jerked his arm away and stepped back. The guard swung his fist wildly, aiming for his face, but Tallin ducked before the guard's fist could make contact.

Tallin heard the other guards laughing behind him. Apparently, they didn't get much excitement in their daily lives.

Suddenly, Tallin felt his dragon stone grow warm against his chest. His fingers fluttered upward to touch it, and he heard the faintest whisper of Duskeye's voice. From somewhere far away, he heard his friend's frantic voice.

"Hold on, Tallin! We are near! We're coming to save you!"

The shock of hearing Duskeye's voice left Tallin distracted long enough for the guard to twist himself around and hit him in the head with his fist. Tallin stumbled and fell to one knee.

The priest's sneering laughter sounded through the chamber. "That's it! Just kneel, dwarf!"

The guard grabbed the back of Tallin's shirt and dragged him across the floor.

Four more guards stepped forward to subdue him. Tallin knew that he was physically outmatched. Without the ability to use *any* type of defensive spell, there was no way he could defeat all the guards inside the chamber. He was weak from his imprisonment, and his strength was failing.

Still, there was one thing he could try. *Did he dare risk it?* His mind raced.

Skera-Kina said that the spirits would be forced to strike if anyone attacked the High Priest. But what if the spirits were merely *freed?* Would they react differently?

Tallin said a silent prayer and hoped that his faded recollection of his dark magic classes at Aonach Tower were correct. If the spirits did not react as he expected them to, he was a dead man. The gamble was desperate, but so was his situation.

"Kneel! Kneel before me, or die!" the High Priest commanded.

"Never," Tallin spat. He hunched over on one knee, his face streaked with sweat. He touched his dragon stone and felt the magic pulsing within. It was now or never!

Tallin tore the glowing stone from his chest, groaning in pain as the implant was ripped away from his skin. Frightened murmurs rose around him as the guards backed away.

The tiles in the room quivered and hummed beneath Tallin's feet. Instinct helped him push away his pain and fatigue.

The High Priest's mouth dropped open. "W-what are you doing with that?" A tinge of fear had crept into his voice.

Tallin's voice was low and steady as he replied. "I *told* you that spirit prisons become unstable over time. The bonds that hold the spirits inside these tiles become weaker and weaker as the years pass. After a while, the prisons can be shattered using a magical object—like the one I have in my hand." He opened his bloody palm and revealed the glowing dragon stone in the center of it.

The priest's eyes widened. "Don't try anything,

dwarf! You cannot attack me inside this chamber!" he screeched. "You will die!"

The guards inched back involuntarily. No doubt they had heard tales of the dragon riders, perhaps even highly exaggerated ones. Tallin was thankful for that small blessing.

"You don't seem to understand," he said, to the now visibly-nervous priest. "I'm not going to attack you... at least not *directly.*"

Tallin raised the dragon stone high above his head, ignoring the blood that ran down his arm and dripped off his elbow. He brought the stone down in an arc, shattering the tiles directly beneath his feet.

The tiles exploded outward with a ferocious burst of energy. The reaction was so violent that his body was catapulted through the air and thrown back against the back wall of the vast chamber, which he hit with a sickening crunch.

The sharp odor of sulfur rose in the air. Tallin blinked, and his vision slowly came into focus. One by one, grey shadows rose up from the shattered floor. The ghosts twisted in a macabre dance and moved slowly toward the guards and the now-trembling High Priest.

Tallin held his breath, crouched in a dark corner of the room, and covered himself with a tapestry. His desperate gamble had paid off. *Now* he just had to figure out how to stay alive.

Dozens of spirits filled the room. Some of the souls left immediately, escaping through an open window, but a few stayed behind to mete out their long-awaited revenge.

The High Priest screamed, and the guards turned to run, but it was already too late.

Tallin hadn't performed any direct spells against the High Priest, so while the spirits were now freed from their prisons, they were not compelled to attack anyone in particular. Instead, the spirits were now free to choose their victim. Tallin desperately hoped they would attack those who had trapped them for so long instead of him.

The spirits fell upon the terrified guardsmen first. The guards screamed as the furious spirits tore into their flesh. Arms and legs went flying everywhere, some of them unattached to their owners. A few guards made it to the door, only to be yanked back and torn apart.

The carnage seemed to go on forever, although it couldn't have been more than a few minutes. Eventually, the spirits turned on the High Priest, who was now cowering behind his chair.

Tallin watched as one of the spirits floated up to the priest and poked him, only to be repelled by the heavy warding tattoos that covered the priest's chest. It tried again, and the old man flinched, but the wards held.

The spirit howled in frustration and retreated back to where the other spirits were waiting. The spirits ignored Tallin completely. Either they hadn't noticed his presence yet, or they had decided to leave him alone. Tallin gripped his dragon stone tightly in his palm, thankful that his plan had worked. He wasn't performing any direct magic, so as long as he stayed quiet and out of sight, he was safe—at least for the moment.

The spirits huddled together and whispered to one another quietly.

On the other side of the room, Skera-Kina entered with Mugla and the elves behind her. The elves looked somewhat improved; the wire had been removed from their ears, but their eyes were still glazed over, and they were still shackled with iron chains. Skera-Kina's mouth dropped open in shock when she saw the destruction in the room.

Mugla gasped and then breathed a sigh of relief when she spied Tallin hiding in the corner.

"Skera-Kina, help me!" the High Priest cried. "You must protect me!"

Skera-Kina frowned and stepped forward. "Yes, Your Grace." She sounded frustrated. She turned to the spirits and spoke without enthusiasm. "Leave now, darkshades, or I'll be forced to destroy you."

The spirits parted from their huddle, examined Skera-Kina up and down, and took a moment to determine their next move. Several more decided to exit, leaving only three spirits remaining in the chamber.

The largest one spoke, its voice rasping and stiff. "This priest has kept us trapped against our will for centuries. His life is forfeit. His death belongs to us."

Two spots of color spread on Skera-Kina's cheeks. "I shall not warn you again. Leave this place now."

Two spirits moved toward Skera-Kina, surrounding her. They reached out to touch her with their icy fingers, but she struck first, wrapping one of them in a thin whip of pure energy; it shot out like a glowing string from her fingertip. She tightened the lash until the shade cried out in pain. The creature howled and strained against the bonds, but it could not break free.

The second spirit reached out boldly, striking a tiny patch of bare flesh on Skera-Kina's shoulder. The area was small, but untattooed, so the jab drew blood. The spirit gave a squeal of triumph. Skera-Kina drew a sharp intake of breath, but she didn't move. The third spirit stepped forward and struck her other shoulder, drawing blood again. She hissed with each strike to her flesh. Blood flowed from her wounds, which were small but deep. Eventually, she would fall.

The first spirit was still trapped in front of her, held fast by her magical whip.

Tallin watched as the cowardly High Priest stood back, trembling behind his chair as Skera-Kina suffered blow after blow without flinching. Her arms streamed with blood. She seemed reluctant to perform any more spells.

She glanced in Tallin's direction and saw him hiding in the corner. She said nothing but implored him with her eyes.

Tallin decided he'd seen enough. He stood up, tucked his dragon stone into his pocket, and walked over to where Skera-Kina stood. Tallin reached down and pulled out the tiny light crystal that he had hidden in his boot and put it in the center of his palm.

"Attention, spirits! Do you know what this is?"

The three shades stopped moving and looked at him with cloudy white eyes.

"It's a crystal trap," hissed one of them. "I can feel its power."

Tallin opened his hand. A tiny purple stone glittered in his palm. "You're right," he said, without hiding his smile. "It's a crystal trap. I usually use this stone as a light crystal, but it has other uses as well. For instance, it can also trap spirit creatures, such as yourselves."

The smallest shade narrowed its eyes at him. "It's a small trap—it can't possibly hold all three of us."

Tallin smiled thinly. "Perhaps you're right. It may not be large enough for all of you—but it's certainly large enough to hold one of you, maybe even two. So which one of you would like to volunteer to be trapped again? Or was hundreds of years imprisoned inside this floor long enough for you?"

The shades exchanged worried looks. They knew they were beaten. In unison, the spirits lowered their arms and stood still. Skera-Kina released her spell, and the strand holding one of them dissipated. Then, one by one, they floated out the window without looking back.

Skera-Kina wiped the blood from her arms with a handkerchief that she pulled from her waistband, but the jagged cuts in her shoulders remained open and visible.

The High Priest crawled out from behind his chair. "Is it safe to come out now?"

"Yes, Your Grace," Skera-Kina replied in a flat voice. "You may come out."

The High Priest looked down at the ragged group assembled below. All his guards were unconscious or dead, their bodies scattered about the throne room.

The old man scowled. He had completely lost control of the situation. He struggled to salvage what little dignity he could by directing his anger at Skera-Kina. "Why are you just standing there, Skera-Kina? Do something!"

Skera-Kina looked at the priest with hooded eyes. "You aren't in any danger at the moment, Your Grace."

The High Priest's face turned so red that his nose flushed dark purple. "I don't care about that! Look at my chamber. Look at my guards! The room is destroyed. Kill him! In fact, kill them all!" His whole body shook with anger.

Skera-Kina looked at Tallin and then back at the High Priest. She stood silently as she struggled to make a decision. There was no doubt that Tallin had saved her life. Finally, after what seemed like an eternity, she said, "No. I shall not kill the dwarf. If you want him dead, get someone else to do it, or do it yourself."

The High Priest recoiled as if he had been struck in the face. "What?" he asked with an outraged whisper. "You *dare* refuse a direct order from me?"

"Yes...I refuse," she replied, swallowing heavily.

"Your refusal to obey is a death sentence, Skera-Kina! You shall be stripped of your office! Stripped of your honor!"

"So be it," she replied. "You may execute me, but I will no longer be manipulated by you. I will no longer be used."

The High Priest glared at her. "I am deeply disappointed in you, Skera-Kina. Very, very disappointed. I believe that I chose poorly when I promoted you to Blood Master. Now I must correct my mistake."

The far door swung open, and a fresh group of guardsmen entered the chamber. The High Priest motioned to the new guards. "Soldiers! Take these prisoners to the main square! Skera-Kina, too. Tie them to the dog posts and wait for me there. The executions shall begin at sundown!"

The guards moved forward to arrest them. Skera-Kina clenched her fists tightly at her sides. One of the guards touched her injured shoulder. She jerked away but otherwise did not attempt to fight. When the guards moved to surround Tallin, he braced for a fight, but there were too many of them. He decided not to resist.

As the guards led all of them out of the wrecked chamber, the High Priest's voice could be heard echoing behind them. "Blast it! Call my servants in here to clean up this mess. Move these bodies out of here! By the gods, my chambers are ruined!"

Tallin, the elves, and Mugla walked out of the chamber surrounded by guards. Skera-Kina lagged several steps behind them, flanked by even more guards, all of whom wore frightened expressions on their faces.

Tallin looked back at Skera-Kina, and as he did, he saw her face change. On her countenance, he saw a look of sorrow but also of liberation.

They locked eyes for a moment, and Tallin felt a connection he could not explain. Skera-Kina's lips parted, and she mouthed silently, *"In death, I shall finally be free."*

2. THE HANGMAN'S SQUARE

T he soldiers led their prisoners into the city square to await the High Priest's orders. The square itself was a massive open space filled with merchant's booths, soldiers, and slaves. Apparently, the Balborites mixed slavery and death with commerce, and no one blinked an eye.

One side of the plaza was dominated by the Temple. On the other side stood an extravagantly-designed town hall, surrounded by gleaming copper statues of former priests.

Cobbled roads branched outward from the plaza in every direction and led to other parts of the city. The square looked a great deal like the plazas in Parthos and Morholt—or, it would have, if not for one ghoulish detail.

The very center of the plaza held a giant executioner's circle.

The merchants kept clear of it; they set up their booths along the plaza's perimeter, avoiding the gallows. A thick wooden beam with attached nooses ran across the stage, designed for public hangings. The structure was undecorated and painted black. Hooded and silent, an executioner waited on the platform.

Under the gallows, there was a set of wooden stairs and a set of steel cages, each of them just large enough to hold a single man. There was also a line of wooden posts with iron loops attached to them.

Behind the gallows, an enormous fire pit belched black smoke. As Tallin's group approached, the executioner cut a dead prisoner down from the gallows and threw the corpse into the fire pit, which flared up as it consumed the dead.

The soldiers led the captives underneath the platform to wait. The elves were chained with iron shackles around their hands, feet, and necks. Tallin and Mugla were tied to a wooden post with ropes, but this time, the guards didn't bother to enchant them. There wasn't anywhere for them to go—there was no escape.

Skera-Kina was escorted out a few minutes later. Unlike the others, she was locked inside one of the steel cages. Guards carried the pen to the center of the square, where they placed Skera-Kina on a smaller stage near the gallows—in a position that was in clear sight of the crowd.

Tallin recognized Skera-Kina's apprentice, Gron, standing in the crowd. His arm was in a sling. The young man was smiling—he was enjoying Skera-Kina's humiliation.

Now that they were out in the fresh air, the elves looked more alert. Amandila blinked her eyes as if she were awakening from a trance. "What's happening to us? Are these men going to kill us?"

"We are in danger," Tallin said, "but all is not

lost." He turned to his aunt, who was tied to the post nearest to him. Her face was gaunt with fatigue and hunger. "Aunt, do you have any idea what they plan to do to us? How much time do we have?"

Mugla sighed. "At sunset, they'll kill us. The High Priest usually doesn't bother to attend executions, but I'm sure he'll be present for this one. At sunset, he'll come down to the plaza and issue a public judgment before the crowd. Then we'll be hanged from the gallows. In the morning, the executioner will cut down our bodies and incinerate them in the pit."

A small crowd had formed around Skera-Kina's cage. A soldier spat at her and hooked a painted sign onto the bars.

"What does the sign say?" Tallin asked. "I don't recognize the script."

"The sign says *'oath breaker'* in their language," Mugla replied. "Treason is the worst crime imaginable—a traitor is the only person who has a lower social rank than a slave. Skera-Kina's refusal to obey the High Priest is considered a terrible offense."

The crowd began pelting Skera-Kina with clods of earth and rotten food. She crouched motionless inside her cell. She didn't flinch when objects hit her through the bars.

"She'll be humiliated and then killed," said Mugla. "This is a common type of spectacle here."

Tallin watched the scene with growing revulsion. Across the plaza, his eyes locked onto her face. There was no anger in her eyes. Only resignation.

He felt a storm of conflicting emotions rising within him. He tried to remind himself that Skera-Kina had caused a great deal of havoc and suffering—and so many deaths. She was a murderer.

So why did he feel pity for her now?

As the minutes passed, the crowd grew larger. People started chanting obscenities at Skera-Kina, shaking the cage and spitting on her. Skera-Kina remained quiet and did not utter a single cry.

The sun began to dip below the horizon. It grew noticeably colder, and their breaths turned into white vapor. A slow drizzle started to fall, but the crowd did not disperse. The moisture turned to steam on the closely huddled bodies in the plaza and created an eerie, misty cloud. The atmosphere took on an ominous quality, like a scene from a nightmare.

Finally, a horn sounded, and everything went silent. From the western side of the plaza, the High Priest entered the square accompanied by a vast entourage of guards, attendants, and slaves. Together with his entourage, he moved toward the gallows in the center of the square.

The High Priest stepped forward and took his position on the stage, flanked on either side by two other high-ranking priests—officials dressed in garish costumes complete with flowing red robes, shiny black stockings, and powdered wigs piled high on their heads. The High Priest didn't wear a wig or a hat, but he did wear a lavishly embroidered white robe and a flowing fur cape. The entire ensemble glittered with tiny gemstones.

"All this ceremony for an execution? These people are insane," Tallin said.

"Aye," said Mugla. "Killing is a communal spectacle here."

The elves had started to look more alert.

Amandila blinked and shook her head. "It seems that the entire city has come to watch us die."

Mugla nodded her head with disgust. "This is completely normal for them. Their preferred entertainment is public violence, and their bloodlust is encouraged by the priests. They're all eager for the slaughter."

The crowd grew rowdier as the people became excited by the prospect of violence. Scattered fights erupted. More guards were brought into to pull unruly citizens away from one another and to calm the gathering.

The High Priest raised his staff into the air, and the crowd quieted down. "This woman is an *oathbreaker!* She has defied me and threatened my life! She is an enemy of the state!" The priest turned to Skera-Kina and addressed her directly. "Prisoner! How do you plead?"

A sardonic smile drifted across Skera-Kina's face. "Why would I plead when you have already decided my fate, Your Grace?"

Her words drew a chorus of jeers from the crowd.

With a scowl, the High Priest lifted his staff again to silence them. "The charges are true and correct! You are guilty! Guilty of treason!"

After a moment of tense silence, the crowd erupted into cheers. The High Priest nodded solemnly and then started toward the gallows.

"Now what?" Tallin asked.

"Now they hang us," said Mugla.

Fëanor piped up. "They won't kill me that easily —I'm not surrendering without a fight."

Mugla shook her head. "Can ye break the bonds of cold iron, elf? They know yer weakness. They won't remove yer shackles, not even after ye are dead. There's no escape."

Fëanor's shoulders slumped, and Amandila started to cry.

Tallin felt the glowing warmth of his dragon stone inside his pocket. In all the commotion, the guards had forgotten to take it from him. "Don't despair," he said quietly. "There's still hope. Duskeye sent me a message. He's coming to rescue us!"

Mugla's eyes grew wide. "No, Tallin. No! Tell him he can't. He'll be killed! Any dragons crossin' the island perimeter will activate the protective wards. There are wards *specifically* designed to stop dragons from coming to this island. Without protection, he'll be torn apart in the sky!"

Tallin's face went white. "What? You never told me that! Who would set wards specifically against dragons? Oh no!" He felt fear rising up within him. Would Duskeye die trying to save them?

"Duskeye might be able to circumvent the wards," said Fëanor, a bit cryptically, "*if* he was smart enough to get help from my queen."

Tallin looked at the elf. "Explain yourself. And I mean right now."

Fëanor cleared his throat. "The Balborites didn't set the wards upon this island. Their spellcasters aren't skilled enough to set wards of that size. The elves did it, thousands of years ago, as part of an ancient compact. The only way to bypass the more dangerous wards is by using a special key—a *shadowkey*—and our Queen has it in her possession."

Tallin grasped at this small glimmer of hope. "What is it? I've never heard of such a thing."

"A *shadowkey* doesn't look like a regular key," said the elf. "But it works similarly. It's an enchanted object, but more powerful than any enchanted object in the human realm. A shadowkey will allow anyone to bypass the wards with ease, including dragons."

"I've heard of shadowkeys, but I've never seen one myself," said Mugla.

Fëanor continued. "There aren't any shadowkeys left in the mortal lands. The elves destroyed most of them eons ago. Any remaining shadowkeys are kept in Brighthollow. There are several shadowkeys in Queen Xiiltharra's possession. A few were made by humans, and others were crafted by other races, but the spells required to create them have been lost to mortals."

Tallin's eyes narrowed. "Why didn't you mention this *earlier*, when we were still on the mainland?"

The elf paused, as if surprised by the question.

"The information is rather sensitive. Knowledge of the shadowkeys is restricted to elves only. The keys themselves are an abomination. The knowledge of their creation has been lost to mortals for some time, which is as it should be. To create a key like this, you have to slay a dragon and then anoint the key with the sacrificial blood of the creature. Killing a dragon is not something that my people take lightly."

Disgust flashed in Tallin's eyes. "You have to *kill* a dragon to create a shadowkey? So the elves slaughtered a dragon to create this key?"

Fëanor looked uncomfortable. "Yes. One was made by the elves long ago after the Balborites were barred from breeding dragons. Long ago, the Balborites had their own dragons and dragon riders. The elves put a stop to that."

Tallin sneered. "Unbelievable! Your queen gets to determine what we have a right to know, even if it costs us our lives? We're your allies! We should be helping each other. Wait—let me ask you this —would Xiiltharra actually let you *die* here, rather than risk us having access to a shadowkey?"

Fëanor raised his chin defiantly. "Perhaps, but despite everything that's happened, I support my queen, even if I am forced to die here. You mortals act like children! Spoiled children! How could you ever be trusted with something as powerful as a shadowkey? Mortals *cannot* be trusted—not with all their pettiness and constant warmongering. What is happening here is proof of that fact."

Tallin shook his head. "You elves don't have the right to force the other races of Durn to bend to your will."

Mugla interrupted them. "Shush now, stop fightin'. Your bickerin' isn't helpin' things. Look... they're bringin' Skera-Kina this way."

Shouts echoed through the plaza as the priest's slaves dragged Skera-Kina's cage over to the gallows. The entourage followed the priest up the stairs.

A group of blackbirds started gathering in the trees around the square. A single red-crested raven was sitting at a distance from the other birds, bouncing back and forth on the branches of a tree. It was larger than the other birds and seemed to be waiting for something. When Skera-Kina passed, it cawed loudly, and she looked up at the raven with visible sorrow in her eyes. It was the first time she had showed any emotion.

When the soldiers reached the gallows, they left Skera-Kina's cage under the steps, near the other prisoners. Tallin caught Skera-Kina's eye again. Her voice floated across the short distance between them.

"It is almost over, brother," she said quietly. "I'll be the first to be killed, so this is farewell."

Tallin looked up into the darkening sky. "There's hope yet," he whispered quietly to himself, "but it had better come soon."

Mugla laughed suddenly. "I should warn ye, nephew, if I'm to die today, I'm plannin' to take a few of these buggers with me. I've still got a few tricks up my sleeve, and iron shackles won't stop *me*."

Tallin smiled despite himself. His aunt was as feisty as ever. Even the fear of death didn't break her spirit.

The High Priest ascended the steps and pointed at Skera-Kina's cage. Four guards went beneath the platform, removed Skera-Kina from the cage, and escorted her roughly up the stairs. Several more guards looked on, ready to strike if Skera-Kina made any sudden moves or attempted to escape.

The executioner stepped back and grabbed a wire whip that was lying behind him. The whip had dozens of filaments, and each one had a sharp barb at the end of it.

"Thirty lashes for the *oathbreaker*!" cried the High Priest, and the crowd cheered again.

The executioner swirled his arm in the air in a theatrical way and then brought the whip down on Skera-Kina's back. She flinched but did not cry out. Although her warding tattoos offered some protection, any of her skin that was not tattooed was vulnerable to the sharp barbs. It wasn't long before her back was streaming with blood.

"She isn't going to fight back? Not even a little?" asked Tallin. "She's just going to let them do this to her?"

"She cannot fight them," said Mugla. "She's taken a blood oath. She can't *harm* the High Priest, either directly or indirectly. She can only refuse to obey him. Blood oaths are what bind the assassins to their masters. If she attempted to hurt the High Priest in any way, it would cause her blindin' pain. Death is her only escape. I guess she is finally tired of being his chattel. Even her position as a Blood Master wasn't enough to make such bondage worthwhile."

Despite everything that had passed between them, Tallin felt saddened by Skera-Kina's impending death. "I actually feel sorry for her."

Minutes later, the flogging was over. Everyone watched as the executioner bound Skera-Kina's hands behind her back.

Mugla sighed. "Skera-Kina never had a chance at a normal life. Slavery and bondage are all she's ever known. Life is unfair, Tallin. Sometimes people are victims of circumstances that they don't deserve." She hesitated, then continued softly, "I'm not proud of the fact that some of this is my fault. She's my family, too."

The crowd cheered as the hangman's noose was fitted around Skera-Kina's neck. A black sack was placed over her head. Skera-Kina stood motionless as she waited for the inevitable. There were thousands of people packed into the square now, and every face was upturned with morbid anticipation.

The High Priest was waiting until the last possible moment to give the final order—drawing out the spectacle. He beamed down at the crowd, enjoying their chants.

The High Priest raised his right arm to give the final order, and the executioner placed his hand on the lever to release the trap door.

Tallin held his breath.

All of a sudden, there was a bright flash in the sky. A dazzling explosion split the air, causing a sound like thunder. It was so loud that it rattled the ground beneath their feet. A few people in the crowd screamed, but others applauded, thinking that it was all part of the show.

"What's going on?" whispered Amandila.

Tallin smiled. "The dragons are coming to save us. I can feel it. Somehow, Duskeye made it past the wards." A feeling of intense relief washed over him. *Duskeye was alive!*

Through a cloud of fog and scattered dust, four huge dragons materialized in the sky. The High Priest looked up and screamed.

Leading the pack was the elf queen, Xiiltharra. She was riding on the back of a magnificent emerald dragon that Tallin didn't recognize.

Duskeye, Nagendra, and Blacktooth followed behind her in a triangular formation. Blacktooth opened his mouth and sent a river of fire toward the crowd. The people screamed and scattered like frightened rabbits.

"Guards! Guards!" the High Priest shrieked. "Arrest them! Stop them!" Dozens of soldiers ran up the stairs to defend the hysterical old man.

Duskeye pulled his wings in tight and landed on the platform with his forelegs outstretched. He roared, swiping at a guard with one enormous clawed foot. Blacktooth joined him, and together, the two dragons fought the stream of soldiers bounding up the stage.

Forgotten by the guards in the chaos, Tallin and Mugla muttered release spells, causing their ropes to fall away. Mugla smiled, but she was clearly exhausted from lack of food and sleep.

Tallin reached out to help his aunt, but she waved him off. "Don't help me! Go help Skera-Kina! I'll free the elves—I'm strong enough to do that."

Tallin ran up the stairs and attacked a guard, stripping him of his sword. The guard fell backward and knocked the lever back for the trap door, causing Skera-Kina to fall through it. Her body jerked violently as the hangman's rope went taut around her neck.

Tallin rushed forward to grab her and support her weight. Her body was limp and slippery; her back and shoulders still slick with blood from the vicious whipping. Tallin reached up and severed the rope around her neck. He removed the black bag from her face and laid her limp body on the floor.

"Skera-Kina? Can you hear me?" he said, slapping her cheeks. She did not respond. Her eyes stared forward blankly, and her face and lips were blue.

Tallin tried to check for a pulse, but someone pulled his leg sharply and knocked him to the ground. He glanced over his shoulder to see a soldier with a sword aimed at his head.

Tallin twisted his body and avoided the killing stroke by rolling out of reach. The soldier swung again, and this time, Tallin rolled off the platform, spinning in midair to land on his feet on the ground below. The soldier growled at him from above and jumped down with his sword in his hand, ready to fight.

Tallin ran towards the guard and thrust his stolen sword into the man's chest. The guard collapsed, shocked at the speed with which he'd been cut down.

Mugla freed both of the elves. They were all fighting side-by-side now, holding back an endless stream of guards trying to get on the platform. Mugla was holding on, but her face was ashen. The elves still looked dazed from the iron poisoning, but they fought fearlessly all the same.

Mugla then remembered the magical sleeping powder Chua had given her, still hidden in her bosom. She drew the little pouch out quickly and poured the bright silver powder into her palm.

A dozen more guards approached them, and she waited until they were just footsteps away before she flung out her hand, casting the powder into their eyes. "Take that, ye dirty buggers!"

The sleeping powder hit the guards in varying degrees. Two merely stumbled, but the rest collapsed to the floor as if they had been struck over the head with a mallet.

Above them, Xiiltharra and her emerald dragon remained in the sky, throwing fireballs and lightning bolts down at the terrified crowd below. More people fell, consumed by dragonfire. Others were trampled by the screaming crowd trying to flee the square. It was complete pandemonium.

Finally, the elf queen circled down and landed on the platform. She raised one ivory hand. "Enough!" The word echoed into the distance. Her voice seemed amplified somehow.

Everyone on the platform froze. The remaining crowd fled away from the square. Only a few guards, two assassins, and the High Priest remained. All of the High Priest's entourage had abandoned him.

Tallin kicked another soldier to the ground and barreled up the stairs again. This time, he was able to reach Duskeye and embrace him. "You're a sight for sore eyes, old friend! That was a close call! How did you find us?"

Duskeye licked his scaly blue lips. *"You can thank the elves for that! Xiiltharra is the one who contacted me—her powers are very strong."* The dragon actually managed to sound impressed. *"I was waiting for you on the coast like you asked me to, unsure of what I should do. I heard Xiiltharra's voice in my head, and soon enough, I saw her riding her dragon in the sky. I followed her here with the others."*

"Xiiltharra is a dragon rider? For how long?" It was a shock.

Duskeye's great blue head dipped down low. *"For some time, now, apparently. Her dragon's name is Atejul. As you can see, he's gigantic—quite difficult to miss. I've never seen an emerald dragon so large. Nagendra and Blacktooth were accompanying them."*

Tallin looked over at Xiiltharra's dragon. "I don't understand—was Atejul simply hiding in Brighthollow this whole time?"

Duskeye chuckled. *"No, you've seen him before. You just don't remember."*

Tallin gave Duskeye a quizzical look. "I honestly don't remember—no. He looks so young. Did he flee the desert before the war?"

Duskeye shook his head. *"Atejul is Nagendra's hatchling. You met him in the desert when he was just a fledgling, remember?"*

Tallin's jaw dropped open. "Nagendra's hatchling —well, by *Baghra,* then he's your son!"

Duskeye nodded, and the look on his face displayed the great pride he felt. Female dragons almost never revealed their mates, but since there were so few male dragons left, it was obvious who Atejul's father was.

"Amazing," said Tallin. He remembered his dragon stone and pulled it out of his pocket. He placed it against his chest and flinched as the stone embedded itself once again into his tender skin. Despite the pain, it felt good to be whole again.

At that moment, the other dragons, Nagendra and Blacktooth, flew below and reunited themselves with their riders. The dragons purred and nuzzled the elves, who laughed so elatedly that it seemed they would burst with happiness.

Everyone paused and waited as the elf queen slid delicately from her dragon's saddle. Xiiltharra was very tall, and she towered over everyone else by at least a head. She wore a rich emerald-tinted gown that shimmered with gold as she moved. The garment seemed designed specially to display the dragon stone embedded near her throat. The glittering emerald caught the dim light with a fiery luster. Xiiltharra's strawberry-blonde hair fell in loose waves down her shoulders. Her skin was pale, but her lips were very red. Her eyes were such a light shade of blue that they looked colorless from a distance.

Xiiltharra looked like a young woman, but she was hundreds, perhaps even thousands of years old. Mugla stepped over the bodies of the guards and walked up the stairs. She went over to Skera-Kina, knelt down, and placed two fingers on her neck to check for a pulse.

Tallin headed over to his aunt. "Is she still alive?"

Mugla nodded gravely. "She's still alive, but barely. Her neck is broken, and she's lost so much blood. It's beyond my power to heal injuries this severe."

Xiiltharra tried to walk over to where Skera-Kina was lying down, but she was blocked by several guards. The elf queen expelled an irritated breath. She turned to the High Priest. "Call off your guards. Now."

Despite his fear, the priest shook his head. "I will not! Who are you to speak to the High Priest of Balbor in such a manner?"

The elf queen's jaw clenched, and her eyes narrowed. "I am Xiiltharra, Queen of Faerie, and by the terms of the Brighthollow Pact, I am your sovereign! You will obey me, whether you like it or not!"

She waved her hand in the air, and all the guards flew backward off the platform as if they had been struck by an invisible fist. They hit the ground below with a hollow thud.

The queen then turned to face two assassins who were standing before the priest.

"Now get rid of these two," she ordered.

The High Priest recoiled in fear, but he did not obey. Instead, he pushed the assassins forward. "Kill the elf witch! You must protect me!"

The first assassin drew a poisoned knife and pointed it at her.

Xiiltharra chuckled lightly. "A poisoned blade? Against me? You must be joking." She made a circular motion in the air with her index finger. The assassin twirled around rapidly before she cast him down to the street below. The attacker landed on his head with a loud crack and did not rise again.

Xiiltharra addressed the High Priest again. "You are trying my *patience*, priest. Call off your last man, or I'll kill him, too."

The remaining assassin moved forward cautiously.

Tallin stepped forward to help, but Mugla grabbed his elbow. "Don't move—Xiiltharra doesn't need your help, believe me."

The last assassin proved more determined than the other one. He struck out and was able to graze Xiiltharra's sleeve with his dagger. The blade made a tiny slice in her clothing. She stared at her ruined sleeve with a look of shocked disgust. The damage to her gown seemed to infuriate her more than the attack itself.

"*Kala!*" she shouted, her voice booming through the cold air. The assassin shrieked and stumbled back. A blue spark shot from Xiiltharra's palm and embedded itself in a tiny spot of untattooed flesh on the man's shoulder.

Icy frost formed on the assassin's skin where the spark had touched him. The ice expanded instantly and spread across his skin. He screamed once with shock and pain. Seconds later, his entire body was frozen.

The queen swept by and pushed his frozen body as she passed. She watched emotionlessly as the assassin's frozen body tumbled to the ground and shattered like a block of ice.

The elf queen smoothed her dress and walked toward the High Priest, who was trembling violently. Her expression had smoothed into a tranquil mask. "That's much better. Now we won't be interrupted. Tell me, priest, what is your given name? The name you were born with?"

The High Priest said nothing. He was trembling and mute with fear.

"Answer me, or I'll rip your tongue out of your mouth," she said. Her expression remained totally calm.

"Fereroaz! My name... is Fereroaz," he croaked.

"Fereroaz, eh?" She rolled her gaze upward and tapped her chin with her forefinger. "And what of Civodous? What happened to him?"

The High Priest looked confused for a moment. "Civodous? Why, Civodous was my great-grand-father. He died many years ago."

The elf queen clucked her tongue. "So soon? Ah, you mortals. Your lives are so short. You don't live very long at all."

"I don't understand," said the priest. "What do you want from me?"

"In due time, my dear. Be patient. For right now, I just want you to be quiet." Xiiltharra paused and looked around. "Where is the daughter of Carnesîr? I know that she is here."

"That's her," said Tallin, pointing in Skera-Kina's direction. "She's badly injured." Skera-Kina was lying on the ground, her breathing shallow and hoarse.

The elf queen walked over to where Skera-Kina lay unconscious. She reached down and touched Skera-Kina on the cheek. "She is still alive. That is good."

Xiiltharra drew a small vial of white liquid from her bosom and poured several drops into Skera-Kina's mouth. "Rise, forgotten daughter of Carnesîr, *elfling* child."

At that moment, Fëanor rushed up the stairs. He looked alarmed. "Your Royal Highness! Stop! This woman is a murderer. She's the one who killed Carnesîr!"

Xiiltharra shot him a sharp look. "I know that, Fëanor. Are you questioning my judgment?"

"Uh...no," said Fëanor, looking confused. "It is

just that I do not want you to make a mistake... and get injured, Your Highness," he finished lamely.

The elf queen smiled. "I do not make mistakes. This female is an *elfling*, a product of an elf mating. She carries our blood, even though she is tainted with the blood of a dwarf. I warned Carnesîr *countless* times about his little indiscretions. He made a choice to lie with mortal women. And worse, he did it under a magical glamour. I warned him not to trifle with mortal women, and *this* is why."

"But why would you save her life?" Fëanor sputtered. "She's a danger to us all!"

Xiiltharra continued as if she hadn't heard him. "I've decided that Skera-Kina shall live. She will be a living reminder for all of you. Carnesîr's actions had consequences. He did not understand the price of his recklessness until it was too late. It seems fitting that Carnesîr's coquetries cost him his life. Carnesîr's child will live a very long life and remain a constant reminder of his foolishness. *That* is Carnesîr's legacy and his eternal shame."

Fëanor lowered his head. "I—I understand, my lady. If I may ask, how did you learn of Carnesîr's death?"

"Carnesîr's dragon, Poth, felt his partner's death from afar. Poth collapsed and died in Brighthollow from the shock. That's when I decided to intervene. I called the dragons to me, and we crossed the sea. We passed through Balbor's wards with the shadowkey."

Fëanor stepped back and said nothing more. Behind them, the moon was rising over the top of a jagged cliff, its light turning the sky a creamy blue.

Skera-Kina's eyes fluttered open. "Where am I? What happened?" Her voice was barely a whisper, husky from the grip of the noose. The rope had left a bright purple bruise around her neck.

"You were hanged," said Tallin. "Your neck was broken. The elf queen saved your life."

Xiiltharra smiled. "Nonsense! Don't scare the poor girl. It wasn't as bad as all that." Gently, the queen put her hand on Skera-Kina's back and guided her to an upright position. "There now, my pet, let's sit you up."

Skera-Kina stared at the queen with disbelief. "Who are you? Why did you save my life?"

Xiiltharra smiled in a way that was probably intended to be motherly, but which only looked frightening. "I am Queen Xiiltharra, monarch of Brighthollow and the northern lands, daughter of King Llewellenir. I am also your sovereign leader, by the terms of the Brighthollow Pact."

Skera-Kina looked even more confused. "Who am I to you, then?"

Xiiltharra smiled again. "You are a means to an end. Each person has a unique purpose. That includes you, Skera-Kina. Your purpose is about to be fulfilled. Observe, and you shall understand the wisdom of my decision."

Xiiltharra turned her attention back to the High Priest. "I am here under the terms of our Pact. This is the *second* time in the last thousand years that

I've had to return to this forsaken island in order to enforce our agreement. I grow weary of this endless game."

The High Priest stared at her in horror. "The Brighthollow Pact? I thought that was only a myth!"

Xiiltharra's feral blue eyes narrowed. "Yes, that's what one of your predecessors said too, before I killed him. I will teach you your place, as I did him. The Balborites are *strictly forbidden* from owning, breeding, or raising dragons. The pact is *explicit* and *binding*, and yet you have attempted *once again* to steal dragon eggs for your foul breeding experiments. That is a direct violation of our pact. As such, your life is forfeit."

"But I didn't know," the High Priest whined. "I didn't know!"

Xiiltharra went on as if she hadn't heard him. "I loathe to meddle in mortal affairs, but I cannot allow this crime to go unpunished."

Skera-Kina stood up and touched her swollen throat. She walked over to the elf queen and addressed her without fear. "Why did you save me? I chose this path, and my oaths cannot be broken. I no longer wish to serve the priests...or anyone else, for that matter."

Xiiltharra smirked at her. "I think I can convince you to change your mind."

"I took a blood oath—it cannot be broken. I am forced to serve the Temple until the end of my life. My only escape from this bondage is death."

Xiiltharra held up her other hand to silence her.

"You *misunderstand* your oath. It is not set in stone and can be changed. Today, you will get to choose between slavery and freedom." Then she turned to the High Priest. "You have broken the pact with faerie by attempting to steal dragon eggs. Your crime is indefensible, and frankly, I have indulged the stupidity of your people long enough. Thankfully, though, I believe I've found a solution to all my problems."

"By the gods! What are you going to do to me?" he cried.

Xiiltharra lifted a finger, and the High Priest's mouth clamped shut like a vise. "Silence. Do not speak." The High Priest tried to open his mouth to respond, but all that escaped from his lips was a choking sound.

Xiiltharra removed a silver necklace from around her neck. A black key, carved from volcanic glass, hung at the end of the chain. It seemed to radiate darkness. Xiiltharra slipped the key from the chain and pressed it into Skera-Kina's palm.

Skera-Kina examined the key in her palm. She didn't look fearful, only curious. "What is this object? I feel dark magic clinging to it."

Xiiltharra smiled again. "This is the shadowkey of Balbor. I created it myself, eons ago, when the Brighthollow Pact was signed. I slew the last of Balbor's tainted dragons to make it. It is rare that I have an occasion to create a shadowkey and even rarer that I should have to use it. Study it closely, for it is unlikely that you shall ever see another in your lifetime."

"But what is it *for?*" asked Skera-Kina.

"You'll understand in a moment." Xiiltharra pointed at the High Priest. "Remove your robe and step forward, Fereroaz."

The priest didn't move.

Xiiltharra's expression hardened. "I *ordered* you to take off your robe and step forward. Now *do it.*"

The priest remained frozen with fear, and the last remnants of Xiiltharra's patience withered away. Her face became a mask of fury.

"Obey me, mortal filth!" She curled her finger into a claw and jerked it forward. The old man stumbled forward like a fish on a hook, and his fancy robe dropped to the floor. Now his chest and arms were bare.

The elf queen rubbed her hands together. "That's much better." Xiiltharra continued. "Now, here's your choice, Skera-Kina. You took a blood oath to protect the Temple. Unfortunately, that oath cannot be broken, so you are bound to protect this island and its citizenry until your death. However, your oath to protect the High Priest is somewhat more... *flexible.* Since the High Priest can die or be replaced, your oath to him is not forever-binding. The oath binding you to him is weaker, so it may be shattered, with the right tools." Xiiltharra pointed at the shadowkey in Skera-Kina's hand. "Now listen carefully. To break the oath, you must kill the priest with this shadowkey. Take the key and pierce his heart. He will die, and you may take his place."

The High Priest almost collapsed with fear. He was now so pale that he seemed to be drained of all blood. Down on the street below, a small crowd had started to creep back into the square. There were a few soldiers too, but they kept their distance. Everyone was afraid but curious.

Skera-Kina touched the key with her fingertips. "So if I kill the High Priest… then what? I would replace him? For how long? Forever?"

Xiiltharra nodded. "You would replace him, but only until the end of your mortal life. In the afterlife, you may do whatever you wish. So, make your choice, child."

The High Priest gurgled awkwardly, attempting to speak. His words came out in a strangled whisper between clenched teeth. "Skera-Kina is a slave. She isn't fit to hold any royal office. You cannot kill me, Skera-Kina! Breaking your oath will destroy your body—it will turn you into a wraith!"

Xiiltharra interrupted him. "Shut up, you old fool," she hissed, "or I shall kill you myself—and believe me, your death shall be decidedly unpleasant!"

A long moment of silence followed the queen's words. Skera-Kina studied the shadowkey, contemplating her decision. Then she looked up and nodded. "I accept your offer."

Moving like lightning, Skera-Kina struck the High Priest with the sharpened end of the key, stabbing him through his heart. The High Priest screamed and clawed at the air, but he was powerless against Skera-Kina's superior strength.

The old man pitched forward on his face, twitching horribly. The priest gasped one final time and then lay still.

Xiiltharra stepped forward and pried the bloody key from Skera-Kina's grip. "Excellent job, my dear. I'll take this now."

When Xiiltharra removed the key from her hand, Skera-Kina collapsed, her body writhing in pain. "I can't breathe!" she cried, gasping for air. "I can't breathe!"

Xiiltharra nodded. "Yes, that's a normal reaction. Your body is fighting itself. It's like a war being waged in two directions—the key protects you, while the magic of the blood oath attacks you. Just be patient, it's only temporary. I shall help you."

The elf queen knelt down by Skera-Kina's side and scraped her neck with the key, drawing blood. Then, Xiiltharra placed the key against Skera-Kina's chest.

The elf queen's hand glowed pink against Skera-Kina's tattooed skin, and she muttered a long incantation. There was a sharp smell of burning flesh. When Xiiltharra pulled her hand away, the key was fused to Skera-Kina's chest.

Skera-Kina's breathing steadied. She inhaled and sat up slowly. She glanced down at her chest and touched the implanted key. Her face registered neither discomfort nor fear, just surprise.

Xiiltharra swatted Skera-Kina's hand away. "Do not attempt to remove it. Not ever. The implant must remain for the rest of your life. As long as the shadowkey remains in your physical possession, you shall live without pain. The scars will diminish over time. How do you feel?"

"Good. Better than I've felt in a long time, in fact." Skera-Kina wiped a streak of blood from her arm and stood up. "What happens now?"

Xiiltharra smiled. "Now, we leave you. As long as you respect our pact, you won't see me again." She flicked a dismissive glance toward Fereroaz's dead body. "I suggest you check this idiot priest's secret library and make yourself familiar with the Brighthollow Scroll. All the terms of our treaty are outlined there. I made certain that the scroll survived. I've deactivated the wards on the island as a measure of our good faith."

As the elf queen descended the steps, she called out to her dragon, who was waiting for her below. "Atejul! Come to me."

"*Yes, Mistress,*" the green dragon growled, slithering forward and lowering his neck so the queen could climb into the saddle. Fëanor and Amandila took their cue from the queen and mounted their own dragons.

Tallin walked over to Skera-Kina. He gave her an awkward nod. "Are you pleased with this arrangement?"

Skera-Kina shrugged. "The outcome is not what I expected, but I find it acceptable."

"Are we finished then?" he asked.

"I believe so," Skera-Kina answered. "We are even, you and I. If the gods have decided that we shall be adversaries in this life, I shall accept that as well." She returned his gaze, and he was surprised to see no sign of resentment in her face. "I suggest that you leave now, while you still can. A crowd has started to gather again, and under the circumstances, I cannot guarantee your safety. There is bound to be a great deal of upheaval here in the next few weeks."

"Let's go, Tallin," said Mugla, walking up behind him. She looked at Skera-Kina sadly. "I wish I could go back and change the past, but I can't. I should have saved ye when ye were a baby. Please forgive me."

Skera-Kina took a deep breath. "I cannot forgive you, but I have no wish to punish you, either. This is the life I've been given. I must accept it."

They knew it was pointless to say anything else, so Tallin and Mugla turned around and walked down the stairs. Duskeye and the elves were waiting for them below.

Duskeye lowered his neck so Tallin and Mugla could both mount his saddle. Before takeoff, Tallin turned to Xiiltharra and spoke to her. "Thank you for saving us, Your Grace."

The elf queen almost sneered at him. "I didn't do it for you, *dwarf*." She glanced at Skera-Kina, who was now standing at the edge of the platform addressing the people below. "We've been having problems with Balbor for quite some time now. I deduced the main problem was that the priests were all human—they die much too quickly. Mortals have very short memories. They forget things quickly and break promises as easily as one breaks an egg. Skera-Kina solves this trifling problem for me. She is half-elf and half-dwarf. Although she is still mortal, she may very well rule this island for thousands of years. Now I don't have to worry about returning to this horrible place for a long time. It's a very elegant solution, don't you think?"

Tallin's lips tightened with resentment, but he didn't respond. The elf queen had already turned away and was crooning softly into her dragon's ear.

Mugla tapped his shoulder gently. "Let's go, my dear."

Tallin shook his head. "This mission was always about making Xiiltharra's life easier—she was simply tired of being... *inconvenienced*," he said.

Mugla nodded. "Yes, well, that's true, my dear. It's their nature, and ye shouldn't be surprised. I've told ye that before. She may have known all along how this would turn out, even Carnesîr's death."

Tallin hadn't even considered the possibility that Xiiltharra knowingly sent Carnesîr to his death. It was frightening to think that Xiiltharra regarded even her *own people* as expendable.

"They're *elves*, Tallin. They don't need a reason for anything that they do." Mugla looked up. The elves had already taken off and were flying upwards into the starry night. "Come now, let's catch up with them."

Before they flew away, Skera-Kina called out to him. "Tallin!" It was the first time she had called him by his name.

Tallin turned and looked over his shoulder. "Yes?"

"I'm keeping the *Sword of Sedaria*," she said. "It belongs to me now. After all, it is a *family* sword, isn't it? And I am of the family."

Tallin nodded. She was right. She *was* family. What else could he say? He tightened his stirrup straps and tapped Duskeye's shoulder. "Let's go, old friend. It will be good to leave this place of death."

Duskeye spread his sapphire wings and took off into the sky, following the elves away from the island of Balbor.

Behind him, Skera-Kina had already picked up the High Priest's staff. She raised it to the heavens. The people stood by, watching Skera-Kina speak. Despite everything she had endured that night, her eyes were bright and clear. She was already giving orders. The guards looked confused for a moment but then started to clean up the square as she commanded.

The people gathered below the platform looked fearful but also ready to obey.

The citizens of Balbor had been governed by a dictator for so long that they didn't understand any other way of life. They were willing to accept anyone who would lead them.

Tallin knew, right then and there, that Skera-Kina's leadership would not be questioned. Her rise to power would be swift and unchallenged.

After that, Tallin didn't look back. He felt very

tired.

3. THE FALL OF MOUNT VELIK

On the other side of the continent, deep inside the caverns of Mount Velik, a battle was raging between the dwarves and the orcs. Though Mount Velik had been threatened several times by orcs through the ages, the greenskins had never breached the city's gates. The dwarves had always prevailed, and Mount Velik had always remained safe.

But not this time.

For the first time in history, orcs had breached the city, and they poured in like rats to destroy it. The dwarves bravely held the central passage into the city for a few days, but they could not maintain the position. Despite having superior weapons and armor, the dwarves were vastly outnumbered, and they were eventually overrun. The city succumbed to the invading army, and the pillaging and destruction began.

The dwarves retreated into the deepest parts of the mountain, and the order was given that the women and children hiding in the lower caverns should evacuate. The terrified survivors escaped using secret underground passages to exit the mountain.

A few soldiers stayed behind to cover their escape. Small bands of armed dwarves stationed themselves inside strategic passageways, fighting off the orcs as best they could. They drove the orcs back several times, but never for long.

The dragon riders Sela and Elias patrolled the sky overhead. After the main gates collapsed, there wasn't much they could do to help defend the city. The orcs' numbers were simply too great. Sela and Elias decided to remain behind to help cover the dwarves' escape using concealment spells.

Small clashes continued inside the mountain. In one of them, Skemtun, leader of the dwarf mining clan, jumped back and only narrowly escaped the downward slash of an orc's sword. He turned around and brought his axe around in a smooth arc and pierced the creature's green flesh. A stinking gush of black blood sprayed across his wrist. The beast collapsed to the ground, roaring in pain with Skemtun's weapon jutting out of his shoulder.

By his side, Kathir, the mercenary, blocked a blow that had been aimed at Skemtun's head. Kathir killed the orc by slicing through its neck.

"More greenskins are coming this way!" one of the men shouted.

In the narrow confines of the tunnel, Skemtun saw another of his men cut down. They were losing too many.

Although the orcs were physically stronger, they were clumsier and slower than the dwarves. And because of their size, the orcs couldn't flank them in such a narrow space. Skemtun pressed close and killed any who gave him the slightest opening. The flurry of violence was followed by another swift withdrawal.

The orcs fell back, running to gather more reinforcements. Skemtun snorted with disgust and turned around to see what was left of his battered contingent. They had lost two more men.

Skemtun walked over to Kathir. "The orcs are stronger than I thought," he said quietly. He took off his hat and wiped his brow with his handkerchief.

"They're aggressive, but they have their weaknesses too," Kathir said. "We're pretty deep inside the mountain, and the passages are getting narrower. As long as we keep moving, we'll be able to defend ourselves. But you should start thinking about how you're going to save the few men that are left."

"How much time do we have, you think?" Skemtun asked.

Kathir shrugged. "Your guess is as good as mine. The orcs are ransacking the lower caverns right now. King Nar will eventually send out smaller forces to rout all the remaining dwarves in the mountain. He won't give us a chance to regroup." The deep scars on his cheeks only emphasized his grim expression.

Skemtun coughed violently as he sucked dusty air into his tired lungs. He looked around. They were in one of the smaller tunnels. Behind him, half a dozen of his men were visible in the dim torchlight. Most of the men were injured.

"They'll be back. And in greater numbers," said Kathir. "We need to retreat before another wave of reinforcements arrives."

Skemtun kicked the body of a dead orc. "Filthy greenskins! I've killed so many, but they just keep coming, like vermin out of the forest during a fire."

"Things have changed," said Kathir. "There's more of them now. I've never seen their numbers so large. We never stood a chance once the orcs breached the main gate."

The dwarves had always triumphed in the past, but now the clans were fragmented and weak. King Hergung was dead, and the Vardmiter clan had abandoned them, splitting their numbers in half. The dwarves were like a rudderless ship—they had no strong leadership, and no direction. They were fighting a losing battle, and not just the immediate one against the orcs.

"We should pull back into the deepest part of the mountain," Kathir said. "This passage is no longer defensible."

Skemtun picked up his axe and his sword and slipped them back into his belt. "Alright, we'll move back, but I think we can defend against one more wave."

Kathir shook his head and pointed at the dead bodies surrounding them. "It's too risky. Your men are past the point of exhaustion. We must retreat."

Skemtun sighed. His bodyguard had a point. "All right, lads!" he said. "Back to the next chokepoint.

Quickly now! Follow me!"

The dwarves ran for a long time, stopping at a point where the tunnel narrowed again. Skemtun spotted a young dwarf carrying a stack of boxes down the shaft. He grabbed the boy by the collar and jerked him around.

"What are you *doing* here, boy?" Skemtun demanded. "Didn't you hear the order? You should be moving outside with the others!"

"Hey!" cried the boy. "Put me down!" The young dwarf peered up at him with startled eyes. "Lady Bolrakei sent me back inside... to save *Klorra-Kanna's* treasures."

Skemtun's mouth dropped open with surprise. "You've been sent down here... to save Bolrakei's stupid jewels?"

The younger dwarf's face reddened. "They're not *stupid*. We must preserve our clan's treasures."

Skemtun snorted with disgust. "I shouldn't be surprised. After all, ye're a member of Klorra-Kanna. Greedy bastards! Risking yer life to save a few gemstones seems like a perfectly reasonable thing to do."

The boy frowned and raised his chin. "I don't have to listen to you! Lady Bolrakei is my leader."

"Be quiet, ye fool! Go sit over there and don't say another word," Skemtun ordered, slapping the side of the boy's head with his palm. The young dwarf sulked over to the wall and plopped down on the floor.

"We need to find a way to stop the greenskins

from following us," said Kathir, "and then we need to get out of here."

Skemtun walked over to a spot where the roof was supported by ancient wood props. "Look here. See these props? They hold up this part of the tunnel. If we can bring the roof down, it'll block this entire passage. This is one of the few tunnels that leads outside. We could seal it, then we can escape."

Kathir looked up at the roof. "Isn't there a risk that the entire tunnel will collapse? I don't want to be buried under solid rock."

Skemtun smiled at him. "That's very unlikely if we do it right. I'm not an expert on many things, but minin' and tunnels are two things that I understand really well."

Kathir's expression warmed a little. "I trust you, but I don't want to find myself trapped between two mountains of rubble. It doesn't sound like a good way to die."

"It isn't," Skemtun said, with the certainty of someone who had seen mining collapses before. "But it won't come to that." He pointed up at a narrower beam on the ceiling. "See this section here? It's not braced on either side. If we destroy these four supports, the roof will come down, but only in this spot." He turned to his men and raised his voice. "Lads! Everyone, get yer axes and come over here! I want you to chip away at these props. Quickly now!"

The soldiers leaped into action, striking at the wooden beams in perfect rhythm. The wood was brittle, and large chunks flew off into the air.

The young dwarf from Klorra-Kanna stood up and tried to creep away, but Skemtun grabbed him. "Hey! Where do you think ye're going?"

The young dwarf pointed back toward the other end of the tunnel. "I've got to go back inside the caves. I've got to save my clan's treasury."

"Are you *stupid*, boy?" Skemtun demanded, jabbing at the boy's temple.

"Ow!" cried the young man, trying to swat away Skemtun's hand. "That hurts!"

Skemtun released him. "I've got dwarves cutting away the only thing that's holding up the roof. That means this tunnel is coming down, and anyone on the wrong side of it won't be getting through. Now, which side of it do you want to be on when it caves in? The side with the *exit*, or the side with the *orcs?*"

The young dwarf's face paled, but he still tried to move away. "Please! Lady Bolrakei sent me on this mission *personally*. She'll be very displeased if I return without everything she asked for."

"Forget yer stupid orders!" Skemtun snapped. "I'm tryin' to save yer life! Bolrakei's an idiot for sending you down here. Mark my words, boy—if you go down that passage, you won't ever come back!" He shoved the young man back in the opposite direction. "Now get a move on! I won't have your death on my conscience!"

The youngster frowned but didn't argue any further.

Skemtun turned to Kathir and pointed his finger

at the boy. "If you catch this young fool trying to go back down this tunnel again, tie him up. I'll carry him out on my shoulder if I have to."

"Understood," Kathir said, smiling.

The young dwarf gnawed at his lower lip. "Bolrakei won't be pleased when I tell her about this."

Skemtun fixed him with a withering stare. "Well, Bolrakei isn't *here*, is she? She ran off with the first rush of dwarves escaping the mountain. If she wants her precious gemstones that much, she should come and get them herself!"

"Bolrakei sent this boy back into the mountain by himself?" Kathir asked quietly. "That seems quite... *unscrupulous* of her."

Skemtun grunted. "Bolrakei isn't really known for her *scruples*."

Bolrakei always acted selfishly, but she was the leader of the wealthiest dwarf clan. She didn't get there by accident—she got there by being ruthless. Skemtun hated Bolrakei's self-serving attitude, but he wasn't about to make a fuss about it right now, not when their lives were at stake. He had to concentrate on the task in front of him.

A loud crack sounded behind him, and a cloud of dust fell from the ceiling. "Stop! That's enough, lads!"

The soldiers stepped back. Skemtun took a length of rope from his rucksack, knotted it carefully around the largest beam, and then walked back to where Kathir and the others were standing.

They were just in time. Skemtun could see the

flicker of grease torches in the distance. The orcs grunted and howled at each other to communicate, and there was no doubt that their voices were getting closer. Another group was coming, and it was larger than the last one—too many for them to fight.

"Everyone grab the end of this rope and form a line," Skemtun barked. "Hurry up! We don't have much time!" The others quickly grabbed the rope and formed a line behind their leader. "When I shout, everyone pull the rope as hard as you can! All at the same time. Got it?"

They all nodded in agreement.

"Now pull! Pull!" he yelled and strained his aching muscles against the weight of the beam. "Pull the rope! Pull harder!" Skemtun bellowed, throwing every scrap of strength he had against the rope. He could feel the others doing the same behind him. With a loud crash, the first prop finally gave way.

The other damaged beams also splintered and fell, but the roof did not collapse. For a few tense seconds, the dwarves stood frozen in place. The orcs were screaming and charging down the tunnel now. The orcs were so large that they had to crouch to fit inside the passageway.

Just then, there was another loud cracking noise, and a shower of pebbles fell down. The orcs stopped and looked up. The roof of the tunnel shook, then the entire roof crashed down all at once, in one giant slab. The cave-in seemed to happen in slow motion.

The orcs screamed as they disappeared beneath

the rubble. Thick dust clouded the air, blinding the dwarves for several minutes. But slowly, the dust began to settle, and soon the dwarves could see that the pile of rubble ended about ten paces in front of them.

"Did it work?" asked Kathir, between coughs.

Skemtun nodded. "Yup. It worked. The tunnel's blocked. There's no way back now."

He was pleased that his plan had worked, but he also felt guilty—how many of his people were still trapped inside the city? Mount Velik was in absolute chaos, and he had just blocked one of the few exits they had left. If any of the survivors inside tried to escape using this passageway, they would be trapped and killed.

Kathir noted Skemtun's unhappy expression. "Don't beat yourself up over this," he said quietly. "None of this is your fault. This needed to be done. We can't leave any of these passages open for the orcs to use."

"I know," said Skemtun, as he swallowed the lump in his throat. He'd spent his whole life mining and building in these tunnels—building them to last for generations—and now he was forced to destroy them. It went against everything he had ever believed in. But he had to accept it—the city was a complete loss. Now his only concern was the safety of his men.

"Come on," Kathir said. "We should get moving."

Skemtun nodded. "Aye, let's go. This tunnel snakes through the entire mountain, so it's a long way to the outside. If we're lucky, we'll reach the exit before sunrise."

"And then what?" asked one of the soldiers. "Where do we go from here?"

Skemtun sighed. "We must go north," he said. "As much as I hate to admit it, we must seek refuge with the Vardmiters. The clans are homeless—and we've got nowhere else to go."

It took Skemtun and his men hours of walking to reach the small, concealed exit leading out of Mount Velik. The ragged band of survivors crawled out of the tiny opening and emerged on the south side of the mountain, about two leagues away from the main road. It was dawn when they finally reached the outside.

The exit was so small that Kathir had to disrobe and squeeze through like a caterpillar to fit. But they all made it out alive.

Sela saw them exiting the mountain while she was patrolling. She and Brinsop landed nearby and covered them with a concealment spell so they could escape to the tree line unseen. Luckily, most of the orcs were stationed on the other side of the mountain, near the front gate, so they were able to make it into the forest relatively easily.

"Sela, do you have any news for us?" asked Skemtun.

Sela nodded. "Most of the women and children

were able to escape, but the orcs are tracking them. I believe that Nar is planning to send out raiding parties. Elias and Nydeired are trying to help as much as they can, but there's only so much they can do. Elias is already tending dozens of wounded in a ravine nearby. He has his hands full as it is. Nydeired has scared off several roving bands of orcs, but there's so many of them—we can't possibly root them all out. Eventually, these people are going to be attacked."

"And what of our men?" asked Skemtun "How many of our soldiers survived?"

"It's difficult to say," said Sela. "An accurate count would be impossible now. Your general, Baltas, is dead, along with his entire contingent."

"*None* of his men survived?" whispered Skemtun.

"No," said Sela. "None of them surrendered. None of them turned back. Baltas held the main passage for two days, which was a feat in itself. He died bravely with his men beside him. All of your spellcasters are probably dead, too. I haven't seen any of them leave the mountain."

Skemtun shook his head sadly. "This is terrible news for us to hear. Hundreds of men, all dead. All the dwarf spellcasters—gone. My people..." He put his face in his hands and wept softly.

Sela placed her hand on his shoulder. "I'm sorry, Skemtun. I know this is difficult for you. What's worse, the road to Highport will be rough, and there are almost no soldiers to cover your escape. The survivors are on their own."

"Thank ye, for all ye've done for us," said Skemtun, wiping his nose on his sleeve. "We'd best get moving."

Skemtun asked if Sela and Elias could remain at the mountain for at least a few more days, just in case other survivors needed their help to escape. Sela nodded and mounted her dragon saddle.

"I'll cover you until you get a little deeper inside the forest, and then I'll go back to the mountain. Elias has a few ponies in the ravine nearby; you can take them and catch up with the rest of your group."

As soon as Skemtun and his men were safely in the trees, Sela raced back to resume her patrols.

Everyone was exhausted, but they couldn't stop and rest. They had to catch up to the rest of the survivors. The remaining soldiers would need to protect them.

Kathir and Skemtun retrieved two ponies from Elias so they could ride ahead. Moving at a swift pace, they caught up to the straggling dwarf refugees in a matter of hours.

"By the gods, look at all these people!" Kathir said, shaking his head.

A long line of people snaked through the mountain trails—mostly women, children, the elderly, and the wounded. Some carried small bundles or packs, but most had nothing but the clothes on their backs. The dwarves trudged along in scattered groups, their heads bowed with shame and grief. A small contingent of battered soldiers brought up the rear to protect them.

Skemtun rode up behind the line and spoke with

one of the soldiers.

"Hey there, boy!" Skemtun hollered at him.

The young man paused. He looked exhausted. "Skemtun, is that you?"

"Aye, it's me," he replied. "How are ye gettin' along?"

"Not too good. The greenskins attacked us last night. About twenty orcs came out of the forest in a nighttime raid. None of us has been able to get any rest."

"Did they steal anything?" asked Skemtun. "Supplies, or horses?"

The soldier shook his head. "No... they seem to be doing it for sport. The orcs killed a woman and five men. We chased 'em off, but they'll be back again. The women and children are terrified."

"How are we on supplies? Do we have enough food and water?"

"Enough for six days, give or take. We've got water, but we've already started rationing food. We didn't have much to begin with—only what people could carry with them. We've been tryin' to forage in the forest as we walk, but there isn't much here. The orcs did a lot of damage when they marched through. A few men offered to go hunting, but they disappeared and didn't return. We think the orcs got 'em. After that, our captain told everyone to stay together and keep walkin'. It's too dangerous to go out alone."

Skemtun looked around. "Were you able to save any of the livestock? That would have helped us along the way."

"Not much, sir." The young man pointed toward the front of the line. "We saved some ponies and a few mules. The ponies are carrying the wounded, and the mules are carrying the food supplies." Skemtun could see the mules moving slowly in the distance. The pack animals were laden with supplies. "That's all we've got. Everyone is tired of walking."

Skemtun reached down and patted the young dwarf's shoulder. "Thank ye, son. Just try to keep movin'. The farther away we get from the greenskins, the safer we'll be."

The soldier's voice dropped, and he lowered his eyes. "We're going to Highport, aren't we?"

"Aye," said Skemtun quietly. "There's nowhere else for us to go, lad. We'll have to take our chances with the Vardmiters."

"That's what I figured." The soldier scratched behind his ear. There was a crust of blood near his hairline, and his hand was wrapped with a bandage. "Oh, I forgot to mention—I also saw a messenger ride up earlier. He gave a scroll to Bolrakei. She's riding a mule up at the front of the line."

Skemtun was about to ask more questions, but he was interrupted by a sudden shout. A raiding party of orcs emerged from the forest and attacked. The women and children started screaming and scattered into the trees.

"Let's go, men!" Skemtun called out as he charged forward. Kathir followed behind him on his pony.

He looked up into the sky—the dragon riders were nowhere in sight. They were on their own.

They rode into the fray, already drawing their weapons. Skemtun raised his axe, swung as hard as he could, and severed an orc's hand. The orc screamed like a wild animal and clasped his wrist. Blood spurted outward, splattering Skemtun's face and chest. He wiped his face with his sleeve and raised his axe to strike again.

As fast as lightning, Kathir sank his sword into the throat of another orc. He ducked and felt a spear whiz over his head, grazing his hair. He turned to see Skemtun's axe embedded in another orc's skull.

From a short distance away, dwarf soldiers fired their arrows into the band of orcs as quickly as they could. More dwarves ran forward, joining the fight with their crossbows, slings, and axes. Skemtun and Kathir stood in the center of the battle, their weapons swinging.

Minutes later, the orcs retreated back into the forest. The dwarves watched them go, and then went to recover their precious arrows from the bodies of the slain. No dwarves had been killed—not this time. There were five dead orcs on the ground, and several more that had been wounded and escaped.

"Good job, lads!" Skemtun called out to his men. He tried to give the dwarves the confidence to keep fighting, but everyone could hear the weariness in his voice.

Skemtun climbed on top of a boulder to give

himself a better view of the trees. "The orcs are gone. We're safe for now."

"Your men did a good job," Kathir said, passing him a water skin.

Skemtun uncorked the skin and poured a little water into his mouth. "We were lucky," he said softly. "We've got to be prepared for more attacks."

"You're right," agreed Kathir. "Scuffles like this will continue for a while. Fortunately, it's late in the year, and we're moving north. Orcs don't like the snow; they're cold-blooded, and freezing weather makes them sluggish. There's already snow on the ground in the plains. Once we reach the forest's edge, your people should be relatively safe."

Skemtun nodded. "I hope ye're right. In the meantime, we've got to keep moving. I can see that these raids are takin' a toll on everyone. All the men look exhausted."

"Things are hard right now," said Kathir, "but it's going to be all right. You're doing a good job leading your people. I'm proud to be fighting by your side."

Skemtun raised an eyebrow. "Ye say that, but ye're a mercenary. Aren't ye gettin' *paid* to be here? Miklagard is still paying ye, aren't they?"

Kathir shrugged. "So? What of it? I'm not going to apologize for being a mercenary. It's my job. I can be proud of what I'm doing and get paid to do it at the same time."

"That's an odd perspective, my friend," replied Skemtun.

Kathir smiled, but he didn't argue. Instead, he

looked out upon the dwarves. The women and children had returned from their hiding spots and were walking on the trail again. They stretched out into a rough column along the path.

It was obvious that the dwarves had never expected Mount Velik to fall. They had failed to prepare for the worst. There had been no time to gather proper supplies for a long journey. That was their worst mistake, and now they were paying for it. They moved with the painful slowness of people who were losing hope.

The days passed as the dwarves trudged ahead. Some started collapsing from fatigue, and so the hard decision was made to stop to rest for a night. They set up a makeshift camp, and Skemtun set up a perimeter of armed guards. Everyone took turns sleeping on the hard ground. Thankfully, the orcs didn't attack them during the night.

They broke camp and moved on the next morning. As they continued onward, they found themselves without any shelter. There were no caves as they moved further north, so they were left vulnerable to the wind, the cold, and the rain.

After a few days, their food provisions began to dwindle. The women scavenged what they could, collecting mushrooms and wild berries, but it wasn't enough for everyone to get a meal. They found very little to eat in the forest, and even their water was running low.

Some of the wounded died along the way and had to be buried in shallow graves. There was no time to grieve properly.

The days were hard, but there were some bright spots. As they moved further north, hunting became easier, and they were able to catch small game on a regular basis. Everyone searched for food; even the youngest boys hunted with slingshots and caught smaller animals like birds, rats, and snakes. They ate everything—nothing was wasted.

One day, Kathir got lucky and shot a huge bear with his crossbow. With the dwarves' help, he used ropes to hoist and hang the carcass up in a tree. Trembling with excitement, they dressed the bear and then cooked the meat over several campfires. The dwarves were so thankful that they threw a makeshift party right then and there. That night, everybody ate and slept well.

The days turned into weeks, and finally, the snow-capped Highport Mountains became visible in the distance. A vast plain of snow broken only by occasional trees extended into the distance in front of them.

The temperatures dropped, and the snow on the ground froze into a solid crust. Their supplies were depleted, and everyone was cold and hungry. Everyone knew this last stretch would be the most challenging part of their journey. And yet, people were still hopeful—after everything they had been through, their quarrels with the Vardmiters seemed easily forgotten.

Reaching Highport would be like crossing the finish line at last.

"It's colder than usual for this time of year. Even if the Vardmiters accept us with open arms, it's going to be a hard winter for everyone," said Skemtun.

"At least the trail is clear," said Kathir. "That's a blessing. Do you anticipate the Vardmiters to accept all your survivors?"

Skemtun shook his head sadly. "I hope they do, but I'm not sure what to expect—not after everything that's happened between the clans."

Skemtun didn't say anything else. He rode up to the front to get a better look at the trail. When he made it up to the front line, he spotted Bolrakei and stopped. They hadn't spoken much in the last few weeks. Skemtun had tried to avoid her. He'd told himself it was because he was busy with his leadership duties, but he knew in his heart that was a lie.

Bolrakei rode a mule while everyone around her walked. Somehow she'd managed to remain quite fat, despite their lack of food. Her neck and wrists glittered with the jewels her people had been able to retrieve from the mountain during the siege.

Bolrakei turned around and eyed Skemtun with disapproval. "What are you doing up here? Aren't you supposed to be safeguarding the back of the line?"

"The orcs haven't attacked us in days," Skemtun said. "They're leaving us alone for now, so I decided to ride upfront for a while. Your clan members have some nice weapons. Perhaps some of them would like to take a turn fighting in the back for a while."

"Not a chance!" she snapped. "I need all my guards up here! Who will guard my gemstones? Someone has to protect the last bit of wealth we have! Without me, the clans would have *nothing!*"

Bolrakei's words stirred up intense anger within him. "What good are yer gemstones here, Bolrakei? Look around ye! Can't ye see that everyone is starving? People are only interested in bread to fill their bellies. Maybe if ye'd spent less time obsessing about yer money and yer jewelry, this march wouldn't have been so hard on everyone!"

"You don't know anything!" Bolrakei snapped. "We'll certainly need my treasures if the Vardmiters don't allow us to stay with them! Have you thought about that? How will we buy food or supplies? How will we purchase land? It will fall on *my clan* to purchase those things, since *my clan* is the only one with anything of value!"

Skemtun's frowned. "Yer clan is no more important than mine, Bolrakei. We're equals."

"Ha!" she snorted. "I'm high-born and have a long line of royal ancestors. You're nothing more than a miner's son, and a *lucky* one, at that! You're low by birth, and I'm destined to be the next queen."

"Don't be so sure about that, *'princess,'*" said Skemtun, with sarcasm. "Ye don't wear a crown yet, thank goodness."

Bolrakei's expression became even uglier. "You

watch your mouth! I *will* be the next queen! You can bet on it!"

"Ye know, I wouldn't take that bet myself!" he snorted, turning his pony around. Bolrakei screamed obscenities at his retreating back. He just kept moving until he couldn't hear her anymore.

Kathir rode up behind him. "I can tell from your expression that your little chat with Bolrakei didn't go very well."

"No… it didn't," Skemtun admitted. "I let my anger get the best of me. She just kept pushin' and pushin', and I finally exploded. But I know how she is, and I really shouldn't antagonize her like that. It's distressin' for the others to us bickerin' like children. We're supposed to set an example."

"As you say," Kathir said, "I agree with you, but I also understand the temptation to fight with Bolrakei. I've been tempted to sock her in the mouth a few times myself."

"Now that's a diplomatic answer," Skemtun chuckled.

"Come on, you know that she's not fit to be a clan leader, much less a queen. She's insufferable, greedy, and self-centered. I realize that her clan holds most of the wealth, but that doesn't excuse her behavior."

Skemtun remained silent for a moment. "Aye, well… let her do what she wants, for now. As long as my people are safe, it doesn't really matter."

There was no wind, but there was a strange haze in the air, and it was growing dark. In the distance, they could see lightning flash on the horizon, the sign of a coming storm.

Kathir opened his mouth to make a comment about the weather, but an alert from the back of the line told him that orcs had been spotted. "Again? I thought this was over!"

They both turned, spurring their mounts to the blast of the horn.

"The orcs have followed us onto the plains!" shouted Kathir, and the dwarves scrambled to defend the camp.

By the time Skemtun and Kathir reached the rear, dozens of dwarves were already fighting for their lives. It was another roving band of orcs, and this time, they were mounted on *drask*, the oversized venomous lizards the orcs rode into battle.

"They've got *drask* with them!" shouted Skemtun.

The horn sounded again, with three short bursts: a warning to the women and children to run and hide.

The drask lined up in a single row—clicking and snapping their jaws. The foul smell of the lizards was so strong that they had to stifle the urge to vomit.

Kathir set a bolt in his crossbow. He hoped that he would be able to keep himself and Skemtun alive, but the odds were certainly stacked against them this time.

As he let loose the first arrow, a large shadow moved overhead. The dwarves looked up to see two large shapes in the clouds. The dwarves cheered: the dragon riders had finally arrived to help them—and just in time.

The dragons roared as they swooped down from the sky, sending thick streams of dragonfire towards the orcs. The drask scattered, running in every direction. For an instant, the fire engulfed everything around them, and the dwarves felt fear as the incredible heat scorched their skin.

Ear-piercing screams carried through the air as the drask died in the flames. The orcs jumped from their terrified mounts and ran, screaming as they tried to escape, but there was no cover for them. The dragon riders continued their attack. Minutes later, it was over.

Once they were sure that all the orcs were either scattered or dead, the dragon riders swooped down and landed near the dwarves. They were all cheering like mad.

Elias and Sela slid from their saddles, and the dwarves surrounded them instantly.

"You two are a wonderful sight!" Kathir shouted gratefully. He really meant it. None of the dwarves had been hurt.

"Who's in charge here?" Sela asked.

"I am!" Bolrakei shouted, trotting up on her mule while pushing her way through the crowd. "I'm in charge!"

Skemtun maneuvered his pony beside her and said in a loud voice, "I'm here, too." He crossed his arms over his chest and shot Bolrakei an irritated look.

Sela smiled. "I'm glad to see that both of you made it. We came as soon as we could. How is everyone else doing?"

Skemtun shrugged. "As well as can be expected, I suppose. We've made it this far, and most of us survived."

Sela nodded and looked Skemtun directly in the eye. "You've done a good job leading your people." Then she turned to address Kathir. "I'm surprised you're still here, mercenary. Why haven't you gone back to Miklagard?" Her tone was curious but not accusatory.

Kathir gave her a slight smile. "Because my contract is still active. It's my job to guard Skemtun and bring him to safety. If he doesn't make it to Highport alive, then I don't get paid."

"Ah, I see," she replied carefully.

"Kathir's been very helpful," Skemtun said. "He's helped us all along the way." Then his expression grew anxious. "You and Elias stayed behind at Mount Velik for a long time. What happened back there? Were there any more survivors?"

Sela nodded. "Yes, a few every day. We would have come to help you sooner, but survivors kept coming out, usually in ones and twos. We continued to search for survivors and checked all the exits several times a day. Many of your people were badly injured and could not be saved. We stayed behind as long as we could, but I eventually called off the search and we flew here. If any unlucky souls are still trapped inside Mount Velik, they are all surely dead by now."

Skemtun looked down sadly. The news was terrible, but not unexpected. "What happened to the rest of the survivors?"

"Some chose to make the journey through the forest alone," said Sela. "Elias flew the ones who were the sickest to Ironport. I assume they will catch up to your group eventually."

"Well, that's good news..." said Skemtun. "Are you staying with us? It would be a real help to us if ye stayed with us until we reached Highport. We could use help finding food, too."

Sela nodded. "We'll help any way we can. Brinsop and I will monitor the skies. Elias will tend to your sick, and Nydeired will go hunting and find some food. Nydeired is very strong; he is capable of carrying large game. In the meantime, your people should keep moving. There's a storm coming, and it's too cold to make camp. Your people will freeze to death out here." She pointed north. "There's a large cave just a few leagues away. It will give your people some shelter for the night, and keep you out of the storm. I'll show you the location when you reach the slopes. You should be able to make it to the cave by this evening, if you move quickly."

"Thank ye for helpin' my people," said Skemtun. "It means a lot to us."

Sela nodded and returned to the air, where she and Elias circled overhead and watched for orcs. Everyone seemed more at ease with the dragons flying above them—they felt safer, and the relief on their tired faces was palpable.

Skemtun turned to Bolrakei. "Look, do us all a favor and spread the word that everyone needs to move faster if we're going to make it to that cave by tonight. Everyone'll be thankful for some real shelter for a change."

Bolrakei huffed a bit, but she didn't argue. She set off and returned to her place at the front of the column.

Skemtun took his place at the back of the line again. He turned to Kathir. "The young dragon rider —Elias—I saw the way ye looked at each other. Do ye know him?"

Kathir paused for a moment, considering his words. "We're not friends, if that's what you're asking. It's a little complicated. I met him years ago, under different circumstances. He was part of a contract job I did, unfortunately." He cleared his throat. "I don't really want to talk about it. A good mercenary learns to keep quiet about his previous jobs. It's not good for business."

Skemtun scratched his chin. "Humph. Ye're a strange one, ye know that? I don't know anything about ye—not really. But then... I guess ye've saved my life enough times that I should probably trust ye anyway."

"Thanks." Kathir smiled. It was an odd feeling, being trusted. For most of his life, he had been loathed or merely tolerated. As a slave, he was treated like an animal. When he became a dragon hunter out of necessity, he was despised by everyone. Even as a mercenary, he was treated with contempt by most people. No one seemed to like him; they just hired him to do their dirty work.

But things were different with Skemtun. The dwarf seemed to trust him, and Kathir found that he liked traveling with him. It felt good to help people, and he felt like he fit in, even though he wasn't a dwarf. He looked onto the horizon. A cave came into view in the distance.

"Woo-hoo!" shouted Skemtun. "There's the cave! That's exactly what we need."

Kathir nodded. A warm cave to sleep in would be good for everyone. If the dragons got lucky hunting, maybe they would have a nice meal, too.

Filled with a strange excitement, the dwarves hurried forward, reaching for their goal.

They reached the cave just in time. The rain started coming down in torrents as soon as they arrived. The dwarves clawed up the final slope and dashed inside the cave to safety.

The dwarves were so grateful to sleep inside a cave again that no one complained about how crowded it was. Despite their cramped quarters, the temperature inside was comfortable. The air smelled cleanly of mud and clay.

The dwarves made camp on the clean sand floor, lighting fires to cook and heat water. After tying their pack animals inside the cave, they all settled down to rest and relax.

Nydeired caught two wild boars, so they even had a filling meal that night. Everyone's spirits were lifted, and it was one of the best nights the dwarves had had in a long while. The next morning, they packed up their things and continued their journey well-rested and in much better spirits.

But soon, reality set in. As the refugees began the final leg of their ascent up the mountain, it became clear that the Vardmiters would not be welcoming them. In the distance, the solid lines of the Vardmiter army stretched out across the slopes of Highport.

The Vardmiters could have sent a messenger, but instead, they sent their entire defensive force out to meet them.

It was not a good sign.

There was a lack of order in the Vardmiters' front lines that showed they were not well-trained soldiers. Most of them were armed with farm tools, rather than conventional weapons. The Vardmiters were farmers and laborers, not warriors. Even so, they looked ready to fight.

Despite their lack of formal training, the ragged group of refugees from Mount Velik would be no match for the Vardmiters, who were all fresh, well-rested, and healthy.

The refugees paused a short distance away from the Vardmiters, not willing to move forward any further.

Bolrakei looked frantic. "Their army is waiting to attack us! Can you believe it? Our own people! How could they do this to us after everything we've been through? Don't they know we were invaded by the orcs?"

"I have to defuse this tension before things get out of hand," Skemtun murmured. He approached the front lines, and the Vardmiters tensed and shifted their weapons.

Sitting on her mule, Bolrakei cried out, "The Vardmiters mean to destroy us! They're traitors! We should take this mountain for ourselves!"

An alarmed murmur ran through the lines of refugees.

Just then, Bolrakei's mule tossed its head and reared back, depositing her unceremoniously in the mud. The animal snorted happily and trotted off in the opposite direction, pleased to be free of his burden. Scattered laughter went through both sides of the crowd. Bolrakei wiped futilely at her dirty face and hair and then screamed at Skemtun. "Don't just stand there! Do something!"

"Be *quiet,* Bolrakei," Skemtun hissed. "What do ye want me to do? Attack them? Our people are exhausted. If we attack, people will die on both sides. Is that what you want?"

"We've got to do something!" she screeched. "I haven't come all this way to be treated like this!"

Kathir interrupted her. "Skemtun is right. Everyone's tired from marching, and you've lost your best warriors fighting the orcs. The Vardmiters could massacre us if they wanted to." He tried to speak as dispassionately as he could, but his words still caused Bolrakei to glare at him intensely.

Bolrakei spun towards Kathir with unmasked

rage. "Shut up, mercenary! You don't get to make decisions for my people!"

"And ye don't have the right to commit our people to a suicidal charge!" said Skemtun. "We came here to forge a compromise with the Vardmiters, not to fight them."

"I'm a clan leader!" Bolrakei screamed. "And my clan ranking is higher than yours!"

As Bolrakei and Skemtun continued to argue, Kathir scanned the Vardmiter ranks. They seemed frozen in place. Kathir could see one dark-haired dwarf in front; he was heavily armed and the only one wearing fine armor. He was obviously in charge.

It was Utan, the leader of the Vardmiter clan, and now, their king. Utan watched the drama unfolding in front of him calmly, without saying anything. He didn't order his men to attack. He merely watched and waited.

The dragon riders arrived next on the scene, circling down to land so they were positioned between the two groups of dwarves.

Sela stepped forward and addressed both groups. "It seems we are at an impasse. Are you going to speak to each other?"

There were nods and murmurs of agreement from both sides.

Skemtun heaved a sigh. "I'll go talk to Utan."

"Stop!" yelled Bolrakei, grabbing his sleeve. "What are you doing? They sent their army out to meet us!"

He shook her off. "Arguin' with me isn't going to

help the situation. Our people are starvin' and tired. We can't go back to Mount Velik now. We've no place to live, so I'm going to talk to Utan and see if we can come to a compromise."

"They're not trying to welcome us, can't you see that?"

Skemtun frowned. "It doesn't matter. We don't have any choice in this, so I have to try."

Her eyes narrowed into angry slits. "I wouldn't do it, Skemtun."

Skemtun rolled his eyes. "I'm still a clan leader, and ye don't have the authority to boss me around. Ye're not a queen—not yet, anyway. Now, I'm going over to talk with Utan. Ye can come along, or ye can stay here, sulking in the mud. I don't care either way." He dismounted and started walking up the hill.

He hadn't gone far before Bolrakei ran up behind him, panting as she jogged. "Wait! I'm coming! I'm coming!"

Utan stepped forward, flanked by two armed guards. Sela and Elias stood nearby, but they did not attempt to interfere. Utan addressed Sela and Elias first. "Thank you for being here. I appreciate the dragon riders' presence during this difficult time." Then he gave a curt nod to Skemtun and Bolrakei.

"Don't try to sweet-talk us, Utan! I remember what your clan did! Don't forget that!" Bolrakei snapped.

Utan bristled at Bolrakei's disrespectful tone.

Skemtun sighed in frustration. "Please, Bolrakei!

Ye're only makin' things worse!"

"He's right," said Utan gravely. "No one is arguing here except *you*."

Bolrakei blinked hard, gritted her teeth, and turned her head in defiance. "Humph!" But then she was silent.

"We didn't come here to fight with anybody," said Skemtun. "We came here to talk. That's all."

"Who's fighting here? It certainly isn't us," said Utan. "But we *have* been hearing rumors about how you intended to come here and teach us a lesson—how you planned your revenge against us. We came here to make a new life for ourselves. All we want is to be left in peace, and now you've shown up outside our gates! I figured you planned to attack. You can't blame us for taking precautions."

Skemtun pointed to the gaunt women and children behind him. "Utan, look at us. Do we *look* like we're in any shape to attack anyone? Almost half our men are dead. All our spellcasters are gone. The greenskins completely destroyed our home."

Utan shot a sympathetic glance towards the women and children. "I'm sorry about your losses... I heard that the greenskins attacked Mount Velik, but I never thought the city would fall. Honestly... I'm sorry about what your clans went through, but you should have been better prepared for the siege. As for your difficult journey, well, every Vardmiter knows how hard the journey from Mount Velik is. We all had to make that trip ourselves when we left."

"No one forced ye to leave our mountain," Skemtun said quietly. "Ye decided that all by yerself."

"Right," Utan said bitterly. "Just like it was yer idea to treat us like dirt! We didn't have any choice but to leave! Can't ye see that? It was either *leave* or continue to be treated like vermin. So we left, and created a *new* life for ourselves. And now you've come here, begging for help. What would you do in my shoes?"

Skemtun paused for a moment, ignoring the fact that Bolrakei was seething silently beside him, watching his every move. "We're askin' for help, Utan. That much *is* true. We need a safe place for our women and children, at least until we can decide what to do next. Is that too much to ask?"

Utan glanced back at his own soldiers. "I'm not sure if my people are ready to forgive how badly they were treated. Why should I make an effort to help you, after everything that your clans have done to mine?"

"We're yer people, too, Utan," said Skemtun quietly. "If ye leave us to fend for ourselves, more of us will die. Is that what ye want?"

Utan fell silent, his resolve wavering. "Aye, no.... I don't want that."

"Please help us," Skemtun continued, "I can't do anythin' about the past, and I'm sorry about that, but if ye turn us away now, ye're killin' us as surely as if ye take axes to our skulls. Ye can see how weak and hungry most of us are. The orcs have been harassin' us for the entire journey. We were attacked again just yesterday, and if the dragon riders hadn't come to our rescue, even more of us would 'ave died."

Utan sighed deeply. "Alright, alright. I'll help you, but that doesn't mean I'll let you all inside our mountain. There simply isn't enough *space* for all of you here; most of our caves are still unfinished, and it's cramped enough as it is."

When Skemtun looked surprised, Utan snorted. "What did you expect? Do you think that all your clans could just show up outside this mountain and have my clan provide for you like before? That's not going to happen! The Vardmiter clan is independent now. If anything, we're better off without any of you here."

Bolrakei clenched her fists. "How dare you speak to us this way!"

Utan's bottled outrage sputtered to the surface. "Did everyone hear that? That's *exactly* the type of response that I would expect from this shrew! You're here *begging* for us to help, and ye still have the nerve to insult me. After everything that's happened, ye still think ye're better than us." There was a moment of sharp silence as he turned to walk away. "Bah! I'm finished with the lot of ye."

Skemtun shot Bolrakei a furious glare before shouting, "Wait! Please, wait!"

Utan didn't stop. He didn't look back.

"Utan, PLEASE," Skemtun yelled, stumbling after him.

This time Utan paused and turned slowly

around. "Just what do you want?"

Skemtun grabbed his sleeve desperately. "Look," he pleaded, "Don't listen to Bolrakei. I know she's rotten and stupid and mean, but she doesn't speak for the rest of us. And I'll admit that I've mistreated your clan in the past. There are many things we need to talk through, but my people need food and shelter *now*. If that means beggin' at yer feet..." The old dwarf battled his pride for a moment. "Then I'll do it." Skemtun got down on his knees and clasped Utan's hands in his own. "*Please* help us. At least the women and children."

Utan stared down at him with a shocked expression. He paused for a long moment before finally speaking. "You can stand up. Begging won't be necessary. My people will bring out food and blankets for you. We'll help your people construct some proper shelters tomorrow."

"We can't come inside?" Skemtun asked.

Utan shook his head firmly. "No. I'll help you, and I'll feed you, but your clans are *not* welcome inside the Highport Caverns. This is *our* territory now. Is that understood? Anyone who doesn't like it is certainly welcome to leave." Then he turned and left.

The rest of the Vardmiters trailed back inside the mountain, with only a few guards remaining posted at the main gate.

Skemtun sighed and lowered his head. It wasn't the outcome he'd hoped for, but it was better than nothing.

Skemtun walked back to his clan and explained the situation. Some were happy that they would have food and blankets, but more than a few dwarves—and most of Bolrakei's clan—were angry that they hadn't been invited inside the mountain.

After a moment, Bolrakei went up to Skemtun and poked his chest. "That didn't go very well. We're in the same position as when we got here—stuck outside like wild animals."

"No thanks to you!" Skemtun spat.

"Humph!" she grunted. "It's obvious to me that the Vardmiters haven't learned any respect or any ground rules for civilized behavior."

"Don't you dare do *anything* to disrupt things here," warned Skemtun.

"Oh, don't worry," Bolrakei said. "I'm not going to start any more arguments, at least not now. They can help us, alright. But afterwards, when we're stronger, we'll put the Vardmiters back in their proper place." She turned around and stomped back to her friends.

Once Bolrakei was out of earshot, Kathir muttered angrily, "Life would be a lot easier for everyone if the orcs had killed her."

Skemtun shot him a look. "Be quiet! Please don't talk about her like that—someone could overhear ye. Things are difficult enough as it is."

"She's intolerable," said Kathir.

Skemtun nodded. "I know, I know. I'll have to keep an eye on her. I can't let her ruin things."

At least they both agreed on that. Whatever

nasty tricks she was planning, neither one of them was about to let her get away with it.

4. NEGOTIATIONS

The clans agreed to hold peace talks a few days later. Bolrakei, Skemtun, and the dragon riders were invited inside the Highport Caverns for the first time. Most of the smaller caves were still unfinished but were at least livable. The main hall was enormous and nearly completed.

Huge stalagmites and uneven floors made for strenuous walking, and none of the footpaths were paved. The sound of dripping water in the background followed them wherever they went.

Inside the caves, the temperature was cool, and the air smelled faintly of moss and smoke. Torches lined the walls, but only a few of them were lit, to conserve fuel. There was also the ever-present odor of animal dung and pig meal.

"Where is all your livestock?" asked Skemtun.

"We only raise pigs," Utan replied. "The pens are outside the mountain, on the banks of the creek. It's easier to feed and care for them there. Plus, the smell is less bothersome when their pens are outside."

Utan led them to a small meeting room close to the gates, and they all sat down at a rough-hewn table. The floor of the cave was covered with fine sand.

Kathir leaned against the wall and prepared to watch the proceedings in silence. As an outsider with no rank, Kathir was barred from speaking. Bolrakei had tried to block Kathir's entry into the negotiation, but Skemtun had insisted that he be allowed to observe, since Bolrakei insisted on bringing several of her "advisors."

The dragon riders, Sela and Elias, were also present, but only as observers.

Once they all sat down, it didn't take long for the dwarves to start arguing.

"...I'm just saying that everyone needs to pull their own weight," Utan said.

"My clan can't spend their time doing menial labor," Bolrakei sniffed. "We're highly-skilled artisans. We earn more money cutting gemstones and making jewelry. That's what we're *trained* to do. We would be most useful in that role."

Silence hung in the room for a moment.

Utan shook his head. "I won't allow that. You just want things to go back to how they were before. We have no use for your baubles and gewgaws here. What we *really* need is more farmers and laborers."

"You're being unreasonable!" Bolrakei sputtered.

"I'm not being unreasonable," argued Utan. "If you want to share this mountain with us, Klorra-Kanna must do their share of the hard labor, just like everybody else."

"That's ridiculous!" she replied, her voice rising to a shout.

Skemtun sat between them, not responding. He

didn't know what to say.

"You think that shouting will get you what you want," Utan continued. "Well, it won't work! Not here. My people can wait inside this mountain forever, and we don't *ever* have to allow you inside. Shout until you're blue in the face, for all I care. You're the ones who need our help, not the other way around."

Bolrakei pounded her fist on the table. "You forget yourself! My ancestry is royal—do you even understand what that means?"

Utan's eyes locked onto hers. "Your bloodline means nothing to me, Bolrakei, and it never has. There aren't any princesses here."

"How dare you speak to me so disrespectfully— how dare you!" Bolrakei cried, springing to her feet. "I come from royal blood. I deserve to be queen by right! I am from the highest family, and your father was nothing more than a lowly peasant farmer!"

Utan gasped. "How dare ye insult my family! I'm done here! This negotiation is over!"

"Wait—are ye sure you want to give up so quickly?" asked Skemtun, finally speaking.

"I'm leaving," said Utan. "I didn't come here to be insulted. The guards will escort you out."

Skemtun sighed and put his face in his hands. He knew that the negotiations couldn't continue without Utan. If he wouldn't agree to a treaty, then they were stuck at a stalemate.

Utan gave the dragon riders a respectful nod and left the negotiation room. "The dragon riders are welcome to stay. The rest of you can leave."

Bolrakei spun on her heel and left, followed by her advisors.

"This is hopeless," Skemtun muttered. "Bolrakei is ruining everything."

"We'll try again in a few days," said Kathir quietly. "Maybe the dragon riders can talk some sense into her."

"Maybe," said Skemtun, but he was doubtful. It was frustrating to have to return to his people without any good news to report.

Bolrakei was the problem, but at least half the dwarves supported her unquestioningly—partly because of her high birth, but also because of her unwavering belief in the superiority of the "old ways."

Even under these difficult circumstances, most of the clans still considered the Vardmiters beneath them, and they *expected* the Vardmiters to capitulate to their demands.

Old prejudices were hard to break. Skemtun was learning that the hard way.

They walked outside, and Skemtun paused on the hillside to view the camp. The refugee camp sprawled before them on the lower slopes of the mountain. Many dwarves were constructing outdoor shelters with whatever materials they could find. There were a few large tents, wooden lean-tos, and simple shacks. Skemtun didn't like the idea of living the rest of his life *outside* a mountain; it just wasn't the way dwarves should live.

Bolrakei and a few of her advisors had claimed

a nicer section of the camp for themselves. She had also bullied other dwarves into building her a large shelter so she could protect her jewel boxes.

"We need to find a way to break this deadlock," said Skemtun quietly as they headed back toward the camp. "The longer this goes on, the harder it'll be to change anything."

"*Lady* Bolrakei is the main problem," replied Kathir. "Utan dislikes her intensely, and I can't say I blame him. Can't you just overrule her?"

Skemtun shook his head. "It's not that simple. I can't oppose her directly without splitting the clans even further. She's got powerful supporters, and she's descended from a very important family. Her lineage means a lot, especially within her own clan. Many dwarves believe exactly as she does— that the Vardmiters are beneath us. I'll admit that I used to feel the same way myself."

"You'll have to work something out soon," Kathir said. "How long can your people live exposed on this side of a mountain? There's a blanket of snow on the ground, and it's getting colder every day."

"At least we have enough to eat." Skemtun tried to remain positive, but he knew that things were bad. Two more of his clan had died last night. Even with enough food, Highport was a harsh place.

"I don't understand what Bolrakei is gaining from this," Kathir said.

"She's very prideful, but she isn't stupid. Klorra-Kanna became the richest clan in dwarvish history under her rule—she's rich beyond all imagining, even now. The boxes she brought with her are probably full of diamonds and gold. If there's one thing Bolrakei knows how to do well, it's how to make money."

Skemtun and Kathir kept walking through the camp. They went silent for a moment as they approached a group of dwarves huddled in a circle. They cooked a freshly-skinned rabbit over a small campfire. Skemtun stopped to greet them.

Kathir stepped back a respectful distance and took some time to think. He'd spent a lot of time working for influential people who manipulated those around them.

Once they resumed walking, he asked Skemtun, "What if Bolrakei's motives are more sinister? Maybe creating obstacles is part of her plan. Could she aggravate things until a final battle occurs?"

"It's possible, I suppose."

Kathir looked at his friend. "What happens when your clans are so sick and tired of freezing outside that they attempt to take this mountain by force?"

Skemtun sighed. "Most of our soldiers are dead, and the Vardmiters don't have any military trainin'. A battle between the clans would be a disaster. Both sides would suffer heavy casualties."

Kathir frowned. "We know that, but does Bolrakei? Does she even *care*?"

"She sees the Vardmiters as a bunch of misfits, so deep down, she believes we can beat them. She's blinded by her arrogance and prejudice."

"You have to stop her," Kathir insisted.

The old dwarf sighed. "I know that, but what would ye have me do? I can't oppose her, at least not openly. Her clan is too powerful."

"Come on, man! Take charge here. Go talk to Utan. Alone."

"And what if Bolrakei discovers that I went behind her back?" Skemtun countered. "I'm not a king! I'm just a clan leader. I don't have more authority than she does. In fact, I have *less*."

Kathir shook his head. He said quietly, "Don't be afraid of her. You can strike your *own* deal with Utan. Negotiate for *your* people. Her followers can stay outside on the mountain if they want. Anyone who decides to follow you can just join your clan inside."

"If I try something underhanded like that, Bolrakei will try to have me stripped of my office."

Kathir rolled his eyes in exasperation. "Come on! That's just bloody politics talking! Your people are freezing to death out here!" Kathir paused and took a deep breath. "You have to ask yourself which is more important—politics or your people."

Skemtun flinched, and Kathir could tell that his words had hit a nerve. Skemtun paused and looked up at the mountain. Grey clouds swirled overhead. It was the middle of the afternoon, but dark and gloomy in the woods. The weather would be freezing tonight.

"All right," he said finally. "Ye're right. The lives of my people are what's important. I don't know how much good it will do, but I'll talk to Utan. But I can't be seen going inside the mountain by myself! That will cause too much suspicion. Listen, why don't *you* talk to him—as my representative? Go speak to Utan for me."

"What do you want me to say to him?" Kathir asked.

Skemtun rapped his finger on his chin. "Tell Utan that my people are prepared to do their share of the work. We'll be farmers, or laborers, or miners—whatever he wants us to do, we'll do it. We'll carve our own sleepin' caves inside the mountain, and we'll do any work that we need to. In return, we get our share of the food, as well as shelter inside the mountain until our sleepin' caves are finished."

"There'll be other questions," Kathir said. "Questions about leadership and the way decisions are made."

Skemtun spread his hands. "Let's take this one step at a time. We can negotiate the rest of it as we go along. Now go. But go quietly, and try not to call too much attention to yourself!"

Kathir nodded. "Don't worry. I'm very good at moving through forests without being noticed." Kathir slipped back through the camp and into a layer of trees. He made his way back toward the front gates, but not directly. He paused for a moment when he spotted a member of Bolrakei's personal entourage walking nearby. He recognized him as one of Bolrakei's private guards, but he was wearing a hooded cloak and scruffier clothing than usual, as if he were trying to blend in with the crowds.

The dwarf moved furtively around the camp and stopped every now and then and to look back and see if he was being followed. Kathir jogged behind him and ducked behind a tree so that he could continue to watch the dwarf. He would walk a few steps through the camp, pause at a tent or a tree, look back, and then go forward rapidly again. He moved cautiously, studying his surroundings very carefully.

Kathir narrowed his eyes. No question about it, he definitely looked suspicious. He decided to temporarily abandon his mission and follow the guard instead.

Kathir was tall enough that he stood out, so he had to move carefully to conceal himself. He stayed just outside the camp perimeter, watching from the tree line. A few times, Kathir was afraid that the dwarf would spot him, but he never did.

Kathir followed the hooded dwarf to a secluded area in the northern part of the camp. Ten dwarves were gathered around a fire, cooking their meat rations over the flame. They looked up and waved. "Gorri! Come over and join us. Any fresh news?"

Gorri went to the fire and rubbed his hands before sitting down near the group.

"There's not much to tell," Gorri said. "It's the same story as always."

"Utan still won't budge?" the first dwarf asked him. "He won't let us inside his mountain?"

Gorri shook his head. "Nay, and what's more, Bolrakei had to stop Utan from sending soldiers to attack our camp. She saved us again."

A gasp went around the circle. "Utan wouldn't dare attack us!"

"Of course he would," Gorri snorted. "They had an army out to meet us when we arrived, didn't they? Not exactly welcoming, was it? Instead of being thankful that we're here, the Vardmiters are trying to fight us. The only reason Utan hasn't attacked us already is because he's scared of Bolrakei."

"That sounds right. She's got powerful connections, thank goodness," said one of the others. There was nodding all around.

"Right now, Utan's just biding his time. He's waiting for the dragon riders to leave." Gorri went on. "Then he'll try and starve us. But don't ye worry— Bolrakei is a true leader. She'll get you bread, and more food is coming."

"What about Skemtun?" the dwarf closest to the fire asked. "Hasn't he tried to help?"

"Skemtun's useless—as always!" Gorri said with contempt in his voice. "He's too scared to do anything. During the meetings, he just sits there like a mute, saying nothing while Bolrakei negotiates for all of us. Think about it—how much has he *really* done? He spends most of his time gossiping and hiding behind that human bodyguard of his."

Kathir listened to the exchange with growing indignation. Gorri made some more disparaging comments about Skemtun and then excused himself, waving goodbye. He walked through the forest until he arrived at another group of dwarves on the out-skirts of the camp.

Kathir followed the dwarf to another camp-fire, where he repeated the same story. Sometimes, Gorri handed over small coin pouches or made promises about the delivery of bread or meat. How-ever, it wasn't until Gorri turned around and headed up toward the entrance to the mountain that Kathir really saw the true extent of Bolrakei's treachery.

There were two Vardmiter guards posted at the entrance, but they didn't stop Gorri. Instead, they smiled and shook his hand as if they were old friends. Kathir couldn't get close enough to hear the details of what they said, but he could see that their conversation was friendly.

Gorri passed two money pouches to the guards and slipped inside the mountain. He came back a few minutes later with a huge basket filled with bread and sausages. Gorri covered the basket with a blanket and winked at the guards. Then he made his way back to Bolrakei's campsite with a smug look on his face.

Kathir was shocked. Was all that food for Bol-rakei? Or was it for bribes? Bolrakei was buying sup-port with food and money while defaming Utan and Skemtun. The pieces fit together so neatly. She was trying to stir up animosity against the Vardmiters while manipulating the clans into supporting her.

Kathir turned and ran towards the main camp. He needed to warn Skemtun right away.

He paused and saw that wagons were approaching in the distance. They were painted brilliant white and had an image of a crystal dome on the side. Kathir knew immediately who was inside them. Skemtun spotted him and waved him over.

"There ye are!" Skemtun said. He lowered his voice. "Did ye manage to set up a meetin' with Utan?"

Kathir shook his head. "No, not yet—there's something else I have to tell you; we need to talk in private."

"It'll have to wait," Skemtun said, gesturing over to the wagons. "Look who's coming. What is the High Council of Miklagard doing here?"

"I don't know," Kathir admitted. "Whatever it is, it must be important. Miklagard doesn't send the High Council outside the crystal shield without good reason." Inside, he felt his stomach twisting with worry. *Why had the High Council come here? What did they want?*

A crowd gathered along the dirt road as the carriages arrived.

Kathir leaned close to Skemtun and whispered in his ear. "I *really* need to talk to you about Bolrakei."

Skemtun nodded but gestured at the crowd. "Not yet. Later... in private. There are too many people here who might overhear us."

The carriages grew closer. Sela and Elias flew down to meet them. Bolrakei seemed to magically appear, wearing a bright purple gown and a silver cape. She had apparently decided to make an impression based on the sheer gaudiness of her clothing. She pushed her way to the front of the crowd with her attendants.

The carriages drew to a halt outside the main gates.

The first man who stepped out was white-haired and wore dark, fur-lined robes. Two younger mage-borns, a man and a woman, helped him step out of the carriage. The two attendants quietly guided the old man to the front gates.

"We've stopped?" the white-haired man asked with a confused look on his face. "Where am I again?"

"Councilor Komu, we've arrived at our destination. This is Highport. We're here to talk to the dwarves, remember?" the woman said.

"Yes, yes... of course," the old man said. "I remember. You don't need to repeat things to me all the time, you know."

Kathir leaned over to Skemtun. "That's Komu. He's the eldest of the High Council. He's still an influential member of the council, but he's grown rather befuddled with age. He's a decent man, from what I've gathered. Just don't expect him to remember who you are from one meeting to the next. His condition has worsened in recent years."

"And the other two with him?" Skemtun asked.

"They're his personal assistants. They're mage-borns too. The woman is named Issani, and the man is called Blias. I don't know either of them very well," Kathir admitted. "I work for the High Council, but they don't introduce me to their inner circle." There was an edge of bitterness in his voice that he couldn't entirely conceal. The Miklagard High Council was happy to use his services, but they never accepted him as an equal. Despite his hard work, Kathir was never appreciated; the slave marks on his cheeks made him inferior in their eyes.

Kathir returned his attention to the carriages, watching as a second carriage stopped behind the first. Two figures descended from it.

A middle-aged man stepped down into the dirt. He had a round belly and a short dark beard. He was dressed similarly to Komu, but his robes were heavier and had gold embroidery on the collar.

"That's Councilor Delthen," Kathir said. "He seems nice enough on the surface, but don't let his pleasant demeanor fool you. It's an act. When pushed, he can be downright nasty. He's got a rotten temper when crossed."

Kathir watched another figure jump down from the carriage. The man was muscular, with a full head of jet-black hair, just turning silver at the temples. Unlike the other two men, he was dressed in a practical tunic and riding leathers, but the shine of silver jewelry made it clear that he had wealth.

"That third man looks familiar," Skemtun said. "Do you know him?"

Kathir nodded. "That's Druknor Theoric. If he's come here, then he must have a good reason, and it probably has to do with money. He normally doesn't travel far from his fortress. He prefers to just sit like a spider at the center of his web. He's a slaver and smuggler."

Skemtun's jaw dropped. "He's a *slaver?* Then what's he doing with Miklagard's High Council?"

Kathir shook his head. "Druknor is one of those talented politicians who knows how to keep his hands clean while still committing crimes. He hides his criminal activities behind various legitimate businesses. I don't know why he's here, but it's bad news. He's a dangerous man."

Skemtun nodded, and they headed forward to join the small knot of people going to greet the High Council. The dragon riders moved forward first.

"Welcome, Councilors," said Sela, with a note of caution in her voice. "What a surprise to see you here."

Komu stared at Sela with a blank expression. Then one of his assistants leaned over and whispered in his ear. "Sela? Ah, yes! I remember you! Did I ever tell you about that time I fought in the war?"

"Please... allow me, Komu." Councilor Delthen swept forward with an elegant bow. He took Sela's hand and kissed it, as if he were greeting a princess. "Hello, Mistress Sela! It's pleasing to see our esteemed allies, the dragon riders, here to help these poor dwarves. Miklagard has also heard of their plight and wishes to help."

Sela's eyebrows rose. "I see," she replied gravely, jerking her hand away. "We weren't expecting Miklagard to send representatives here, much less actual members of the High Council." Sela shot a scathing look in Druknor Theoric's direction. "Why is he here?"

Druknor's expression darkened.

Councilor Delthen swept a hand in Druknor's direction. "Druknor is our valuable ally, and he is here to observe the proceedings and promote trade in this region. I expect that he will be treated with all due courtesy."

"Oh, I'll give him every courtesy he's due," Sela replied coldly.

"Lady Sela," Druknor said with a frozen smile. "I hope I haven't offended you in some way?"

Sela stared at him with narrowed eyes. She knew the truth about Druknor, but she couldn't prove anything against him, so she was forced to be diplomatic.

"Druknor has been able to provide us with invaluable information on this region," Councilor Delthen continued. "He has also helped us identify potential mageborn students for our training school. His network of contacts has been quite helpful."

Druknor gave her a sly smile. "I'm here to help. I have financial resources, and my fortress isn't far from here. Besides, I'm a businessman, and this situation is rich with business opportunities. Wouldn't you agree?"

"This isn't a peddler's market!" said Sela. "There's a war going on. The greenskins have taken Mount Velik, and people are *dying*. Truly, this is not the time or place to discuss business affairs."

Druknor's smile became a grimace. "My lady,

please...we should be friends. Perhaps when this is all over, you will come to Sut-Burr. I would love to welcome you there as an honored guest."

"I would rather eat dirt than—" Sela started.

Councilor Delthen interrupted before Sela could finish. "Ah! Enough of this chitchat! We are all tired from our long travels and wish to rest. Perhaps it is best if we finish this conversation inside?"

Councilor Komu circled the group, looking a bit confused. "Now, let's all get inside, shall we? It's cold out here. Where can I get some tea?"

"Utan isn't letting anyone in," Skemtun said.

"He isn't letting any of *your* clan in, I'd imagine," Councilor Delthen replied. "But we are not dwarves. We are the High Council of Miklagard, and we've never been denied entry into any allied stronghold." Then Delthen smiled, but the smile did not reach his eyes. "However, friend, if you do not object, could I borrow your bodyguard for a moment, so we can speak in private?"

Kathir stiffened but said nothing.

"Yes, yes, of course," Skemtun replied, looking slightly surprised. "He's your man after all, isn't he?"

Councilor Delthen ignored the question and replied, "Thank you. I appreciate it." With a small frown, he fixed his eyes on Kathir and waited for him to follow him.

Kathir nodded and led the delegation up to the mountain's entrance. Delthen walked beside him and spoke quietly.

"I want your report," Delthen murmured.

"I've protected Skemtun, as you ordered," said Kathir. "There've been several attempts on his life."

"What happened during the siege? Nobody was expecting Mount Velik to fall so quickly—if at all."

"I tried to persuade them to strengthen their defenses, but it was too late by the time I arrived. The dwarves were unprepared, and the orcs greatly outnumbered them. King Nar was more clever than anyone anticipated. The next thing I knew, we were fighting for our lives. I did what I could to evacuate the mountain and to escort the survivors safely here."

"So, the city is a complete loss?" Delthen asked.

"Yes," Kathir responded, sighing. "Mount Velik is gone."

"This whole thing is a *disaster*," Delthen hissed. "How can we prevent the orcs from invading the rest of the continent? The greenskins are spreading like the plague, and you've done almost nothing to stop it."

"I did the best I could, under the circumstances," Kathir replied.

The councilor stared him in the eye. "You may have saved a few dwarves, but that wasn't your primary mission. We need to salvage this situation any way we can. The dwarf clans must reunite and take back Mount Velik; it's the only solution. The Vardmiters have greater numbers; they might be strong enough to raise an army by themselves."

"The clans aren't ready for reunification. There's too much animosity between them," Kathir said.

"I don't care about their petty squabbles! There's more at stake here. The clans *must* agree to a treaty. If that means getting rid of Utan and Skemtun to make it happen, so be it! We *cannot* allow the orcs to spread any further. The dwarves must reclaim Mount Velik before next winter. Otherwise, the entire eastern territory will be at risk of conquest by the greenskins!"

Kathir didn't respond. He didn't see any hope of success in Delthen's plan. Even if all the clans were to join together, they still couldn't defeat the orcs in open combat. "I thought you wanted Skemtun to be the leader of the clans."

"The situation has changed," Delthen said. "When the dwarves controlled Mount Velik, Skemtun was the best choice for the job. But if he can't support our needs now, then the High Council must shift their support to a more… suitable leader."

"You want me to start guarding *Bolrakei* instead of Skemtun?" Kathir asked incredulously.

"No," Councilor Delthen replied. "She's not an appropriate choice, either." Delthen paused and Kathir could tell he was choosing his words carefully. "Let's just say that she's not as open to *persuasion* as we'd like. You shall continue to guard Skemtun until we deem that it is more advantageous for you *not* to guard him. At some point, we'll find someone to replace him. Do you understand?"

Kathir understood. At some point, the High Council expected him to step aside and actually let Skemtun *die,* so that he could be replaced with a leader more to *their* liking.

Delthen reached into his robes and drew out a large pouch that clinked with coins inside. "Here's your payment." Delthen handed him the bag, and Kathir shoved it into his pocket. For the first time ever, taking the money made him feel dirty and deceitful.

Delthen cleared his throat and spoke loud enough for everyone to hear. "Thank you, Kathir. I believe we can find our way beyond this point." He gave Kathir a wave of dismissal and turned his back.

Druknor walked past him without so much as a passing glance, as did Komu's aides, but the old man himself paused. Slowly, with the discomfort of age, Komu bent to pick up a coin that had fallen and placed it in Kathir's palm. "You dropped something, young man."

"Thank you," Kathir replied, somewhat surprised.

"Oh, think nothing of it," said the ancient mage. His eyes were cloudy with cataracts, and Kathir wondered how much he could actually see. "So... you spoke to Delthen?"

Kathir struggled to understand why Komu was even talking to him. "Actually, our chat was quite brief."

"I see." For a second, Komu's bewildered look dissolved and his gaze became sharp and focused. "Listen to me, boy. Delthen forgets that he doesn't speak for the whole council." Komu patted him on the wrist. "Consider this payment for saving the dwarves. You did a good job."

"Thank you," Kathir said, looking at him strangely.

"You know," Komu said. "Things aren't always what they seem. This isn't where it ends. The future is falling into place."

"What do you mean by that?" asked Kathir, taken aback.

Komu didn't answer. His two aides rushed back and grabbed him gently by his arms, guiding him away. Komu started babbling about the weather again, and his aides nodded vaguely.

Kathir just stood there, unsure of what all of it meant.

5. PARTHOS

Tallin and the elves flew over the Death Sands. They flew without stopping until finally, at sunset on the second day, they saw the city of Parthos ahead in the distance. The landscape had changed in the short time that they were away.

"The desert's in bloom," Tallin murmured. A sea of flowers reflected the brilliant sunlight from the sky. Bright purple cactus blossoms struck a brilliant contrast to the ruddy color of the sand. The scenery was magnificent, but the elves said nothing. They stared ahead and did not speak to anyone.

Fëanor and Amandila flew near their queen but remained respectfully behind her.

"It's odd to see Fëanor defer so much to his queen," Tallin said.

"Elves don't have a high opinion of mortals, but their own queen is another story," said Mugla, sitting behind her nephew.

"And her dragon is *huge*. Atejul is the largest emerald dragon that I've ever seen. He's almost as large as Nydeired."

"*Atejul flies very fast*," Duskeye blurted out proudly. "*Just look at that wingspan of his!*"

Dragons didn't usually discuss their offspring, but it was clear that Duskeye was proud of having fathered such a large and powerful son.

"I wonder why they don't just fly on ahead," Mugla said. "With Duskeye carrying both of us, their dragons could outdistance us easily."

"I was wondering that myself. We've nearly reached Parthos," Tallin said.

The desert city sparkled like a bright green jewel on the horizon. Its hanging gardens were an engineering marvel, maintained by underground wells. The plants weren't just decorative; most of them were also edible.

The city supported a population that was much larger than one might expect, given its location in the harsh desert. "The elves will probably stop in Parthos before they return to Brighthollow."

Through their telepathic connection, Tallin could sense that Duskeye was eager to see his current mate, Shesha, and her clutch of eggs.

"Shesha is waiting for us," Duskeye added. *"I told her to seek refuge in Parthos so that her eggs would be safe. She resisted the idea at first but eventually agreed. I gave her one of my saddlebags to carry the eggs."*

When they initially left for Balbor, the wild dragon Shesha had been guarding her eggs in the forest. The whole reason for their trip to Balbor had been to protect her eggs from the Balborite High Priest, who desired to steal them. Now that the High Priest was dead, Shesha's eggs were safe. When these eggs finally hatched, the dragon race could finally begin its slow recovery.

The city of Parthos grew larger as they approached. Finally, the four dragons crossed into the city perimeter and flew down to land on the castle ramparts. They were greeted with waves and cheers by the Parthinian guards. Tallin slid down from Duskeye's back and then helped Mugla climb from the saddle.

Xiiltharra, Fëanor, and Amandila also dismounted.

The teenage twins, Galti and Holf Thallan, ran up to greet them. Galti and Holf were the youngest of the dragon riders, and they had almost completed their apprentice training. They usually stayed behind to help guard the city when the other dragon riders were away.

Shesha, who before hated cities and feared humans, was lying calmly near Orshek and Karela, the two black dragons that were joined to Galti and Holf.

Shesha's tail was curled protectively around her eggs. Duskeye crawled over to Shesha, purring softly. He moved cautiously, even though Shesha was his mate, since nesting females were often unpredictable. Duskeye touched his snout against hers, and she snapped at him playfully. Duskeye hopped back, but he was happy.

Galti and Holf greeted Tallin with a warm handshake.

"How were things while we were away?" asked Tallin.

"Exciting!" Galti said. "We caught a Balborite assassin in the desert a week ago. I spotted him when we were on patrol. We alerted the guards and sealed all the city entrances. We waited a few days and then decided to go out and find him ourselves. Shesha came along too—*she's* the one that found him the second time."

Tallin's eyebrows shot up. "That was a hazardous thing to do."

"*The painted human was coming here to steal my eggs!*" Shesha said in the dragon-tongue. "*I knew it was true, so I offered to help. We caught him in the canyon nearby. The young fleshlings fought the painted human and killed him.*"

Tallin looked at Galti and Holf with stunned approval. "You managed to kill a Balborite assassin by yourselves? I'm impressed."

"Orshek and Karela did most of the work," Galti said. "They trapped him inside a fire circle. He... kind of got burnt to a crisp."

The two black dragons raised their heads and yawned.

"We persuaded Shesha that the palace rooftop was the best place for her and her eggs," Holf added. "It's so warm up here. And look how happy she is!"

Shesha sent a small flame bursting from her nose. "*Humph! I was not persuaded by these little fleshlings. I made the decision myself to stay up here, because it's nice and hot on the roof... plus there are always chickens to eat.*" She jerked her chin toward the palace chickens, pecking away at their feed nearby.

Fëanor edged toward Shesha to catch a glimpse at her eggs, but Shesha growled and snapped at him.

"Get back, elf! I don't trust your kind."

Fëanor looked at his queen, who shook her head slightly.

Tallin's eyes narrowed. It was an odd exchange. After everything that had happened, maybe the elves were still hoping they could take some of the eggs back to Brighthollow.

Xiiltharra seemed to know what he was thinking, because she said, "There's no need to worry about the eggs now. The Balborites have been dealt with, so there's no danger to the nest."

"So, you're going to allow Shesha to keep her eggs?" Tallin asked. "How thoughtful of you."

If Xiiltharra heard the sarcasm in his voice, she decided to ignore it. "Yes, of course. I'm pleased that we were able to work together to protect this nest."

Galti decided that it was time to interrupt so that he could play host. "Is everyone ready to eat? We sent a message to the kitchens for food when we saw you coming. They've set up a nice buffet downstairs."

"Great!" said Mugla. "I'm starvin'!"

After such a long journey, they were all famished and exhausted. "Do you have meat for our dragons?" asked Fëanor.

"The cook slaughtered a few camels for them," said Holf. "They're dressing the beasts now. I'll have the meat brought up."

Tallin looked at the elves. "You are all welcome to dine with us, of course." He tried to be friendly, but he couldn't keep the edge out of his voice.

"Thank you, *halfling*," Xiiltharra said with a sharp smile. "We accept."

The elves seemed happy enough to follow them into the dining hall. Their sharp eyes scanned everything around them. Galti and Holf excused themselves to notify the kitchens that their guests were ready to eat.

As they walked through the palace, the servants greeted Tallin but gasped in surprise when they saw the elves walking behind him. A few maids swooned, almost falling over, as the elves passed. The elves weren't even *trying* to enchant anyone, but it was happening anyway. Their very presence was disruptive.

When they reached the hall, Xiiltharra headed to the front and took the seat at the head of the table. The elves sat next to their queen, talking in low voices.

Tallin and Mugla sat several seats down from them. Servants brought the food out in two or three courses, and each course included several dishes.

Mugla reached out and grabbed a chicken leg and began to eat it with relish. "The elves are so aloof, even after everythin' that's happened," she whispered between bites.

"It's not surprising to me," replied Tallin quietly. "I wonder how they really view us. Long after we're gone, they'll still be alive. You heard Xiiltharra on the island—a thousand years is *nothing* to her. I can't imagine what life is like from their perspective."

The elves ate little, whispering to each other between bites. Galti and Holf came back a while later to see if they needed anything else.

Their entrance into the room broke the tension, and Tallin spoke. "Do you have news from Sela? I was tempted to contact her myself along the way, but I wanted to save my strength just in case we ran into trouble again."

Galti nodded. "Sela's been contacting me every few days." He was a naturally-gifted telepath. "Once Mount Velik fell, she and Elias traveled to Highport with the survivors. Both of them are there now. They're trying to negotiate a treaty between the clans."

"Mount Velik has fallen to the orcs?" Mugla gasped. "I can't believe it! We were gone less than a few weeks!"

"I'm sorry I didn't mention it sooner—I thought you knew," Galti said apologetically. "Most of the women and children escaped, but the dwarf army was destroyed. The refugees traveled to Highport to request sanctuary, but the Vardmiters won't let them inside their mountain."

Mugla sighed. "What a disaster. This news is unfortunate. All the clans are still my bloodkin. They should try to cooperate with one another."

For a moment, Tallin did nothing but try to absorb the shocking news. Mount Velik had fallen? All the clans were in Highport?

So many things had happened while they were stuck on Balbor. Only the elves seemed unsurprised by the news.

Tallin turned on Xiiltharra. "Did you know about this?" He couldn't keep the bite out of his voice.

"Careful, halfling," Fëanor said, his voice low. "This is our queen. Show some respect."

Xiiltharra stretched in her chair like a cat. Then she smiled and held up one perfectly shaped hand. "I can speak for myself, Fëanor. The halfling's gruff manner does not bother me; I find it rather amusing, actually."

Xiiltharra paused to pluck a grape from a plate of fruit in front of her. "Although the animosity between the dwarf clans does not interest me, it *does* worry me that the orcs have conquered the dwarf stronghold." She popped the grape into her mouth and chewed slowly, then swallowed. "I am *somewhat* concerned about the situation at Mount Velik. The orcs are a plague, even to us, and my people do not wish to see the greenskins spread their vileness any further. I originally believed that the dwarves had the situation under control. The dwarves haven't fallen to the orcs in untold millennia, so we did not believe they would lose. By the time I learned of the clans' defeat, I was already on my way to Balbor. There was nothing we could do to help them at that point. The elves can't be everywhere at once, you know."

Tallin sighed. "I've only just arrived back home, and now I have to go to Highport. I have to help my people."

"I'm comin' with ye," Mugla said immediately.

Tallin rolled his eyes but didn't even try to argue with his aunt this time. He turned his attention back to the elves. He didn't want any of them inside the city, to be honest. "Will you all be leaving now?"

"Why the sudden hurry to push us out of your city, halfling?" snorted Fëanor. "Are you afraid that we might try to pinch your precious dragon's eggs after all?"

Tallin didn't respond, but his face must have betrayed his emotions because Xiiltharra chuckled.

"Don't worry, halfling. My people only wanted to safeguard the eggs from the Balborites. Now that the threat has been removed, it is in our best interest for Shesha's brood to grow up strong and healthy in the desert. This is their natural habitat, after all. So, I'll give you my vow—we won't attempt to take any of Shesha's eggs. However, if any of her offspring should happen to make their way to Brighthollow once they've hatched, then we will accept them into the land of faerie with open arms."

Tallin nodded. He felt better. "So tell me, how did Atejul manage to hatch in faerie? Is all the talk of Brighthollow being dangerous for hatchlings just a myth?"

The queen pursed her lips, as if considering whether or not to answer him. Then she shrugged. "No, it's not a myth. Dragons are creatures of the desert. They breed best in this climate, so this is also the best place for them to rear their young. The magic of Brighthollow affects dragons in a negative way. Female dragons refuse to nest in faerie, and they will not accept a mate there, either. We don't know why."

"Then how did you get Atejul to hatch? Did you use magic?"

"No, that would be impossible. Dragon's eggs are impervious to magic—even ours. When Nagendra fled the desert years ago, she came to us. Physically, she was in a terrible state, but she had already mated with Duskeye. She carried her eggs in her belly across the ocean mists into our hidden land. When she arrived, she was exhausted and badly injured. We nursed her back to health over several months. At the end of her recovery, she laid seven eggs. Although it is rare for dragon's eggs to hatch in Brighthollow, it is not impossible. So we kept the eggs safe and waited for them to hatch, but they did not. Elves offered to carry the eggs back to the desert for a few months to see if the heat would encourage the eggs to hatch, but Nagendra was too afraid. Nagendra was terrified of leaving Brighthollow— her family had been slaughtered by dragon hunters. And who could blame her, after everything she had suffered at mortal hands?"

Tallin's lips thinned, but he said nothing.

She continued, "In the end, only one hatchling emerged from his shell, and that was Atejul. The other eggs went sterile and died. Atejul was weak at first, but we fostered him to health. He eventually grew into the beautiful creature that he is today. We were joined as rider and dragon a while ago, and I must say, it's been a wonderful experience. I have a new perspective now. I want to see the dragons re-cover and flourish. Are you satisfied now, dwarf?" She flashed a dazzling smile.

Tallin smiled with what he hoped looked like genuine gratitude. "Yes, that's comforting news. And congratulations on your joining."

"Thank you. Now that we've settled our lit-tle problem with the Balborites, Atejul and I will return to Brighthollow. However, Amandila and Fëanor shall be traveling to Highport to assist you with *your* little *dwarf* problem."

"W-what?" sputtered Amandila. "But... my queen; I was looking forward to going home. Why must we accompany these dwarves? What are they to us?"

The queen looked at her with a hint of a smile. "I understand your desires, my dear, but circum-stances have changed. We cannot let the greenskins spread; if we do nothing, then they shall eventually become a nuisance, even for us. I want you both to help the dwarves."

"But my queen—" Amandila tried again, but Xiil-tharra cut her off.

The Queen's smile turned frosty. "Are you ques-tioning my orders?"

Amandila bowed her head. "No, your majesty. I apologize."

Xiiltharra gave a slight nod. "Very good. You and Fëanor should make your preparations right away. It's a long journey to Highport." The queen looked at Tallin. "Will you allow us to stock provisions for the trip?"

"Yes, of course," said Tallin. He didn't *like* the elves, but he certainly wasn't going to turn down their help. They couldn't hope to win this battle against the orcs unless they had a lot more people on their side. "I'll notify the stable hands. They'll restock your saddlebags."

They all rose up to prepare. Tallin hadn't expected to be undertaking such a long journey so soon after his last. He'd been hoping to spend some time relaxing, but he couldn't. There was another threat to be taken care of, another battle to fight. At that moment, Tallin felt very tired.

He trudged up to the ramparts with the intention of getting Duskeye ready to leave. Shesha was there with him.

"Where are you going now?" Shesha pouted. *"You've only just arrived."*

Tallin explained the situation at Highport and watched as Shesha grew agitated by the news. Duskeye didn't seem happy either.

"You're leaving so soon?" Shesha asked.

"We have to," Duskeye said. *"It will be a long journey, and I have to carry Tallin's aunt, too. It's tiring for me to carry extra passengers. I'm not as young as I once was."*

"I'm sorry, old friend," Tallin said with a sympathetic smile.

Shesha raised her head. *"I'll come with you, then. I can carry this... aunt."*

"You?" Tallin looked at her with mild shock.

"But what about your eggs?"

"My eggs are safe in Parthos," Shesha said. *"Orshek and Karela have shown me that they can keep my eggs safe—they are my cousins and my kin. Besides, it will be a while yet before they hatch. I won't let Duskeye go into this battle alone."*

Tallin could hear the strength of her determination. Orshek and Karela were still too young to fight in open battle. They were staying behind in the city, so her argument made sense. "Thank you. Having the assistance of another dragon would be helpful. All right, we'll be leaving at dawn. You'll need to be ready by then."

"I'll be ready."

It seemed that the elves were ready as well. As soon as Shesha finished speaking, they all appeared on the ramparts together. Amandila and Fëanor began to ready their dragons for the long journey by removing their saddles and greasing their backs with oil to reduce friction. Nagendra didn't seem any happier about going to Highport than her rider.

Blacktooth and Fëanor remained silent and brooding, mainly keeping to themselves.

Xiiltharra hopped onto Atejul's back. "It's time for me to bid you all farewell. Hopefully, I won't have to leave Brighthollow again for a long time. I would prefer to keep my visits to the mortal lands to a minimum. Away, Atejul!"

The magnificent emerald dragon took to the air and flew north.

"We're stuck with these two elves again, it

seems," said Tallin.

"They're rotten company, but we could use their powers," said Duskeye, *"There's not much sense arguing about it."*

Tallin knew that Duskeye was right. He just hoped that they would be able to get to Highport in time—before it was too late.

6. AMBUSH

B ack at the Highport Mountains, the situation between the clans was getting worse by the day. Snow had started falling incessantly, blanketing the mountainside with freezing white powder. For the dwarves stuck outside, their living conditions became unbearable. The political stalemate continued, with neither side willing to compromise.

Skemtun tried to get things moving by sending Kathir to speak to Utan in secret. Kathir tried to catch Utan on several occasions, but he didn't dare approach the gate when there was no way to be sure which of the guards Bolrakei had bribed.

The only time Kathir actually found Utan outside, Druknor prevented him from talking to him. Druknor wagged a finger at Kathir as if he were chastising a naughty child. "Are you sneaking over there to speak to Utan?"

"No..." Kathir lied.

"Good, I'm glad. We don't want you to interfere in this little political situation, Kathir. That's not what Miklagard pays you for. The High Council hired you for a very specific need."

"I know, I know. I'm just a bodyguard," Kathir finished for him.

"Exactly. I'm glad we understand each other." There was nothing friendly about Druknor's smile. "Now, don't interfere with our plans. Remember who's paying you. Remember why you're here."

Kathir shot him a scowl. "The High Council pays me, not *you*. I know you're chummy with Delthen and the rest of the council, but you don't have the right to give me orders. So tell me...why are *you* here?" Kathir itched to reach for his sword, but that would mean a public fight with Druknor, who was a very powerful man. No matter how badly he wanted to, Kathir couldn't risk actually fighting him, even though he wanted to punch him in the nose. "Don't tell me that you're simply here as Delthen's friend. What does a *slaver* care about what's happening with the dwarf clans?"

Druknor put a hand to his chest, as if deeply offended. "A slaver? Why would you call me that? That's just a vicious rumor, you know. Is it so hard to believe that I would want this situation resolved quickly?"

Kathir's eyes narrowed. "You could have let the High Council deal with this without involving yourself. Why are you really here?"

"Orcs spreading farther north would be bad for Miklagard, but it would be even *worse* for me. *My* little fortress isn't protected by a magical dome. Sut-Burr doesn't have much of a defense against an army of greenskins, so I'm definitely invested in the outcome of this little skirmish. And of course, there are certain... opportunities when such conflicts arise."

"Of course," Kathir snorted. "You saw another opportunity to make a profit—off someone else's misery."

Druknor smiled thinly. "I'm a businessman, not a charity. I see opportunities in many things."

"You're a war profiteer," Kathir retorted. Wars meant captives, refugees, and stranded civilians. For a man like Druknor, it would be a perfect hunting ground to collect more helpless slaves to smuggle and sell like cattle.

Druknor's eyes hardened, but he didn't stop smiling. He stepped forward so that his face almost touched Kathir's. "Those are some tough words, mercenary. What are you going to do about it?"

Kathir clenched his teeth and backed away. He knew it would be foolish to start a fight with Druknor out in the open. He spun on his heel and walked back to the camp, inhaling deeply to calm his pounding nerves.

As he walked through the dwarf camp, the stares were no longer as friendly as they had been while they were on the march. Days ago, the dwarves had considered him a protector and a friend, but now many looked at him with open hostility. It seemed that Bolrakei's negative propaganda was working. People were easily swayed when they were hungry and desperate.

Kathir slipped quietly through the camp, making his way back towards Skemtun's tent, which was just outside the treeline. In the darkness, he saw two dwarves creeping in the same direction.

Both were dressed plainly in simple brown tunics and cloaks. But Kathir also noticed the glint of chainmail under their simple clothing, and each of them carried a dagger in his hand.

"Can I help you?" Kathir said loudly, his hand moving to the hilt of his sword.

The two dwarves jerked back and hissed at Kathir. "It's that bodyguard! Get 'im!" one shouted.

The other dwarf spun and swung his knife at Kathir. Kathir jumped back and slid his sword out of its scabbard. The dwarf swung again, and Kathir managed to block the blow. As he defended himself, he noticed that the other dwarf running toward Skemtun's tent.

"Skemtun," Kathir yelled. "Wake up! They're trying to kill you!"

He parried the next swing and then smashed his head into his attacker's face. The head-butt was risky, but Kathir had size and momentum on his side. He succeeded in knocking his opponent back, sending him stumbling to the ground. Kathir drove his sword into the dwarf's neck to finish him off.

The other dwarf jumped inside Skemtun's tent, his weapon already raised. In his desperation, Kathir grabbed his dagger and threw it. It tumbled end over end before embedding itself in the second attacker's back. The dwarf shrieked, falling back just as Skemtun himself came out, holding his axe and ready for a fight. The attacker fell down on his side awkwardly, and Skemtun jumped on top of him, finishing him off.

"What in *Baghra's name* is going on here?" Skemtun shouted as he rose up.

"I watched these two heading towards your tent," Kathir said. "When I questioned them, they attacked me. They wanted to kill you."

"To kill *me*?" Skemtun asked in disbelief. "Who would attempt somethin' like this now?"

"Who do you think? Do I have to say her name?" Kathir asked.

Skemtun shook his head. "No, I don't believe it. Bolrakei wouldn't dare."

"Open your eyes, man! She *wants* a war! Your death would give her exactly that—she'd blame everything on Utan. Many of these dwarves believe everything she says."

"Aye," Skemtun conceded as he looked down at the two dead dwarves. "But there's no chance provin' any of that with these two dead. We can't question 'em now."

"Sorry," said Kathir. He did have a point.

Skemtun scanned the camp. It was already dark, and his tent was surrounded on all sides by trees, so no one seemed to have noticed the scuffle. "We can't risk anyone findin' out about this. We'd better hide the bodies. It's better if this attack didn't happen."

Kathir nodded, went inside the tent, and returned with a shovel. "It's a grisly business, but it needs to be done."

They wrapped the bodies in sackcloth and dragged them far away from the camp. They dug a hole without speaking. When the hole was deep enough, they slid the bodies into the grave, covering it with gravel and leaves.

After they finished, Kathir explained what he saw happening throughout the camp, as well as Bolrakei's attempt to spread false rumors to increase tensions between the clans. He was vague about the details. *No reason to scare Skemtun any more than necessary*, he told himself.

Skemtun accepted the news almost as if he had been expecting it. He seemed saddened more than shocked by it.

They both ambled back into camp, picking their way over the rocky slopes as they went.

"Did ye talk to Utan yet?" Skemtun asked.

Kathir shook his head. "No, not yet, sorry. I've *tried* several times, but there's always someone around, and I can't trust any of the guards. I want to be discreet. He's a difficult person to get ahold of. "

"I know," Skemtun said quietly. "I'm not good at any of this—ye know—this *political* stuff. I'm just an old miner. I know how to dig caves and find ore. *That's* what I'm good at. Bolrakei's usin' her money to influence everyone around her. I don't have any connections; I don't have any money, so how can I compete with her?"

"Money's not the most important thing in the world. Don't despair. Not yet. Things are going to work out." Kathir tried to sound convincing.

"What would ye do if ye were in my shoes?" asked Skemtun.

Kathir fell silent for a few moments. "I think we

should focus on the High Council. You need to find out what they *really* want. If you can convince the High Council to support you, the rest of the clans might come around. Once the clans unite together in peace, everything will be fine, and Bolrakei's opinion won't matter as much."

Skemtun's shoulders slumped. "I don't have anythin' to offer the High Council. I'm not wealthy or important. And I won't put any more of my people in danger. If they want to kill me, there's really nothin' I can do."

Kathir swallowed nervously. He was a mercenary and a warrior—he would stay by Skemtun's side and protect him—but he couldn't watch him *all* the time. How long could he keep him safe?

The two of them drifted back to camp and watched as the supper food lines started to form.

Sela and Elias were watching over everything, trying to keep order. Everyone was cold and restless, and the atmosphere was negative. It was strange to think that two of the most powerful mageborns on the continent were now charged with supervising the distribution of bread.

Suddenly, an idea popped into Kathir's head. "Skemtun, could you call a meeting where *all* the important people are present? You, Utan, Bolrakei, the High Council, and the dragon riders? Everyone? And could you make it open to the public, so anyone else could be there and witness it?"

"I guess I could," Skemtun said, scratching his chin. "But what good would it do? Bolrakei shouts everyone down. If the High Council is as corrupt as ye say, they won't help us, either. Wouldn't such a meeting be a complete waste of time, just like the others?"

"Not this time. I'm going to speak up," Kathir said, "and tell them the truth. We just have to make sure that enough people are around to hear it."

Skemtun called the meeting the next day. Everyone came together inside Highport's still-unfinished great hall. The dragon riders, the High Council, and representative members of the dwarf clans were all in attendance. Bolrakei came with her entire entourage.

Though the hall was unfinished, it was already impressive and spacious enough for a large crowd. The ceiling was filled with hanging stalactites, and the Vardmiters had carved niches into the rock to hold candles. The room shone with their soft glow.

Skillfully carved tiles filled every inch of the floor space. Stone chairs sat around the edges of a large meeting table. Everyone came in and took their seats.

Kathir stood near the doorway, watching everyone as they entered. The dwarf leaders were each accompanied by a group of supporters. Kathir couldn't help but notice that the little group that came with Skemtun was the smallest in the room.

Councilor Delthen stood next to Druknor, while

Issani and Blias occasionally whispered into Komu's ear.

Elias and Sela left their dragons outside, but even then, both of the dragon riders still had a commanding presence.

Kathir knew how powerful they were. In fact, he was relying on their support.

"Thank you all for attending," Kathir said, as he walked to the middle of the room.

Being the center of attention was uncomfortable for him. Standing there, Kathir couldn't help but think about what everyone looking at him was thinking—he was a former slave, a mercenary— someone with no real authority at all.

Bolrakei scoffed. "Ha! What's this? Your bodyguard's speaking for you now, Skemtun? Unbelievable! It's bad enough that I had to come here to listen to you. Having to listen to some human scum is simply unacceptable!"

"Kathir has important information that he needs to share, and I've agreed to let him speak," Skemtun said. "Ye should listen."

"Fah!" Bolrakei snorted. "What could this miserable human possibly have to say that would be of interest to any of us?"

"She makes a good point," Druknor said, his eyes narrowing dangerously. "This is a gathering of *leaders*. What is your bodyguard doing? I wasn't called here to listen to a commoner."

Kathir bit the inside of his cheek to prevent himself from responding angrily.

To his surprise, Elias spoke up to defend him. "Let the man speak," he said, "let him say what he needs to say."

"Thank you," Kathir said. "I believe I have a way to end the problems here."

"And how would you propose to do that, *mercenary?*" Councilor Delthen said with a sneer. "The rest of us have been trying our best to come up with a solution. How have you succeeded where we have not?"

Kathir took a deep breath. This was the moment where it could all go very wrong. "With all due respect, Councilor, I doubt that you have been trying very hard."

Delthen's brows knitted together, and his voice lowered to a menacing tone. "I don't understand what you mean. If you're looking to get some kind of political advantage out of this little show..."

"I'm not a politician, Councilor," Kathir pointed out. "So I care little for political intrigue. I'm a mercenary, and yes, I'm also a former slave—all of you know this. As for what I have to gain from this— well, I have few possessions in this world, so I have nothing to lose here."

Kathir looked up and addressed the circle of people before him. "The dwarf clans can't reach an agreement on a treaty for their people. That is because Bolrakei has been actively blocking all attempts to forge peace. She wishes to secure enough power to take over all the clans and crown herself queen."

Bolrakei stood up, fiery and furious. "Liar! Liar! You have no proof!"

Kathir continued talking. "It's obvious to everyone that you've been trying to maintain the tensions between the clans. I've seen the evidence with my own eyes. I've seen open bribery, lying, and the list goes on."

"I don't have to sit here and listen to this!" she said, standing up to go.

"If you leave, you won't hear the best part," Kathir said.

She turned back for a moment. "And what would that be?" Her lip curled up in a sneer.

Delthen cleared his throat and spoke. "Kathir, where are you going with this? Everyone is saddened by Mount Velik's fall to the orcs. It was unexpected. But we will work together to stop the spread of the greenskins—and that includes Lady Bolrakei. There's no reason to start a war of slander."

Kathir continued. "This isn't slander. It's more complicated than that. Bolrakei doesn't *want* a quick resolution. She wants to return to Mount Velik and retake the mountain. If that means sending thousands of dwarves to their deaths, so be it. And worst of all, the High Council is complicit in this scheme. Miklagard also wants the orcs to be routed from Mount Velik, even if it means thousands of lives are lost."

The room fell dead silent. Bolrakei's mouth twitched.

Skemtun stood up to speak. "I believe Kathir.

Why is the High Council here, anyway? Why are they involved in our clan struggles all of a sudden?"

Kathir fixed his eyes on Bolrakei. "Tell the truth, Lady Bolrakei. You are more interested in securing power than helping your own people. You want to go back to Mount Velik—and retake it by force, with the Vardmiters on the front lines, as your cannon fodder."

"Yes! Is that so wrong? We must win back our home!" Bolrakei yelled, pounding her meaty fist on the table. "I never *wanted* to come to this freezing wasteland, filled with snow and smelly pigs. Mount Velik belongs to *us,* not those filthy greenskins! We must retake what's ours! We could do it if we had enough men. The Vardmiters could join the fight and help us! They owe us that much!"

"It's a death wish," said Utan quietly. "I've seen the reports. Trust me, there's no way to retake Mount Velik with the numbers we have now—the orcs outnumber the dwarves ten to one. They even brought some of their females to Mount Velik, and they've already started multiplying like rats. Just accept it. Mount Velik is lost to the dwarves forever."

"Oh, you're wrong!" Bolrakei screamed wildly. "You're wrong, wrong, *wrong!* My clan can't live here—not in Highport! Look around you! Cramped, smelly quarters, dripping water, and no raw gemstones to mine! This whole place smells horrible because of all of those filthy pig farms of yours! I can't live like this! It's intolerable! We *must* go back to

Mount Velik."

Druknor was smirking. Of all the people inside the hall, he seemed to be enjoying the chaos the most.

"Does anyone have a solution?" Sela asked. "Even setting aside the enmity between the clans, the dwarves simply aren't strong enough to mount an offensive against the greenskins. Not now. Maybe not for several years. Even with the Vardmiters, the clans simply wouldn't have enough men. Plus, the orcs are vicious. Does anyone doubt that King Nar would sacrifice ten of his orcs to kill a single dwarf?"

Kathir looked directly at Sela, imploring her with his eyes. "But what about the dragon riders? You have powers! With help from the dragon riders, maybe we can drive the orcs out."

Skemtun tilted his head sideways and seemed to consider the idea. "Ye know, he's got a point. If we could drive them out, even temporarily, we *might* be able to retake the mountain. There's still plenty of open tunnels that lead inside. What if a small group could get inside and find a way to collapse the exits—seal them all properly—that would make Mount Velik completely useless to the orcs. Collapsing the tunnels would cause so much chaos and confusion that they would be forced to abandon it as a stronghold."

"Sealing the exits wouldn't be enough; we would have to do more," said Sela. "The orcs have their own mineworkers, and they can create crude tunnels, too. Sealing the exits would only cause momentary disruption."

"There are thousands of orcs occupying the mountain and thousands of tunnels inside," said Bolrakei. "It would be impossible to collapse them all. We must gather support and attack with a proper army."

"But what if we did *more* than that?" said Skemtun. "There's an underground stream that runs underneath the caverns. Mount Velik has been flooded before—on accident. What if we did it on *purpose* this time? Filled all the caves with water, I mean? The orcs would be trapped, and we could drown them all, like mice in a sewer! Could you spellcasters do that?"

A low murmur ran around the table.

Sela thought for a moment, then nodded. "The plan is risky, but it could work, if we had enough spellcasters. I received a message from Tallin a short while ago. He, his aunt Mugla, and two elf dragon riders are coming to Highport. That's four more mageborns. With their help, we *might* be able to do it."

"We should *all* go back to Mount Velik—including the High Council," said Kathir. "They wanted to be involved, so their spellcasters should assist, as well."

"You want us to go to Mount Velik and fight the orcs?" Councilor Delthen asked, his eyes popping. "That's a ridiculous—"

"Sounds like a wonderful idea!" Komu shouted suddenly. He spoke so abruptly that everyone jumped. "Ah, Mount Velik. I remember it well. The festivals, the beautiful caves, and that wonderful food!"

"Mount Velik is full of greenskins now, you doddering old fool!" Delthen snapped, abandoning his carefully maintained facade.

"Full of orcs? Well, that's a terrible shame," said Komu. "Well, that's all the more reason we should help, don't you think?"

Delthen fumed, but he held his tongue.

Kathir was grateful for Komu's outburst. Between the High Council and the dragon riders, they would have a large group of mageborns to help them with their plan.

"The plan is risky, and it could damage the tunnels inside," Bolrakei pouted. "I still think that we should send an army."

Skemtun rolled his eyes at her. "What army? Would ye send our women and children? Our injured soldiers? Wake up, Bolrakei! We don't have enough men!"

Delthen nodded, but he looked unhappy. "As much as I hate to admit it, he's right. The greenskins are too powerful—it would take years to build an army large enough to rout them out of the mountain by brute force. Trapping them all and then killing them inside seems like a more plausible solution. If the dragon riders agree to help, then I'll go, too."

Kathir's eyes sparked. "I'll join the fight, too. Where Skemtun goes, I also go."

Councilor Delthen's expression soured even further. Beside him, Komu smiled and nodded his approval.

Sela stood up and raised her hand. "It seems that we've decided on a course of action. Spellcasters will travel to Mount Velik and will try to neutralize the orc threat. I will contact Tallin and the elves and tell them to join us along the way. If all of us work together, we might be able to overcome the greenskins and take back the mountain."

There was unspoken hope in her voice. The meeting had gone better than anyone expected, but they all knew that the most difficult task was still ahead of them. The orcs had proven themselves resourceful and dangerous, and if they couldn't find a way to deal with them, then they would lose this battle.

Utan clapped his hands to get everyone's attention. "It seems that we have achieved more today than in all the time since the clans arrived. I'm disturbed by *some* of what I've heard here, especially about Mistress Bolrakei." He paused to shoot her a pointed look. "But if there's no actual proof of Bolrakei's treachery, then I'll leave it there."

Skemtun knew there would never be a better moment to ask for more. "What about the dwarves stuck out outside? Will ye allow all the dwarves to come inside now, before the weather turns even colder?"

Utan looked at Skemtun, and the weight of his gaze crushed him like a stone. But then, slowly and deliberately, Utan nodded. "All right... any dwarf who wishes to come into our mountain can carve a place for themselves, as long as they agree to come in peace. But they'll have to do their share of the work—*and* pull their own weight. My people aren't going to do all the hard labor anymore. Those days are over."

Skemtun opened his mouth to say thanks when he felt Kathir's hand on his elbow. "We should leave now," he said softly. "It's best to stop while you're ahead."

They all walked out of the mountain quietly. Although the air was cold, the sun was shining brightly.

"You did well in there," Skemtun said once they were outside.

"Thanks, but we can't get smug about this," Kathir said. "It's only a small victory. Bolrakei will continue to cause trouble, you can bet on that."

"Even if nothing else comes of this, ye still got all the clans inside the mountain. My clan finally has a warm place to sleep, thanks to ye. I won't forget that. And I won't forget the part ye played, either, mate." Skemtun clasped Kathir's forearm in a tight grip. "I'll go now. I have to start packing for the journey."

Kathir watched him go back to his tent. Skemtun held his head a little higher, and his shoulders didn't seem as slumped as before.

Kathir turned and saw Councilor Delthen approaching him out of the corner of his eye. "We won't forget what you did either, mercenary," he spat. "Your smart mouth has caused a lot of trouble here today."

"I helped the dwarves," Kathir replied. "That's what you hired me to do, isn't it?"

"Don't play stupid. That's *not* what we hired you to do—and you know it." Delthen said menacingly. "Better watch yourself. Right now, you're just one wrong move away from having a knife in your back."

"Don't threaten me," Kathir replied.

Delthen looked over his shoulder to make sure there was no one listening. "You must do what we discussed before. You must be ready to step aside when the right moment comes. Skemtun has become a liability for all of us."

"I don't understand. I thought you were getting what you wanted! After all of this, you still want Skemtun dead? But why?"

"Don't question me," Delthen hissed. "I don't pay you to think! I pay you to follow orders."

"You're making a mistake," Kathir insisted.

Delthen's gaze went icy. "You will obey me, or by the gods, I promise that you'll live to regret it."

7. OLD WOUNDS

They set out on their journey the next day. Komu and Delthen's wagons formed the heart of their small convoy and rattled along the roads from Highport with a kind of relentless certainty. Their magnificent black horses never seemed to tire, and the carriage wheels never seemed to get snarled in the mud the way ordinary carriages would have.

They were faster than any carriages that Kathir had ever seen, and he knew that Delthen and Komu were using their magic to speed things along.

Kathir chose to ride his horse rather than sit inside one of the carriages, as he enjoyed the independence that riding alone offered.

Sela and Elias rode their dragons in a circle high in the air. Each dragon was outfitted with armor, which they had carried with them just in case. Nydeired was as white as a pearl, while Brinsop gleamed a rusty red in the dazzling winter sun. The dragon riders monitored the road for threats while they flew overhead. They also hunted occasionally and brought food when their caravan stopped to make camp in the evenings.

Delthen and Druknor occupied the front carriage. To everyone's surprise, Bolrakei joined them.

She had insisted on being a part of the expedition to Mount Velik at the last minute. Bolrakei seemed to get along with them without any problem. Inside the carriage, the three of them colluded and conspired, whispering plans inside the privacy of the coach.

Just before nightfall, the dragon riders signaled that it was time to stop. Typically, they only did so when it was time for the group to rest in the evening, but it was early, and there was still plenty of light to travel by.

"Why are we stopping?" Skemtun called out. "Is there something wrong?"

Kathir shrugged as he reined in his horse. "I don't know. The dragon riders have stopped. Maybe something on the road ahead spooked them."

The carriages followed along the road until they reached a meadow filled with high grasses, where the dragon riders were waiting for them. The clearing was large enough that even the enormous Nydeired didn't look crowded. The massive white dragon stretched his wings in the evening light. Sela stood by Brinsop, looking up at the sky as though she were waiting for something.

"What are we stopping for?" Kathir asked as he rode up to her and dismounted.

"Tallin and the elves are close by," Sela said. "We'll rendezvous with them here." She closed her eyes and pinched the bridge of her nose as though she had a headache.

"Are you all right?" Kathir asked.

"I'll be fine in a minute," she replied. "Tallin sent me a brief telepathic message, and mind-contact is difficult for me. We'll camp here for the night and wait for Tallin and the elves, and then continue on in the morning."

Kathir nodded and helped set up the camp. By now, they had a pretty solid routine in place. The dragon riders collected wood and got the fire going. Komu's aides helped set up the tents while Kathir and Skemtun tended to the animals.

Delthen, Druknor, and Bolrakei usually did nothing to help—they just sat down in a circle and talked. This evening was no different. They watched and spoke together in hushed tones while everyone else toiled.

After the camp was set up, there wasn't much to do but wait, so Kathir decided to explore the surrounding forest.

"I'm going out," Kathir said. "I'll try to catch a rabbit or something." He set off into the forest on foot, glad at the chance to get away from Bolrakei's angry glares.

It wasn't long before he saw fresh tracks and animal droppings. Kathir followed them until he came to the edge of a swollen creek, where he found a small pig stuck belly deep in the mud. Kathir moved towards the terrified animal and brought it down with a well-placed arrow through the heart. He was dragging the animal back to camp when he saw the other dragon riders arrive.

He was surprised to see *four* dragons flying over

the treetops above him. Two were red, one was a deep onyx, and the last one was a bright sapphire-blue. None were as large as Nydeired, but they were still impressive.

Kathir sighed and looked away. It had been a long time since he'd seen so many dragons in one place. It brought back terrible memories—memories that he had tried to forget. Memories of those dark days, years ago, when Kathir was a dragon hunter. His past filled him with great shame.

Kathir had been lucky to walk away from that life, but seeing these dragons now, it was impossible for him not to think back to it. He deeply regretted those days, but he hadn't had much choice back then; as a former slave with obvious slaver's scars, he was forced to take whatever work he was offered.

Kathir picked his way through the forest and rode back to camp. By the time he got there, all the dragons were on the ground with their riders standing beside them. There was a shrunken old dwarf woman there, a much taller halfling with fiery red hair, and two pale-skinned elves, a male and a female. Sela and Elias were talking with the newcomers.

Kathir threw the boar carcass over his shoulder and made his way toward the fire. He patted Skemtun on the back, sat down, and started to dress the boar in silence. He wasn't important enough to warrant the newcomers' attention, and he wanted to spend as little time near Druknor and Bolrakei as possible.

"So, is anyone going to make introductions?" Druknor said. "I'm sure we're all eager to meet the new dragon riders."

Sela gave him a cold stare. Her dislike of Druknor was obvious.

Druknor smiled. He seemed to enjoy her discomfort. "Listen... we're all going to have to get along if we're going to make this happen."

Sela sighed and inclined her head in Tallin's direction. "This is my fellow dragon rider, Tallin Arai," she said. "This is Tallin's aunt, Mugla Hoorlick. She's the oldest and most respected dwarf mageborn, and perhaps the last surviving dwarf mage, unfortunately."

"Not respected by everyone..." Bolrakei muttered.

Sela ignored Bolrakei and continued. "The elves are Fëanor and Amandila. They've been sent to assist us. Tallin and the elves have just returned from their mission on Balbor."

Druknor raised his eyebrows. "You've just returned from *Balbor?* That's quite... surprising. How did you escape the island?"

"It wasn't easy," Tallin admitted. "We barely escaped with our lives. However, we were able to accomplish our mission. The High Priest has been replaced."

Druknor stared at him, puzzled. "A new High Priest? But who—"

Tallin gave a short shrug. "I'm sure you'll find out soon enough. Hopefully, this news will make your slaving business more difficult."

Druknor's mouth dropped open. "I don't—," he sputtered.

"Yeah, you do," Tallin replied coldly. He seemed glad to wipe the look of perpetual arrogance from Druknor's face.

Sela touched Tallin's shoulder and gave him a look of warning. "Not now, Tallin," she said softly. "It's not the right time."

Sela changed the subject and quickly introduced the others. Councilor Delthen gave a courtly bow. Komu talked nonsense about woodland fairies until Issani and Blias quieted him and guided him back to sit at the campfire.

"Lastly, we have Skemtun and Bolrakei. They are clan leaders of the dwarves," Sela said.

Tallin said nothing, but Mugla popped in front of her nephew and jabbed an angry finger at both of them. "So! Skemtun and Bolrakei! Ye helped push the Vardmiters out of Mount Velik, but now the shoe is on the other foot! How does it feel? Perhaps this hardship will teach ye a lesson in kindness and humility."

"What do the *Vardmiters* have to do with *any* of this?" Bolrakei shouted. "We didn't deserve to be attacked by orcs! Mount Velik is rightfully ours!"

Mugla continued, "Bah! Ye've had time to change, but ye're the same as before—greedy and selfish. The mountain gods have punished ye for your wicked nature and yer foolish pride. Ye got what ye deserved!"

Skemtun was calmer. "Please, Mugla. What's done is done. We're here to stop the orcs, not fight amongst ourselves."

"Humph!" said Mugla, scowling.

Sela interrupted their bickering and introduced the dragons last.

"This is Duskeye, Nagendra, and Blacktooth," Sela said as she pointed to each dragon. She looked over at Tallin. "And I assume that the other dragon is Shesha? I've heard so much about you."

Shesha reached out and touched Sela with her snout, sniffing her carefully. Sela touched her cheek gently and whispered a few words in dragon-tongue. Shesha responded with a razor-sharp smile.

"Yes, this is Shesha," Tallin said. "She is not bound to a rider, but she has agreed to help us."

Sela called out to Kathir. Smiling, she waved him over. "And this quiet one is named Kathir," she said. "He's Skemtun's bodyguard."

Kathir stood up and raised a hand in greeting.

Suddenly, Shesha made a deep sound in her throat. Tallin and Sela looked at each other with confused expressions on their faces.

The dragon growled. *"There is something familiar... about this human. Those scars... that smell..."* Then the dragon's eyes went wide with shock and rage. *"Murderer! Murderer! I'll kill you, fleshling!"*

Shesha roared, and that was all the warning Kathir got. His instincts came to life as he threw himself backward. A hot burst of flame struck the spot where he had been standing. The intense heat broke over Kathir as he rolled away. He jumped to his feet and then dove again to avoid a second blast.

"Stop!" cried Kathir, but Shesha kept advancing. The horses were frightened beyond belief and bucked wildly.

Shesha reared up to blast Kathir again.

"*Bjarg-Risa!*" Sela called out, and a wall of frost rose up to stop the next spear of flame. A shield from Elias blocked the next attack, and Nydeired maneuvered his huge body between Shesha and Kathir. Shesha paced back and forth, growling and snapping her jaws, but she couldn't get past Nydeired without hurting him—he was just too huge.

"Shesha," Tallin called out. "Why are you doing this? Calm yourself!"

Kathir looked at Shesha. The dragon looked hauntingly familiar. There was only one thing that would explain her violent reaction to his presence.

"What is it? Why is that dragon acting crazy?" Skemtun demanded. He jumped to Kathir's side, eager to help his friend.

"I think I know the reason," Sela said quietly. Her expression was grave. "Shesha attacked Kathir because she recognized him."

Kathir's shoulders drooped, and he stood up. His face was filled with trepidation. "Yes. It's true. She recognized me from my days as a dragon hunter. Shesha knows me, because... I killed her hatchlings."

8. THE HIGH PRIESTESS

B ack in Balbor, Skera-Kina explored her new suite of private rooms. The former living quarters of the High Priest were far more opulent than those she was used to.

All the rooms were filled with expensive silks, golden ornaments, and soft cushions. Like the rest of the main fortress, it was furnished in a dark, baroque fashion—levels of luxury that bordered on the obscene. Even the room's location seemed to have been chosen more for its beauty than based on any practical sense.

Here, in these decadent rooms, it was easy for Skera-Kina to wonder whether she had ever truly believed any of what the priests had told her.

Skera-Kina walked to her desk and shuffled absently through piles of reports, letters, and missives. A few of the letters were sealed with wax and written in foreign script. Others gave details of spies and bribed officials. Others were more mundane—one letter from a merchant demanded increased prices for his smuggled spices, and another requested more guards to protect a cache of ancient weapons in the northern part of the island. Skera-Kina didn't read through them all. There were too many.

A quiet knock on the outer door interrupted her. "Enter," she said.

Her former apprentice stepped into the room with his head bowed. She noticed that though his arm was still swollen, his shoulder had been set. Perhaps he had done it himself.

"Gron, do you know why I have summoned you here?" Skera-Kina asked.

"No, Mistress." The young man kept his head bowed, but Skera-Kina could still see a faint trembling in his limbs that betrayed his fear. Once, Skera-Kina would have despised him for that weakness, but now she had a different perspective.

Her apprentice wasn't a threat to her now. It might do him good to remind him of his station. Still, she felt no need to be cruel. Not anymore. "You were in the crowd jeering at me when I was a prisoner in that cage."

Her hand fluttered to the hilt of her knife out of habit. There had been a few who had not been willing to accept her rise to High Priestess. The ordinary citizens had accepted her ascension almost without question, but the other mageborns were not so quick to do so.

There were a few challenges to her new authority, but so far, Skera-Kina had come through unscathed.

"Please, Mistress..." he went to his knees.

"You called for my death. Don't bother trying to deny it. I heard your voice in the crowd. So the question becomes—what am I going to do with you?"

The apprentice bowed his head in submission. "I'm sorry, Your Grace. Please, have mercy. I didn't mean it."

Skera-Kina looked down at the unfortunate young man. She could feel the shadowkey pulsing in her chest, protecting her heart. She reached out, grabbing the apprentice's injured shoulder. It was still swollen and bruised. He winced but did not pull away.

"*Curatio.*" It wasn't a spell that Skera-Kina had used much for others, but she used it now. The healing magic flowed from her body, pouring into her former apprentice. She felt his damaged flesh move back into alignment. It was quick. For several seconds after the healing, he just knelt there, panting softly.

"Come now, get up," Skera-Kina said. "You have work to do."

Gron wobbled to his feet. "Work? What kind of work?" He licked his lips nervously.

Skera-Kina gestured to the stacks of letters. "You can read, can't you? I am not going to spend my time going through all this paperwork. I'm appointing you as my personal assistant."

The young man's face brightened immediately. "Oh, that would be a great honor, my lady!" Clearly, this meeting had turned out better than he expected.

"I want you to read through all these reports and letters," Skera-Kina said. "Tell me what's important —anything that requires a real decision to be made.

You will provide me with the information that I need to know, and you will do so *honestly*, because I *will* be checking. And If I ever discover that you have lied to me or have withheld anything from me..."

Gron gulped loudly. He nodded. "I understand."

Skera-Kina left the threat hanging in the air. She knew that she didn't need to finish the sentence. He knew perfectly well that to betray her would mean death, and he wouldn't get a second chance next time.

"When would you like me to begin, Mistress?" Gron asked. He tugged a handkerchief from his pocket and dabbed at the beads of sweat on his forehead.

Skera-Kina went to the window and looked out over the city. "Right now. Today. And have someone bring me the Brighthollow Scroll from the temple library."

"Yes, High Priestess," Gron said, running outside quickly to summon a library messenger.

She turned to face the window. There were so many things to do, but understanding that ancient treaty was her top priority. The elf queen could take back what she had given her so easily. Skera-Kina needed to read the treaty and understand it completely. As long as she followed the terms of the compact, she would be free to rule as she wished. And that was the key to her happiness.

She could now bring someone's life to an end by merely ordering it; no longer was she forced to go out and do the killing herself. Where Skera-Kina was once a blood-soaked hammer, she was now the arm that did the swinging.

The apprentice returned a few moments later. She went over to the desk where he was already organizing the stacks by date; she could already tell that he would be a good addition to her inner circle. "I'm going to my quarters. I'll be back at sunset. Have your first report ready for me by then."

The apprentice bowed. "As you command, Your Grace."

She walked past the set of massive doors which opened into her new sleeping chambers. She frowned and looked around the room; the large tapestry, the gaudy decorations—it was all too much. "It's time to redecorate, I think."

She tore the garish tapestries from the walls, depositing them into a heap on the floor. She knew her servants would take them away later, saying nothing.

She could finally see the stained-glass windows, which had been covered up. They were beautiful. Bright light streamed in through the windows, throwing a kaleidoscope of color against the walls. She opened one of them, and a burst of wind entered the stuffy room. She inhaled deeply, enjoying the fresh air.

She yanked the silk sheets and feather down pillows off the bed, throwing them into the corner with the crumpled tapestries. She would replace them later with linen sheets and plain wool blankets.

The previous High Priest had been paranoid and self-obsessed. Skera-Kina was different. The time for change had come. She would see to that.

The people still needed to be kept in line, the yearly sacrifices still needed to be made, and the death gods still required their due, but Skera-Kina was smart enough to know what was *really* important. She would appoint competent advisors who knew how to rule. All the rest of it—the boring, day-to-day business of running a society—was merely a distraction.

Skera-Kina could see the path of her life stretching before her, and her mission was clear: she would be the one who would return Balbor to its former glory.

The elf queen had saved her, not the High Priest or her own magic. This made her believe that her new leadership role was all part of the prophecy —the prophecy which declared that the Balborites would rise to power once again and that they would become so great that no one would dare to oppose them.

She just had to figure a way to make it happen *without* dragons.

Skera-Kina touched the black key embedded in her flesh. She knew the truth of her own ancestry. She would not have to worry about death's embrace for a long time to come, so she had plenty of time to plan.

Skera-Kina hadn't made her mind up yet about what to do with the countless slaves, the brutal structure of Balborite life, or the endless killing that was the focus of their existence. Changing a whole society was a project that might take generations. But Skera-Kina had the time in which to make those changes. She sat down on the stripped bed and yawned. Minutes later, she was asleep.

She awoke after several hours and noticed that servants had quietly removed the discarded tapestries and bedding. The room had been cleaned, and the doors and windows had been closed again.

She rubbed her eyes and went back into the throne room. The apprentice was sitting in the same position, going through the stacks of paper. He had a steaming mug of tea and a half-eaten bread roll next to him.

"Are you ready to tell me what is happening yet?" Skera-Kina said.

The young man looked up, somewhat startled by her sudden appearance. "Yes, Your Grace. I have gathered some information. There are a few spy reports, many requests, and several private letters. Most of the correspondence is from the priests or from freeborn citizens, but a few are from the mainland. I separated those out. Most of those requests are already outdated, and can probably be ignored. It seems that the former High Priest usually paid them no mind."

"What types of requests are these?"

He held up one of the letters. "Most of them are assassination requests. There is a request here to have the leader of a small village killed," the apprentice said. "The man is suspected of stealing livestock. The sender has offered to pay one hundred gold coins as a bounty."

Skera-Kina waved her hand dismissively. "I'm not going to use my assassins to settle local squabbles. The citizens must learn how to work out those differences amongst themselves."

Skera-Kina remembered too much of her own upbringing, where the violence had been constant and senseless. As a slave, she had no choices. Even as an apprentice, she had to kill or be killed. When she became one of the Blood Masters, she also became an instrument of the priests, who sent her to kill anyone they desired. Skera-Kina's vision for the future included killing—but only when it made sense.

"What else?" Skera-Kina asked.

"There are several letters from Druknor, the governor of Sut-Burr. He says that his prices on future shipments of slaves will rise. He's under closer scrutiny from the dragon riders, and it's becoming more difficult for him to transport them."

Skera-Kina inhaled deeply.

Druknor. Druknor Theoric. Just the sound of his name brought blood roaring into her ears.

In all the excitement since she had become High Priestess, Skera-Kina had managed to forget all about Druknor. More than anyone else, it was Druknor that had doomed her to this life of servitude and violence. Her fists clenched involuntarily. If he had been in the room in that instant, Skera-Kina would have killed him without a second thought.

"Your Grace? Do you wish to reply to this message?"

Skera-Kina gave her assistant a cat-like smile. "Oh, yes... I'm going to reply."

The apprentice nodded obediently. "What do you wish to say? I could compose it for you. I've completed my scribal training."

She paused for a moment. She hadn't been able to act of her own volition before. Of course, there were so many things that needed to be arranged here on Balbor. *There's so much work to do here....* But the memory of Druknor's sneering face gnawed at her— some things couldn't be forgiven.

Of course, she was the High Priestess now; she could simply send someone else to kill him. She had dozens of assassins at her disposal, but it just wouldn't feel the same.

Skera-Kina shook her head. "I prefer to deal with Druknor myself... in person. I'll go to the mainland."

The apprentice didn't seem surprised and merely nodded. "Would you like me to prepare supplies for your journey, Mistress?"

Skera-Kina smiled. "Yes, prepare my bags. I need a fast horse, and send a messenger bird to the shipmaster. Have a small clipper waiting for me on the southern coast. I'll leave tonight."

"As you wish, Mistress," he stood up and bowed again. "Is there anything in particular that you need for your journey?"

"Pack my things for the cold," Skera-Kina said. "I've got one last piece of unfinished business."

9. BAD BLOOD

Tallin stood between Shesha and Kathir, but there was a part of him that wondered why he should. The other dragons had turned against the mercenary now and were growling and snapping along with Shesha. Fëanor and Amandila were standing to the side. He could see that they wouldn't interfere.

Delthen and Komu stepped back from the ruckus, as well. Druknor watched from the sidelines, but he was smirking.

"Kathir is a dragonkiller," Duskeye said. *"He killed our kind."*

"He deserves to die!" Shesha screamed as she lunged forward again. Tallin stopped her with a magical shield, but the other dragons didn't move to assist him. They apparently agreed with Shesha's assessment.

Elias stepped forward. "Kathir is a changed man. Please, everyone, calm down. At least hear him out."

"Calm down? Calm down? After what he has done?" Shesha said. *"He killed my hatchlings!"*

"Please, Shesha," Tallin said. It felt odd, defending him. Five years ago, he would have killed Kathir without a second thought. "Things have changed since the war."

"He's a murderer!" Shesha roared. *"I don't care what you say, I'll kill him!"* She spat a river of flame in Kathir's direction. Tallin's shield blocked it once again, but he could feel the searing heat on his face and arms. He was starting to get tired. He wasn't enthusiastic about it, either.

The other dragons were larger than Shesha, but Blacktooth and Nydeired didn't seem interested in acting against her. Nydeired had moved out of her way. Nagendra, on the other hand, looked ready to pounce on Kathir herself.

Either they needed to find a way to calm Shesha down, or Kathir needed to get away—and fast. Tallin and Sela exchanged nervous glances. Tensions were getting worse.

Komu coughed. "In my day," he said, "an accused man was given a proper trial, not an immediate execution. Are we going to ignore the law?"

"Please, Shesha," said Sela, jumping into the fray. "Stop this! You're not going to kill Kathir. I cannot allow cold-blooded murder."

"He killed my hatchlings! Will you allow this murderer to go free?" Shesha demanded.

"He's openly admitted it," Delthen said. "He *was* a dragon hunter."

"I suppose his confession should carry some weight at trial," Komu murmured, almost to himself, "but that's no reason not to have one. People are entitled to a fair hearing when they are accused of a crime, you know. It's in the books—that's the law, and it should be followed."

"That's the law for our citizens, but he's not a citizen of Miklagard," Delthen pointed out. "He's just a mercenary, remember?"

"Really?" Komu said. "But you claimed him as one of ours, or have you forgotten that? I have an excellent memory for these types of things, you know. Besides, he's been very loyal to us."

"Don't be absurd," said Delthen. "He's a mercenary. Whatever he does, he does for the money."

Again, Komu coughed. "Even so, it isn't fair. How about a vote—there's plenty of important people here, after all. Sela is the regent of Parthos. There are two clan leaders present, two elves, and the governor of Sut-Burr. We should at least *discuss* things before we kill a man in cold blood, don't you agree?"

"Komu's right," Tallin said. He turned to Shesha. "Shesha, what do you remember? Tell us your side of the story first." He hoped that the talking would calm everyone down, at least for the moment.

Shesha finally stopped pacing and sat back, glaring at Kathir. *"What is there to say? I left my nest to hunt. When I came back, I found dragon hunters slaying my clutch. There were a dozen men inside my cave. I killed two, but most of them escaped. This one..."* she pointed a claw at Kathir, *"this one was their leader. I'll never forget his face—the face with two long scars."*

Tallin repeated Shesha's words in the common language for those who didn't understand dragontongue.

Sela nodded. "Thank you, Shesha. And you,

Kathir? What do you have to say for yourself?"

The mercenary stood in the middle of the camp. He hung his head and sighed. "There is nothing I can say. She isn't lying. I don't remember her exactly, but I probably did it. I served the emperor during the war. I hunted dragons, as I was ordered to do. I don't know for sure if it was her hatchlings that I killed, or those of another mother elsewhere, but it doesn't really matter. I'm guilty either way."

Kathir almost sounded like he wanted to die. His face was filled with remorse and shame.

"So we have the facts of it," Bolrakei said, speaking up. "It sounds like Skemtun's little friend deserves everything he's got coming to him." There was a strange eagerness in her voice.

Skemtun cleared his throat and stood up. "I'll speak for Kathir. I didn't know him when he committed these supposed crimes, but I know him now. He came to Mount Velik as a mercenary, but he's done many good things since then. He's saved *countless* lives. He's tried to help solve the crisis between the clans, and I know he wasn't being paid to do *that*. He's a different man today. A better man. A man that I'm proud to call my friend."

Delthen snorted. "That doesn't change the past, does it?"

"No, it doesn't," Elias said. He moved to stand beside Kathir. "But I've seen the way people treat Kathir. Everywhere he goes, he is despised because of the markings on his face—the markings of a former slave. Employers throw his coins in the dirt.

People sneer behind his back or even openly to his face." He fixed Druknor and Bolrakei with a level stare. "I know this man. He was never cruel to me, not even when he held me captive years ago. He's not an evil man, and I have had the chance to see him do some good things to help the dwarves. He protected them, and they aren't even his people."

"Oh, yes... he's a true paragon of virtue," Delthen said, rolling his eyes. His voice dripped with sarcasm.

"There can be no doubt that what Kathir did in the past was terribly wrong," said Elias. "But he is a good man now, and if we give him a chance, I believe that he will be a better man still. It's taken me a long time to understand that, but I believe in second chances."

Elias continued quietly, "Would you rob Kathir of the chance to change? Despite the evil he's done, I also believe that Kathir deserves a second chance. He's a changed man. What good would come of killing him now? He deserves a fair trial, at the very least."

"This is all very touching," Druknor sneered, "but I vote that the mercenary dies for his crimes."

"So do I," Bolrakei piped in.

Delthen nodded. "I agree. The dragon hunter must be punished."

"I vote against," Elias said.

Sela nodded. "As do I."

"Obviously, I do too," Skemtun said.

Amandila tentatively raised her hand in Kathir's

favor. "We might need his help when we reach Mount Velik. I believe we should be merciful."

Fëanor shook his head. "Not I...this dragon killer should die for his crimes. I'd be happy to kill him myself."

Kathir shook his head and sighed. "I'm sorry," he said, "but this isn't about any of you. You don't get to decide." He walked to stand in front of Shesha, who growled as he approached.

Kathir dropped to his knees and looked up at her with pleading eyes. "I know that you can understand my words," he said. "So please hear me out. You're the one I've wronged. I'm sorry. I wish I could take back the past, but I can't. I did many things that I'm ashamed of, but I can't change that now. If you want to kill me, I won't try to stop you. My life is yours. All I can say is... that if you allow me to live, I'll spend the rest of my life trying to make amends for what I've done."

He knelt there, staring up at Shesha. She reared above him, and for a moment, it looked like the dragon would bite him in half. Shesha stood there, poised to strike, breath going in and out in hot waves. Finally, she whirled away, turning her back on him in disgust.

"Do you need this fleshling for your fight against the orcs?" She asked Tallin sharply.

"Yes... he is a trained fighter. He would be helpful to us," Tallin said, amazed that the dragon would seek his opinion. Shesha had always been clear that she only tolerated him for Duskeye's sake.

"Let the mongrel fleshling live, then," she snarled. *"He can do his penance fighting the greenskins."*

10. RETURN TO MOUNT VELIK

T he return journey to Mount Velik dragged on, and the weather grew increasingly cold. There was snow on the ground in many places, and it rained often. The horses strained to push ahead, but the roads became so muddy and treacherous that it was slow-going all the time.

The group eventually made it to the village of Ironport, a city on the west side of the Orvasse River. There was a bridge outside the city, which the wagons would use to cross the river. It was late afternoon when they arrived, and they decided to stop and rest.

Sela found a reasonably clean inn, and they all stayed for the night.

The dragons and the elves chose to stay outside the city walls and sleep in the surrounding forest.

When they entered the inn, the owner's eyes widened until they were as large as saucers; the inn-keeper was ecstatic to have so many "nobles" inside his tiny establishment.

They rested, ate the inn's simple food, and quietly discussed their plans. At sunset, the major-ity of the party retired to their rooms to sleep, but Kathir left the inn to acquire more provisions and to explore the city.

Tallin also left the inn; he headed toward the city center but did not bother to explain the purpose of his errand. He was gone for several hours, and when he returned to the inn, he found the place almost entirely empty.

Kathir was enjoying a mug of hot cider by himself. He noticed Tallin standing in the doorway and waved him over. "Pull up a chair and sit for a while, dragon rider."

"Where are the others?" asked Tallin, as he hung his wet cloak near the fireplace. He sat down next to Kathir and ordered spiced ale for himself.

Kathir shrugged. "Up in their rooms sleeping, I suppose. I couldn't sleep, so I decided to come downstairs and have a little nightcap. Bad news?" he asked, taking a sip from his mug. "You look like you've had a hard day."

Tallin paused for a moment, unsure of how much he should share with the mercenary. They weren't friends by any stretch of the imagination, but they got along. Which was more than he could say about Druknor and Bolrakei, both of whom he could barely stand.

He sighed. "I know several Shadow Grid members in this city, so I went out to get some information. Things are bad here. Very bad." Tallin was unable to keep the bitterness from his voice when he spoke.

"So what's the problem?"

"The greenskins have been attempting nighttime raids on the city walls. The citizens are terrified—the orcs have gotten bolder now that King Nar has a nearby foothold. The mayor has decided to seal the city gates permanently—the gates will never be opened at night again. Merchants will only be allowed to enter the city in the morning. It'll cripple the trade here."

Kathir took a sip of his ale. "That's unfortunate, but it's partially their fault. All of this could have been prevented if the other races of Durn had bothered to help the dwarves. Ironport has a fairly large militia—thousands of men. They could have helped the clans defend the mountain, but now it's too late."

"You're right, the other kingdoms *should* have helped the dwarves. But they didn't," Tallin said. "It's been a terrible year for the dwarf clans, but it's going to get worse for the other races of Durn too."

The barmaid placed another mug in front of them. She winked at Tallin, staring openly at the dragon stone on his chest. The serving girl had blue eyes and pouty lips, which she puckered up into a flirty smile. Tallin shook his head and waved her away.

Kathir raised an eyebrow. "That girl was interested in you. Why did you reject her?"

Tallin shrugged. "Trust me, the extra attention isn't as fun as it seems."

Kathir looked wistful. "I wish I could attract women so easily. Don't you enjoy the touch of a willing woman?"

"Yes... sometimes," Tallin said, looking down at his drink, "I find female company easily enough, but most women are interested in my position, not me. All they care about is that I'm a dragon rider. I'm just a novelty to them. Eventually, the novelty wears off. That becomes tiresome, so now I just avoid the situation altogether."

Kathir snorted. "I would trade places with you in an instant. Most women won't even look at me. They can't see past these scars." His finger traced the marks on his cheeks.

Tallin took a drink before answering. "Everyone's got some scars." He pulled back the neck of his tunic, exposing a long, raised weal that disappeared under his collar. He also raised the cuffs of his sleeves, exposing deep scarring on his wrists and forearms, which he had received while he was held captive during the war.

Kathir gulped and looked away. He'd seen marks like that before, and he knew that Tallin's wounds were probably from struggling against iron cuffs in Vosper's dungeons. "I worked for the emperor during the war," he admitted. "I've done a lot of things that I'm not proud of."

"I know that," said Tallin, shaking down his sleeves. "A few years ago, I would have killed you without a second thought. But times have changed, and so have I. The Dragon Wars are over, and the emperor is dead. What good would it do for me to track down everyone who ever worked for him now? I'd have to kill half the commoners in Morholt." He waved a weary hand. "We have bigger problems on our hands."

"Do you still think about the war?"

Tallin leaned back against the chair with a weary sigh. "Yes. I still think about it. I've tried to forget, but I'm plagued by memories that keep me awake at night. We were tortured and left to die in Vosper's dungeons. It was sheer luck that Duskeye and I escaped."

"That's how I feel about my time as a slave," said Kathir quietly. "I've tried to move on with my life, but the memories just won't go away; it's as if the bad ones are carved in stone."

The two men sat in silence for a moment, watching the flames dance and sputter. The barmaid walked over and added more wood to the fire and then hung her apron and her towel to dry.

Kathir waited until she was out of earshot before he spoke again. "Do you think our plan will work?"

"It's risky," Tallin replied. "There's a lot that could go wrong. But we don't have many options at this point, so we'll just have to take our chances." He looked up at the ancient water clock on the mantle. "It's late. Let's go to sleep. We need to be off before the sun rises."

They both went to their rooms to sleep.

The next morning, their party woke before dawn. They started moving again as soon as the horses were saddled and ready. Soldiers opened the city gates so they could leave.

From Ironport, the carriages moved onward toward their destination. The next few days were cold, but there was no rain or night frosts.

They were approached by bandits several times, but the would-be robbers always ran away as soon as they caught sight of the dragons. Even so, they decided to post guards at night, and the dragon riders took turns on patrol. Because he was awake so much during the night, Tallin often listened to the dragons speaking on the edges of the firelight.

Although the elves remained aloof throughout the journey, their dragons were relatively friendly, although not very talkative. Brinsop and Blacktooth grew closer with each passing night and sometimes paired off alone.

No one was surprised when the two of them slipped off into the dark together one evening around the time of the last watch. Nagendra seemed the shyest of them all; she was not hostile, but she stayed huddled next to her rider Amandila most of the time. Shesha spent much of her time hunting wild pigs in the woods and trying to avoid Kathir.

Everyone grew somber when Mount Velik appeared in the distance. There was a cap of white snow on the mountain, and a belt of grey clouds circled its peak. A dark fog hung around the mountain and clung to the tops of the trees.

Their breath steamed in the cold air, and their horses' footsteps echoed in the silence.

A sense of impending doom seemed to fall over the group, and all idle chatter ceased. Snow and sleeting rain fell intermittently as they rode through the ravaged forest. Evidence of the orc's presence was all around them. Barren trees stood stripped of their bark and branches, and the streams were tainted with ash.

"The countryside looks ravaged," Kathir said quietly.

Skemtun nodded. "The orcs did this. They're scavengers—they don't care about the forest; they'll destroy everything."

"It's difficult to see."

The dwarf nodded. "Yes, it is. The orcs are living inside my home... It just feels so... *wrong.* To be honest, I don't have much hope for this mission. I'm not sure we'll be able to drive them out."

"The dragon riders have a plan, and it's a good one," said Kathir, "you have to give them a chance."

"But the flooding might destroy everything. Then our home will be ruined."

"Don't let that worry you. Everything will work itself out," said Kathir with a sympathetic smile.

A few days later, the roads changed abruptly. The cobbles had been torn up, and the land had been burned in every direction all around them. There was smoke in the air, blackening the skies above, and the pounding of war drums could be heard faintly in the distance.

Late in the evening, the dragon riders saw a raiding party of orcs waiting by the roadside. The travelers redirected their course in order to avoid them, but the discovery put everyone on edge. They moved cautiously along the damaged roads and were always careful to keep themselves hidden.

After a while, the road became too bumpy to use, and they had to make the hard decision to abandon the carriages. They unhitched the horses, and everyone was forced to ride horseback. The dragons burned the wagons to ash so that they wouldn't be discovered. Without the wagons, they were more exposed to the frigid weather, but no one complained about that.

A light rain began falling steadily, and the silence among the travelers was broken only by occasional thunderclaps in the distance.

The next day, the group was attacked by a band of orcs as they were watering the horses. The roving pack of greenskins moved forward warily, grunting and snorting as they stalked them. As usual, Bolrakei and the High Council members stepped back from the fray.

Kathir drew his sword, and Skemtun drew his axe. This time, Druknor decided to join the fight. He pulled a magnificent short sword from his saddlebags.

The dragon riders circled cautiously above the greenskins, waiting for their first move.

Kathir attacked first, galloping forward with his blade raised in the air. He struck the first orc in line, shouting as dark blood spurted forth from its severed arm. The orc howled in agony and fell forward. Druknor stabbed at another with his sword.

Another orc hit Kathir's horse with a flanged mace. The terrible weapon tore mercilessly into the horse's neck. The horse screamed and pitched forward before crumpling to the ground. Kathir rolled away just in time to avoid being crushed. As he struggled to rise, a flash of dragonfire behind him told him that the dragon riders had landed and were joining the battle.

Kathir knelt by his fallen horse, scrabbling to reach inside his saddlebags. The poor animal was in agony. He would have to put it down after the battle, but there was nothing that Kathir could do to help it now.

Kathir drew his crossbow from his bags and swiftly fitted a bolt to the string. He tried to steady his ragged breaths as the orc who had attacked his horse rapidly approached him. Kathir exhaled and let the bolt fly. The orc dropped down dead, a fletched arrow jutting from its eye.

Tallin blinded the orcs with a brilliant flash as he jumped from Duskeye's back with his falchion in one hand and a small shield in the other. One of the orcs staggered forward and swung his sword at Tallin's chest. Tallin parried the blow, twisting his hand to move the sword away from his body. The orc stabbed outward, but Tallin's sword glided along the orc's weapon and hit the creature in the chest, stabbing deeply.

Swinging his axe, Skemtun moved in to join him as the elves and their dragons joined the fight. The elves drew their bows and fired at the greenskins. Several fell from the arrows, but many of them were protected by metal armor.

"They have armor?" gasped Kathir. "Where did they get it?"

"Stolen from Mount Velik," said Skemtun grimly. "That's dwarf armor—they've broken it up into pieces and attached it to their bodies with leather straps."

The orcs struck back and hit the travelers with another vicious assault. An orc fighting Skemtun swung a great club and struck the dwarf in the head so fiercely that he was knocked unconscious. The orc screamed in victory and jumped over Skemtun's body to deliver a killing blow.

"Stop him!" screamed Kathir, who turned just in time to watch a blast of blue flame topple the beast before he could strike. Kathir glanced over to see Councilor Komu looking very pleased with himself. Kathir jumped forward, grabbed Skemtun by the arms and dragged his limp body back to where Komu and Delthen stood behind their shield.

Tallin shouted for everyone to move back. Duskeye reared up on his hind legs and sent a stream of flame in the orc's direction. The other dragons stepped directly behind Duskeye and let loose their own mouthfuls of fire, bringing the battle to an end almost immediately. Several orcs were burned to death, and those that survived ran away in fear.

The two elves jumped on their dragons and pursued the fleeing orcs, killing them before they could return to their camp and give away the convoy's location.

"That was a good shot," Tallin said, walking toward Kathir. "It's a pity about your horse."

"The poor thing," Kathir said, patting the horse's trembling flank. The horse's face was streaked with blood, and its pain-crazed body twisted and turned wildly. Blood pumped from the horse's neck in spurts, leaving crimson splashes on the snow. "Can you do anything for him?"

Tallin shook his head. "I'm sorry, I don't know how to heal horses. Animal healing takes special training—you have to understand the anatomy of the animal to heal a serious injury. I can heal dragons, and minor wounds in some animals, but this injury is beyond my skills."

Kathir sighed. "That's it, then. Poor beast. I must confess, I don't feel good about having to kill this fine horse... but I have to put him out of his misery."

"Wait! Don't be so sure about that," said Komu, tottering forward. The old wizard cracked his knuckles and placed a glowing hand on the terrified animal's neck. "I can save him. This is a chance for me to practice *my* healing skills. I don't get to work with animals very much these days."

Komu kneeled forward and pet the horse's face gently. "There now, boy, you'll feel better in a moment." He pulled a scarf from around his neck and draped it over the terrified horse's eyes like a blindfold. The animal immediately calmed down. There was a flash, then the horse shuddered.

They all watched in amazement as the horse's wounds closed up and then disappeared. Minutes later, the startled horse was back on its feet. Kathir went to it and patted its nose gently. "Astonishing!"

"He's a little worse for wear," said Komu, "but he'll be sound enough to ride, as long as you don't push him too hard."

Even Tallin was impressed. "How did you do it?"

"I studied animal healing in my youth," Komu said, rising stiffly. "I can heal any farm animal. Those skills came in handy when I was younger—my parents were sharecroppers, and their animals were always getting hurt, so I learned how to heal them. We had to do work ourselves, you know. That was a long time ago, but I still remember."

"This is all very touching, really," Druknor quipped, "but shouldn't we get out of here? More greenskins are sure to be nearby." He pulled a handkerchief from his pocket and wiped a blotch of black blood from his face. "For each one we killed, there are ten more out there, and they're just waiting to attack us again."

Druknor was right; they needed to move. Everyone mounted their horses and dragons, and they were off again.

They rode through the day and into the night and rested only when necessary. After a while, the road became a narrow trail that began to slope upwards. And they soon found themselves just a few leagues from Mount Velik.

The elves and the other dragon riders landed

near the horses, and they all gathered together to discuss their strategy. The smoke was even thicker than before, and fiery sparks flew all around them.

Bolrakei coughed and covered her nose with her sleeve. "The smoke smells awful! I can hardly breathe!"

Tallin nodded. "The orcs cleared the forest by slashing trees and burning them. I flew ahead and saw that they've cleared the entire circumference of the mountain. They've burned the ground vegetation, too. The earth is scorched black for leagues. We won't have any cover as we approach, so we'll be forced to use concealment spells for the remainder of the journey. It's too risky to continue in daylight. We should approach at night, since even the strongest concealment spell won't hide our shadows. There's no other option. We can't afford to be seen, heard, or smelled."

Delthen looked shaken. "That'll be exhausting! I can't maintain a high-level concealment spell for that long!"

"I can," said Tallin. "So can the elves. We will help you if your protective shield falters."

"Are we going to stop here for the night?" Kathir asked. "It doesn't seem safe enough."

"Yes," said Tallin. "This is the tree line, and the only place left for us to stop. This is our last chance to sleep, while we still have some forest cover. Everyone's tired, and none of us will be able to maintain a concealment spell if we don't get at least a few hours of rest. We'll continue onward after midnight."

Bolrakei looked around nervously. "Is it safe to stay here? This area must be crawling with orcs!"

"The air is full of smoke. That will conceal us somewhat," Sela said, "There's a small underground cave nearby. I found it while I was patrolling. The entrance is narrow, but the inside is just large enough to hold all of us and the horses. We won't be able to light a fire, but at least everyone will be able to sleep and stay dry. There's no room for the dragons, but they can fly to a safe location further away. We'll tackle the final leg of our journey after we've rested."

Delthen folded his arms. "That's all well and good, but what happens after that? The greenskins are guarding every entrance. How are we going to get inside the mountain?"

It was a practical question and one to which there seemed to be no easy answer. Finally, Mugla spoke up. "I know a secret entrance into the mountain," she said quietly. "I told Tallin and Sela about it when we started this journey."

"Ye know a way inside Mount Velik that I don't?" Skemtun asked, surprised.

Mugla nodded. "This entrance is private and warded. It can't be seen from the outside. It leads directly into the spellcasters' chambers. Hopefully, the wards are still active, and none of the orcs have discovered the chamber. We'll need to leave the dragons outside, though. The passage isn't large enough for animals to squeeze through. It's barely large enough for a human to pass. But they'll be waiting outside if we run into trouble."

Amandila's eyes widened. "Going into Mount Velik without our dragons sounds incredibly dangerous."

"There's no other way to get inside without being seen," said Tallin. "The dragons can wait for us above the caldera, within the cloud cover. We'll rest for the night, and then we'll need to push on to the southern side of the mountain. That's where the spellcasters' entrance is. We will all need to go on horseback from here on. Mugla, Sela, and the elves are lighter than the rest of us—they can share a horse."

Everyone agreed to this plan, and they soon found their way to the cave that Sela had mentioned. The elves volunteered to keep watch, and everyone else fell into an exhausted sleep. They rose shortly after midnight and saddled the horses in the dark.

It had rained heavily while they were asleep, so the smoky air had cleared some, and it was easier to breathe. The mountaintop was visible in the blue moonlight, its snowclad peak rising up into the sky like a glittering white pyramid.

Skemtun hung back so that he could ride alongside Kathir and talk.

"All our caverns are going to be destroyed, I just know it," Skemtun whispered dejectedly. "Thousands of years of hard work—for nothing."

"Don't be so discouraged," said Kathir. "A flood

won't do *that* much permanent damage. You said the caverns had been flooded before."

Skemtun sighed. "Some of the lower ones, yes. But not the entire mountain. I wish there were a way to rout the orcs without damaging our home."

"Just remember all your people waiting for you back at Highport," Kathir said. "The people who used to live in this mountain are more important than the mountain itself."

"Aye, you're right." Skemtun scratched his arms absently. "I feel strange—itchy all over."

"It's a reaction to the concealment spell," said Tallin, who was riding behind them. His face looked strained. "The concealment spell we are using now is much stronger than most—it's of elvish origin. Everyone reacts differently to elvish spells, but the sensation you describe is perfectly normal."

"So we're hidden from view right now? The orcs can't see us, even if they're right in front of us?" asked Skemtun.

Tallin nodded. "That's right. We are completely hidden from sight, smell, and sound. Just stay in close formation. I won't be able to extend the shield much further than this. My power does have limits."

After another hour of careful riding, they left the horses tied up near a patch of scraggly trees and continued on foot.

The dragons flew higher, rising into the sky to hide in the clouds above the mountain. Even with the concealment spell, they moved as quietly as possible and tried to stay hidden within the shadows.

As they walked on, they saw that the land was blackened and burned. Where there were once trees and gardens, now there were just mounds of burnt grass and debris. Charred stumps dotted the blighted terrain. They soon came upon water and saw a large band of orcs dressed in leather armor.

At one point, Bolrakei was so frightened that she started hyperventilating, but Komu, of all people, delivered a sharp slap to her face to shut her up. Bolrakei rubbed her cheek and frowned but said nothing more.

As they walked, more and more orcs came into view. They worked outside in large groups, building their huge war machines.

"Look at all this mud and trash!" whispered Bolrakei.

Tallin cast his gaze around the horizon. The orcs had redirected the water that seeped into the mountain outward to support their building. Seeing so much water *outside* the mountain worried him a great deal, but he decided to keep his concerns to himself for the time being.

They made their way around the orcs cautiously. Sometimes, the orcs were close enough to touch, but the travelers held their breath and kept their distance. Tallin and the elves kept their eyes pinned on the treacherous greenskins. The concealment spells held.

When they made it to the southern side of the mountain, Tallin and Mugla stopped near a patch of twisted rubble. There were no apparent openings in the stone, but there was a black boulder that was darker than the other rocks around it. Tallin shot a small fireball at it. The fireball sparked and bounced off the hidden wards.

"This is it," Tallin whispered. "This is the spellcasters' entrance. Mugla can deactivate the wards. That will take a few minutes. I don't know what it's going to be like inside, but we'll need to stay together. We'll go in, check out the spellcasters' chambers, and then finalize our plans from there. Agreed?"

Everyone nodded. With a series of muttered words, Mugla temporarily deactivated the wards on the entrance. The black stone shimmered briefly and then rolled back, revealing a dark passageway. They were forced to squeeze through one by one. Skemtun was the last one to pass through the warded entrance, which automatically sealed behind him. Although the old dwarf looked nervous, he also had the look of a man coming home.

Tallin led them through the spellcaster's tunnels, using a small mage-flame to light the way.

"Will the orcs be able to see us?" Bolrakei whispered.

Mugla shook her head. "No, this passage is sealed with protective runes. The orcs don't have any mageborns among them, so they won't be able to enter the spellcasters' chambers unless they destroy the walls. But there's no telling what our mages left behind, so be careful where you step."

Collapsed sections of tunnel forced them to change their route several times, and they had to squeeze around various rock falls.

"Skemtun," Tallin called back, as quietly as he could.

The dwarf clan leader squeezed his way to the front of the group. Kathir followed close behind him. It seemed that the mercenary was still focused on keeping Skemtun alive.

"What do ye need?" Skemtun asked.

"These tunnels have changed since I was last in them," Tallin said. "Where are we now?"

Skemtun paused for a moment. "We're descending into the lower caverns. It's a bad thing. Our tunnels shouldn't change. There's a lot of damage here. I'm not sure if it was done by orcs or by our own spellcasters trying to seal the passage."

"Look here," Tallin said, pointing to a section where the floor was strewn with large rocks. "I'm not sure we can pass here. This passage is almost completely blocked. We're running out of detours."

"Aye, well, we had to seal some of the tunnels when we left. That will have affected things. Then again, it is a dead volcano, so there are lots of twists and turns throughout the mountain."

"A volcano?" Amandila asked, with a question in her voice.

Skemtun nodded. "Yes, of course. There's ore in

many places, and the walls of the lower caverns glitter with diamonds and precious stones. Why do ye think there are so many gems for Bolrakei's clan to cut and mine? All our diamonds and rubies come from the mountain's deepest chambers. But like I said, the volcano hasn't been active for centuries."

"Don't be so sure about that, old man," said Mugla. "Ye don't know all the secrets of this mountain. There's still fire in her yet!"

Skemtun looked at her oddly but said nothing.

"Follow me," said Mugla. "We'll get past this section—I know which way to go." She walked along the narrow tunnel until she reached a small opening at the bottom of a stairwell. She got down on her hands and knees to crawl through the opening, and the others followed her through.

Eventually, the passage widened and they were all standing in a vast cave filled with steamy air. A small, circular pool of slow-bubbling magma simmered in the center of the cave floor. The chamber glowed with orange light.

Mugla pointed to the far side of the chamber, where an opening showed the continuation of the tunnel they had been following. "Over there —there's another passage that leads to the spellcasters' chambers."

Skemtun looked dumbfounded. "I've never seen *that* tunnel before. How come I never knew about these passageways?"

Mugla shrugged. "They're not really a secret— but no one comes down here anymore, now that the Vardmiters are gone. They're the only ones who used to service these tunnels, and the other clans never came down here because *they* wanted to avoid the Vardmiters. I'm a lot older than ye, Skemtun. Old enough to remember that Mount Velik is full of secrets. These passages were carved before my great-great-grandmother's time, back when the Kynn Oracle was new. Even I haven't been down here in hundreds of years. The magma pool is still as I remember it."

"We need to find a way around this," Tallin said. He could feel the violent heat of the magma on his face even though he was far away from it.

"Maybe there's another tunnel," said Sela.

"Why go around when we can go across?" Councilor Delthen said. "Magma is hard enough to walk on when it cools, correct?"

Skemtun looked startled, but he nodded. "Yes, of course."

"I assume that everyone here knows how to cast *Bjarg-Risa*?" Even when he was trying to be helpful, Delthen managed to sound patronizing. "A bridge is a good idea, and it wouldn't take much energy to create one."

The other mageborns agreed and stood on the edge together, circling the pool.

"On three," Tallin said. "One, two... three... *Bjarg-Risa!*"

The spell struck and spread, filtering the heat from the magma bit by bit. As the magma cooled, it went from vibrant orange to dull brown, and finally to glossy black.

Tallin stared at what lay in front of him for a second or two. Magma still flowed underneath, but now the pool was covered by a bridge of solid obsidian, which ran straight from one side of the flow to the other.

"Is it safe to walk on? How thick is it, do you think?" Bolrakei asked skeptically. "I don't want to step on there and get cooked like a dinner goose."

"Like anyone would ever eat a goose that tasted like *you*," Skemtun muttered.

Kathir heard the joke and gave a bark of laughter.

Bolrakei shot him a furious glare.

Tallin tapped his foot on the bridge. He could still feel the heat under his boot, but the bridge felt stable enough to cross. "It feels solid enough to me."

"So which of us wants to volunteer to be the first across?" Druknor asked, but he stopped short when he saw that Councilor Komu had already stepped onto the bridge.

"Ah, this reminds me of freezing the ponds in Miklagard when I was a boy so that we could skate," said Komu as he skipped across the magma flow. His assistants followed him to keep him from teetering over the side. The rest of the party crossed one by one.

"This chamber is fascinating. I can't believe I didn't know about this. I might have to rebuild it when we get back," Skemtun said.

Mugla shot Skemtun a strange look but said nothing. The old dwarf mage knew there was a possibility that none of them would be coming back, but Skemtun seemed too excited to accept that fact.

Now Skemtun took the lead at the head of the group. He used his instinct and experience in the tunnels to pick a route through the mountain. "We should be close to the spellcasters' chambers now."

Tallin agreed, but not because of instinct. He could hear faint shouts and the thud of picks against rock in the distance. Occasionally, the beat of marching feet echoed from one of the corridors. They finally reached a dead end, and Mugla stepped forward.

"We're trapped!" said Bolrakei.

"No, the entrance is *warded*, remember?" Mugla explained patiently as though speaking to a child. "This is the western entrance to the spellcasters' chambers. Everyone step back." The wall was carved with ancient runes, and she traced them with her fingertip.

Mugla muttered something under her breath. There was a bright flash, and the chamber was filled with light. "Stay behind me, and don't touch anything!" Mugla closed her eyes and walked into the blinding light. The others followed on her heels.

Once they were all past the spelled door, the light dimmed, so that they could see. The spellcaster's chambers were filled from floor-to-ceiling with piles of gemstones, jewelry, and shining coins. It was an enormous treasure horde.

Druknor's eyes widened. He reached out and

sifted a handful of coins with his hand. "Holy Baghra! Look at all this gold!"

"Don't touch it!" Bolrakei shouted as she slapped his hand away. "That's *our* gold!"

Druknor glared at her.

An overwhelming scent of burnt incense hung in the chamber. The smell was laced with the faint odor of decay. "Something's happened in here," Tallin said ominously.

He walked into the adjacent chamber, which was also filled almost to the ceiling with trunks of gold coins. There was a dead dwarf lying face-down on the chamber floor. Tallin kneeled down and flipped the man over. Chills went down his spine—he recognized this dwarf—it was Graff, one of the dwarf spellcasters. Tallin's stomach was empty, but he felt nauseated all the same.

"That's a shame," said Mugla, standing at the chamber doorway. She approached the body and nudged it. "He's only been dead a few days. The body is just starting to smell."

"He was young...why did he trap himself in here?" Tallin asked, stunned. "Why didn't he try to escape? Why would he seal himself inside this room?"

Mugla shook her head slowly. "Look around ye. Before he became a spellcaster, Graff was a member of *Klorra-Kanna*. He was always a bit greedy, but fear of losing everythin' must have driven him to madness. He died tryin' to save his clan's riches. He must have been goin' back and forth for days inside these tunnels, trying to save these treasures."

Tallin looked down at the dead man and didn't know whether or not he should pity him. "Then what Sela said is true. None of the other dwarf spell-casters survived. You're the last one."

Mugla smiled slightly, but her expression was sad. "Ye're a spellcaster too, my dear."

Tallin frowned. "You're a pureblood. I'm only a *halfling*. It's not the same thing."

Mugla sighed, but she didn't bother to argue with him.

They went back into the adjacent chamber and told the others about the body. Bolrakei shivered and looked away. She didn't look guilty, exactly, but there was something awkward in the way she cleared her throat and shifted her feet.

"So what do we do now?" asked Skemtun.

"Well, we can't stay in here," said Tallin. "We've got to find out what we're facing out there."

They made their way to the chamber exit. Mugla deactivated the exit wards and they stepped out into the orc-occupied mountain. The elves acti-vated their concealment spell again.

"Everyone, stay together, and remain on guard," Tallin whispered. "We can't afford to be dis-covered."

A couple of corridors later, they spotted an orc patrol. There were a half-dozen of them; most wore dark leather armor, and all of them were carrying sharpened spears or maces.

Tallin pressed his back against the wall to avoid

them, and all the other members of their party followed suit. The elves' eyes narrowed dangerously, and they looked ready to attack, but Tallin held up his hand. "Let's observe for a while," he said quietly. "We need to get a better idea of their numbers."

As the orcs stomped past, they were close enough to reach out and touch. Amandila wrinkled her nose and held her breath. The orcs smelled foul and unwashed and were drenched with sweat. Even though the concealment spell masked them completely, it wouldn't conceal their presence if one of them vomited on the floor.

"Thank Baghra," Sela whispered as soon as the orcs walked out of sight. She rubbed her nose. "Those greenskins smell utterly *rancid.*"

Tallin glanced at Amandila and Fëanor. "How long can the two of you hold this spell?"

Amandila exhaled deeply. Her skin looked paler than usual. "Over this many people? While we move? Not very long. An hour, perhaps two."

"Let's find a place to hide. It would be better to conserve our strength for when we really need it," Fëanor said. "We can always cast the spell again when the orcs get close."

"Orcs will be around us constantly now," Tallin said. "But you're right. We can't exhaust ourselves."

Mugla raised her finger. "I have a suggestion. Why don't we cast a more basic concealment? Just to mask our appearance? Then, if orcs get any closer, the elves can use their version so that we disappear completely."

Tallin nodded. "It sounds like a good compromise. Remember, everyone—this spell is weaker. It won't mask your voice or your smell. Don't speak unless it's absolutely necessary."

Tallin cast a weaker spell, extending it to cover Skemtun and Kathir. Elias covered Bolrakei and Druknor. The others all had the skill to conceal themselves.

As the party continued onward, they moved through more open caverns. Orcs worked within the caves, chipping rocks, skinning animals, and crafting iron weapons. Tallin led the way, trying to pick out a route that kept them as far from the orcs as physically possible.

Foul odors and chaos were everywhere. As they reached the center of the mountain, they heard roars from the *drask* in their breeding pits. They paused for a moment near the drask pits. Tallin pointed to the middle of the floor. "Look—the orcs have painted dozens of fighting circles on the ground here. The white chalk outlines are stained with blood from recent battles. But why aren't they fighting now?"

Fëanor spoke. "It is unusual. The orcs use fighting circles to settle even their most basic arguments. So they should be fighting all the time. In fact, there should have been fights breaking out in every room we passed through. They are remarkably... calm." The elf shivered. "It's actually very disconcerting."

Tallin frowned. "King Nar is a stronger leader than I thought," he said. "The orcs are more organized than I've ever seen."

"Maybe the orcs have always been smarter than you've given them credit for," Druknor said.

Tallin's eyebrows rose. "You sound like you admire them."

Druknor shrugged. "No—but I can respect a powerful leader. There is much to admire about any leader ruthless enough to control his people so completely. That does not make him any less my enemy. If anything, it makes Nar more of a threat. Nar must be eliminated. I will *not* allow threats to my interests to survive."

Tallin decided to let it go. For now, he had to focus on getting them to Mount Velik's main hall. Whatever was happening inside the mountain, he was sure that they would find some clue to it at the heart of the city. So they crept along, wrapped in their concealment spells. They kept to the shadows and pressed themselves against the walls whenever any orcs walked past.

When they passed into the main corridor, they got their first clear view of the interior under the caldera. The destruction was awful. The dwarves' carefully planted fields had been trampled into nothingness.

Skemtun's face fell. "They've destroyed our home..." His voice trailed off.

"Wait—more important than that... what's happened to the spring?" asked Mugla. "All the wells are gone."

Tallin's blood ran cold. All the wells had been

covered over and sealed with concrete. The area where the spring had been was now a layer of solid stone. "The orcs *sealed* the spring. That's why we saw so much runoff outside the mountain. They've redirected the water outside." He felt their carefully-laid plans slipping away. How could they flood the caverns without a water source? How else could they drive out the orcs?

"But why?" asked Skemtun. "It doesn't make any sense. Even orcs need a water supply."

"They've got water outside, now. Plus, maybe they never planned to stay," said Fëanor. "Perhaps their goal wasn't to occupy this mountain—only to destroy it... and to destroy the entire dwarf kingdom in the process."

"If that's their plan," said Druknor, "it looks like they've succeeded. The walls are crumbling, the water's polluted, and the surrounding forest is destroyed. And the stench in here is awful—the whole place stinks like a latrine in high summer. Who would want to live here now?"

"Shut up, you wretched fool!" hissed Bolrakei. "You don't know anything! Mount Velik is our home. We can *fix* this—all of this. My people will return to these caverns someday! I swear it!"

Druknor didn't respond, but everyone knew Druknor had spoken the truth. The caverns were in terrible shape. It would take years of rebuilding just to return to the level of development that existed before the orcs took over.

"Come on," said Tallin grimly, "let's keep moving."

Soon, they reached a familiar-looking set of grand doors, which they found guarded by two huge orcs in full armor.

"This is the main hall. We need to get inside," Tallin whispered. "Nar is probably in there, holding court. It would be useful to know what he is planning."

The elves smiled wickedly at each other and stepped forward. "We'll take care of these two guards."

Fëanor and Amandila snuck forward under cover of their spells. They slid two daggers into the orcs simultaneously, so quickly that their movements were almost a blur. The orcs coughed blood and slid down against the wall without making a sound.

Tallin stepped forward to help drag the dead guards into the shadows. By the time they were finished, he turned to see that two perfectly crafted illusions guarded the doors now, giving the impression that everything was the same as before. One even scratched its nose and coughed.

Komu's assistants stood nearby, controlling the two fakes. "We'll stay outside and maintain the illusions—hurry!"

"The illusions *look* perfect—except the other orcs might notice that they don't stink," Tallin pointed out. "So, we'd better hurry."

The others nodded and entered the great hall under the elves' strongest cloaking spell. The group slipped into the great hall and froze, unable to do anything but stare at the nightmare that stood before them.

The great hall was ruined. Every scrap of ornamentation had been torn from the walls. Priceless tapestries had been ripped, leaving only threads hanging from their hooks. Carved tables had been broken up for firewood. The walls were blackened with soot and stained with dried blood.

What had once been a cherished meeting place for the dwarves had become a filthy ironworks for the orcs. Metal forges burned hot along one wall, and endless racks of crude weapons hung along another.

They stood and stared in horror and awe. Everyone's eyes stung from the acrid smoke of the fires, and the whole space was uncomfortably hot.

Skemtun gasped. "They're melting down all our weaponry and armor—those pieces were priceless!"

Bolrakei started sobbing quietly.

Groups of orcs were grinding, sharpening, and hammering the weapons into shape. Other orcs stood at the far end of the hall, testing the finished weapons. In the open space in the middle, more orcs were carving away at massive pieces of wood, wrapping them in iron bands and covering the ends with iron. They were making battering rams. Two orcs working on the floor were shaping wood so that it could be used for a ballista.

"They're getting ready for another siege," Tallin whispered.

"So soon?" asked Skemtun incredulously. "How?

They couldn't possibly have enough soldiers to mount another offensive so quickly. We killed thousands during the *last* siege!"

"Tallin is right," said Fëanor, frowning deeply. "They're still preparing for war. Nar may be too ambitious for his own good. For orcs, this level of organization and preparation is unbelievable. Nar must be getting ready for another assault, probably on Ironport, or maybe even Morholt. He must be stopped."

"Look at this place," Skemtun muttered. "It's a disaster! They've taken all the statutes out of the hall. Those statues were priceless—they were thousands of years old. Where did the orcs put them?"

"They probably melted them down for scrap—to make more weapons," said Tallin.

"This is hard to watch," Mugla said. "They're destroyin' our history."

Bolrakei shook a rigid finger in Mugla's face. "Why do you even care?" she growled, "You and the Vardmiters left us to fend for ourselves! You're probably happy about all this, you traitorous witch!" Tears streamed down her face.

Mugla's nostrils flared with anger, and she opened her mouth to respond, but she stopped when the clamor in the hall ceased. King Nar had entered the room.

He came in through the door that used to lead to the kitchens, accompanied by twelve large, brutal-looking orcs. All were armed with huge knives, and their chain armor had iron spikes sticking out of the shoulders. One of them spotted another orc with his back to the king and shoved him so hard that he flew into the wall.

"That's King Nar's royal guard," whispered Fëanor. "Each of his guards has a symbol on their armor that identifies them. Those twelve green-skins are his protectors, as well as his closest advisors. When the king finally dies or is replaced, his entire guard will follow him onto the funeral pyre so that they can serve him in the next life."

King Nar stood in the middle of the group. He was barrel-chested, his body corded with muscle. His plate armor was blackened with soot and grease and was adorned with skulls taken from his defeated enemies. The bones hanging from his fur cape and chest plate were a grisly reminder of the destruction he had wrought. Around his thick waist hung a sheathed broadsword. A coiled whip hung from his left shoulder, and a huge dagger hung from a strap around his chest.

The darkness made it impossible to read Nar's face, which was covered with black paint. He strode into the room with confidence and poise. When he reached the center of the room, he stepped up onto a stump of wood and roared.

All the orcs stopped their chatter, and the hall fell silent. King Nar began to speak in the guttural tongue of the orcs.

"What's he sayin'?" Skemtun asked, "Can any of ye understand his language?"

Fëanor nodded. "I'll translate. He's saying, '*My*

people! Listen and obey with your heart, and pledge yourselves to me. I am your king, and my wrath is terrible.'"

Tallin stared at the elf. Fëanor's eyes were glazed over, as if he were in a trance.

"'I am pleased with the growth of our army,'" Fëanor continued. *"We took this mountain, and we shall take everything else that we want.'"*

The orcs responded with hoots and roars.

"The humans think that they are safe in their cities," King Nar shouted. *"They believe their walls will protect them. They think that we shall not strike at them, because they have a few dragon riders to protect them. Yet the dwarves had walls, and were they safe? No! We crushed them like ants!"*

There was a rumble of excited chatter around the room.

Nar raised his fist into the air. *"We crushed the dwarves, and we shall do the same to the humans!"*

The orcs roared.

"We are only days from success," Nar went on. *"Even now, more of our brothers are arriving from Mount Heldeofol. We are stronger now than we've ever been! Soon, our armies will sweep down on Morholt. That frail human city shall fall before our armies. We will crush the humans—squash them like mice! Soon, the whole continent will be ours! No one can stop us!"*

Each time Nar spoke, the crowd roared their approval. They bellowed, they shouted, they shook their fists.

Tallin looked at the others. "We should go. We've

heard everything we need to. It's time to get out of here."

They slipped back out of the hall, retracing their steps through the tunnels. They were all quiet as they retreated along corridors and through caverns, looking for the way back out. They made it out of the area and headed back toward the tunnel that led to the exit. It was only when they were almost at the magma chamber that they heard clicking sounds behind them.

"Orcs," Kathir whispered.

"Worse. *Drask*," said Tallin. "They must have caught our scent..." he shook his head. "We've been stupid. The concealment spells masked our scent only sometimes. We've left traces behind us inside the mountain. They're tracking us. Our scent trails will lead the drask right to us!"

They hurried for the exit. Bolrakei, who had been hanging back for most of the way, was suddenly jogging at the front of the group. Amandila and Fëanor started to cast their concealment spell again, but Tallin stopped them with a gesture.

"Don't bother—it's too late for that. Our scent is already all over this area. Save your strength instead —we need to be ready to fight. Try to stay hidden while we move."

They rushed back toward the magma room and were pleased to find that their stone bridge was still there; it was narrower than before, but it still spanned the width of the flow. Bolrakei rushed across without stopping.

"I guess it's still safe to cross," said Tallin, testing the bridge with his foot. "One at a time, though. Hurry, everyone!"

Komu went next, followed by his assistants. Councilor Delthen and Druknor also rushed across. The elves went next. The clicking got louder. Tallin drew his sword.

"Get ready," Sela said, raising her hands. "I can smell the drask—they're almost upon us."

"Skemtun," Tallin said. "You go across next. I'll stay behind with Sela to cover your crossing. Get to the spellcasters' quarters—you'll be safe in there. The orcs won't be able to enter those chambers as long as they're warded."

"I'll stay and fight," said Kathir.

Skemtun opened his mouth to argue, but Kathir silenced him by pushing him onto the bridge. Skemtun skittered across.

The orcs arrived. There were only ten of them, but a pair of drask hissed and snarled beside them.

An orc threw himself at Kathir, and the mercenary parried the attack, digging in his heels to keep from falling towards the edge of the magma pool. Tallin also traded strikes with another orc while Mugla made her way across the bridge.

"Go, Elias!" shouted Tallin as he shot a blue firebolt at one drask.

Elias blasted one of the orcs with a fireball, and then jumped across the bridge while Tallin covered him. Kathir spun and cut down the orc he was fighting before engaging another orc.

Sela flung one of the drask across the cavern with magic, slamming its body against the far wall. The other snapped at her, nearly catching her leg, but she jumped back onto the bridge. Tallin distracted the beast with a stroke of his sword, drawing blood, but only causing a small cut to the animal's leg.

Kathir killed another orc but barely missed getting bitten by the drask.

"Don't let the drask touch you—not even a scratch!" yelled Sela. "Their bite is deadly!"

Kathir nodded and went back to fighting. Sela crossed the bridge. Now only Kathir and Tallin were fighting on the other side of the bridge.

"Go," Kathir said. "*Go*. You're a dragon rider—they can't afford to lose you."

Tallin stared at him for a moment before running across the now failing bridge. An orc ran up on Kathir's left, but a firebolt from Mugla hit it in the chest.

She had been waiting on the other side for Tallin and the others to cross. More magic flared around Kathir, and several more orcs died. He thrust his sword through the heart of another one of the attackers. Then a drask jumped on top of him, snarling and snapping with dripping jaws.

"Don't let it bite you!" Tallin yelled from the other side.

Kathir jammed his sword into the creature's mouth, forcing it back while he scrambled for his dagger with his other hand. He stabbed, but the blade skittered off the drask's hard scales.

"Kathir, get up and run!" shouted Skemtun.

Kathir sprinted for the bridge and felt it give under his feet as he ran. He glanced back and saw that the injured drask was struggling back up to its feet.

Kathir jumped off the bridge onto solid ground just as the drask rose up from the cavern floor. It stepped forward onto the bridge tentatively.

"Quick!" Tallin yelled. "Collapse the bridge! *Bjarg-rammlingr!*"

As the bridge dissolved and collapsed, the drask shrieked, swallowed by the molten rock. The magma flared as it consumed the beast, its final screams echoing through the cavern. All of the orcs were dead, and their bodies were scattered around the room on the other side of the molten pool.

"We can't stay here," Sela said. "More orcs will follow. The magma pool won't stop them for long— they'll find another way to bridge the gap."

"We can't leave here without a plan. We have to stop Nar—before he gathers his forces to attack Morholt," replied Tallin.

Mugla went around the group to treat any wounds they'd received during the fight. "All the injuries were minor," she said. "We've been very lucky."

Remarkably lucky, Tallin decided, remembering the fetid smell of the drask's breath in his face. "Let's go," he said with urgency. "Our plans have changed. After what the orcs have done, there won't be sufficient water pressure for us to flood the caverns. We have to think of something else. We must strike another way, and we need to formulate a new plan by tonight."

They wound back through the tunnels, following the same route. By the time the group made its way back out into the spellcasters' chambers, hours had passed, and the smell from the dead spellcaster was worse than before.

"We should take him outside and bury him," said Mugla. "That poor soul."

"It's too dangerous," said Bolrakei. "Just roll him up in a blanket and set him aside."

"I hate to admit it, but Bolrakei's right," said Tallin. "The man deserves a proper burial, but we'll have to wait. We can't leave the chamber now. It's too risky."

"The orcs know that we're inside the mountain, said Skemtun. "We've lost the element of surprise. What are we going to do?"

"How are we going to stop the greenskins?" Bolrakei wailed. "Their numbers don't seem to have diminished at all. If anything, there are even *more* of them than before!"

They were quiet for a long time. No one seemed willing to begin the difficult conversation that they all knew they needed to have.

"Morholt can't stand against the orcs," Sela said grimly. "Rali is still rebuilding his armies, and the orc's numbers are too great. The city will fall."

"We can't afford to take that chance," said Tallin. "The orcs must be stopped *here and now*—at all costs."

Bolrakei snorted. "Why is *Morholt* so important? Once the orcs leave Mount Velik to march into the south, my people could take back Mount Velik. Let Morholt defend itself—it has its own army. They certainly didn't come and help us when *we* needed it!"

"Are you mad? My son Rali is the king, and I won't risk his life on a gamble," Sela snapped. "The orcs must be stopped *before* they start their march towards the capital city."

"Sela's right," said Elias quietly. "And it's not just the city at risk—it's the thousands of people along the way. All the villages in the greenskins' path will be razed to the ground. We can't allow them to go any further with their plans."

"I agree the orcs must be stopped now," said Delthen. "If the orcs take Morholt, then they will have control of the entire eastern seaboard! Eventually, even Miklagard and even Parthos will be in danger. We cannot allow the greenskins to spread."

"Speaking as the governor of Sut-Burr," Druknor said. "I also agree that the orcs must be stopped at all costs."

"Our queen also agrees," Fëanor said. "I speak for her: the greenskins must be eliminated."

"I think we all understand the gravity of the situation," Tallin said. "The question now is how we are going to stop them. From what Nar said, we only have days before the orcs start their march toward Morholt."

Skemtun held his axe across his knees, looking down at the reflection of his face on its blade. "We can't meet them in open battle. And we can't flood the caverns with water, since the spring is sealed up with rock. What other options do we have to drive them out?"

"We could collapse all the entrances to Mount Velik and trap them inside," Fëanor said with a spark of cruelty in his eyes. "Their food would run out eventually. We could let them starve."

Mugla snorted. "It's a mountain, not some crofter's hut with only one entrance. There's lots of ways to build exits and entrances in this mountain —especially if ye're desperate. Besides, there's no way to seal all the orcs inside. Half of them are pottering about outside, working on their death machines. It wouldn't work."

"Mugla's right," Elias said. "The orcs aren't stupid, like cattle—they would figure out a way to escape eventually. Sealing the mountain would temporarily slow them down, but it wouldn't stop them. They probably have food stores inside, too. They have to be eating *something*."

None of them wanted to think about what that *something* was.

"So you're saying that there's no way to kill them?" Amandila asked, with an edge of hysteria in her voice. "The orcs are going to pour out of Mount Velik like a plague of locusts!"

"Worried that your snobbish queen will be a bit displeased?" Druknor asked. "Some of us stand to lose more than you, elf. We don't have a mystical land that we can all escape to!"

"Everyone, stop arguing." Tallin took a deep breath. "I think I have a solution. But some of you aren't going to like it."

Sela's expression was dark. "Well, let's hear it. What's your plan?"

Tallin looked around the room. "We activate the volcano. It will fill the caverns with magma and smoke. All the orcs will be forced out or killed. It will also destroy all their weaponry."

A surprised murmur rose from around the room. The elves smiled and clapped their hands. Bolrakei's mouth dropped open in shock.

Sela looked thoughtful. "It's so crazy that it just might work."

Bolrakei screamed. "No! You can't do that! It will destroy our home! We will never be able to return."

"At this point, it may be our only option," said Tallin calmly.

"Are you insane?" She was now shrieking. "Destroying our home is not the only way! It's a stupid idea!"

Skemtun raised one hand and spoke. "I don't think it will work. The mountain is dead. It hasn't erupted in thousands of years."

"Right! I've never heard such a ridiculous plan in all my life!" Bolrakei agreed.

"I agree with the old dwarf," said Druknor. "It would never work."

"I think it's possible," replied Sela, "The volcano

isn't dead; it's just inactive. It could be done—if we all worked together and had the dragon's strength, as well."

"The elves have spells that can do this sort of thing—manipulate the natural order of things," Amandila said. "Fëanor is especially gifted in this type of spellcasting. He and I could spark the natural processes of the volcano to create a true eruption... that is, if we had enough help. We just need a catalyst—something with great heat, and runestones to activate the spell."

"Dragonfire could work," Tallin said, astonished how quickly this had gone from a vague possibility to something that now seemed like a solution.

"Stop talking about this ridiculous plan!" Bolrakei snapped. "We should be gathering an army to retake Mount Velik, not plotting to destroy it. The humans and elves can help us! They're our allies, and they owe it to us!"

"It's too late for that, Bolrakei," said Sela quietly. "Stop arguing with us. Mount Velik is lost."

"No!" Bolrakei screamed. "You can't do this! You can't destroy everything we have!"

"There is no other way," Tallin insisted.

"That's a lie!" Bolrakei's fists were clenched, and her face was flushed purple. "I will *not* agree to spend the rest of my life living with the Vardmiters! I will not!"

Skemtun just shook his head. The old dwarf looked defeated.

"This is our home," Bolrakei continued, "This is

where we live and work—it's where our jewels are mined! There's *nothing* for us in the Highport Caverns. Nothing!"

Tallin fought to keep his anger in check. "We're not putting our lives in danger just so *your* clan can continue to dig gemstones out of this mountain. I don't care about your wealth. I care about stopping the greenskins, and this is the only way to do it."

"There's one thing we haven't discussed," said Elias quietly. "If we force the mountain to erupt, we'll kill thousands of orcs. We're talking about taking thousands of lives."

Fëanor snorted. "They're just greenskins. Why does it matter?"

"They're sentient beings. Plus, if there are any humans or dwarves nearby, it might kill them too," Elias said. "Every life counts—even an orc's."

Councilor Komu stretched and yawned. "That is a fine sentiment, young man. Although I doubt the orcs would feel the same way about you."

"With all due respect, sir, that isn't the point," Elias responded.

"I agree... it's horrible," said Sela. "And there are a lot of risks. We might not survive this ourselves. But we don't have another choice. If we don't do something, thousands of innocent people will die. We can't allow the orcs to begin their war march. If there were a way to end this peacefully, we would, but the orcs don't negotiate with anyone. This is our only option. Are we all agreed?"

Everyone except Skemtun and Bolrakei nodded.

"We'll do it, then," Sela said. "Tonight."

Skemtun's shoulders slumped. He stood in silence, staring down at the floor. "My people are more important than this mountain. As long as they are safe, I will agree to help."

"No!" Bolrakei said. "How can you agree to this, Skemtun?"

Skemtun's expression was gloomy. "Because it needs to be done, and I'll do my part."

"This isn't going to be easy," Tallin said.

Mugla smiled beside him. "We're blowin' up a whole mountain, dear. Of course it won't be *easy.*"

11. RUNESTONES AND MARKERS

They rested for a few hours and discussed their plans. Tallin and the elves contacted the dragons and let them know what was happening.

The finer details took some time to work out. There were endless conversations about how to get the dragons inside the mountain and about how to activate the volcano in a controlled manner. All the while, Bolrakei remained furious and silent.

Mugla provided a lot of useful information; she used her extensive knowledge of enchantments to suggest a way to delay the spells while they escaped the danger.

"The idea is simple," Mugla said. "All the spell-casters will pair up and make their way around the caverns under concealment. You must enchant certain critical spots—marking stones at specific points within the mountain. We're laying a linked *web* of spells. They'll remain dormant until we are ready to activate them all. When we're ready, we'll trigger the spells with concentrated blasts of dragonfire from the caldera. Dragonfire has magical properties, so it will increase the strength of the enchantments. The molten rock will erupt upward, which will destroy the caverns and drive the orcs out of the mountain. Does everyone understand?"

Amandila raised her hand. "There's one problem. Rock enchantments take time, and they're rather unstable. We might get a nasty surprise when the time comes to trigger the spells."

"Such risks can't be avoided," Tallin said. "We'll just have to take our chances. When the orcs see the dragons flying into the caldera, they will panic. We won't have much time to act after that."

"We'll need to split up in order to get this done in time," Councilor Delthen said.

"If we split up, each of us will only need to lay two or three spells each," Mugla said. "That should be enough. Then we'll all meet back here before sundown. The dragons will fly in to trigger the enchantments with dragonfire while the rest of us get clear of the mountain."

They all discussed suitable spots to set the spells, so that the enchantments would be spread evenly throughout the caverns. Then they divided into groups. Kathir and Skemtun were paired with Komu and his assistants.

They crept outside the chamber with Skemtun as their guide. Kathir found himself pitying the group that had Bolrakei as a guide, but not too much, since it also included Delthen, Fëanor, and Druknor. If it weren't for the fact that they needed every group to succeed, Kathir would have hoped for them to get lost.

Komu and his assistants used concealment

spells, but they all still held their breath every time an orc came into view. The orcs seemed to be agitated—almost as if they were expecting trouble.

They tiptoed their way along the tunnels, pressing themselves into niches as orcs passed by. Once, Kathir saw an orc sniffing the air around them, and he lunged forward to stab it before the creature could raise the alarm. They dragged the dead orc by its feet into a dark chamber.

"We need to move quicker!" Kathir said. "We aren't safe here."

"We aren't safe anywhere," said Skemtun. "And I'm moving as fast as I can!"

Kathir sighed. He knew it was true. Besides, even with the help of his aides, Komu could only move so quickly.

They stopped inside a darkened alcove. "It's time, Master Komu," Blias whispered.

"Time for what?" asked Komu with a bewildered look on his face.

"The enchantments, Councilor," he reminded him.

"What? Oh yes... of course. The enchantments." At that moment, Komu's features sharpened, and he seemed much more in control. He rubbed his hands together. "Let's get started then."

He began to cast the spell, mumbling under his breath. His fingers touched the rock, which vibrated lightly under his palm. Skemtun and Kathir kept careful watch, making sure that no orcs came near.

The stone under Komu's hand started to glow,

and bright lines of red appeared on it like a spider's web. "There," he said at last. His breath came sharply. "It's done. One more to go, I believe."

The next spot was harder. It was inside a small cave, but a group of orcs were sitting in the middle of the floor, talking in low voices and eating a quick meal. Kathir paused at the entrance, hoping that they would move out, but after a few minutes of waiting, it became evident that the orcs weren't going anywhere.

"It *has* to be in here?" Kathir whispered to the others. "Can we go to another spot?"

"This cave is right in the center of the fourth quadrant. It's in a strategic place," Skemtun said. "It has to be here."

"Then I guess we do this the hard way," Kathir sighed, drew his sword, and charged forward. His body shimmered and became visible as he leaped outside the perimeter of the concealment spell. The startled orcs jumped up from their seated positions, but it was too late.

Kathir's sword sliced the first in the throat, and he was already turning toward the second when Skemtun hit it squarely in the chest with his axe. Their concealment spell gave way entirely as Komu took the last orc down with a well-aimed fireball. The five of them scrambled inside the cave and quickly covered the entrance with an animal skin.

"We need to work quickly," Komu said to his assistants.

Kathir nodded. "Go! We'll keep watch at the

door."

It didn't take long for Komu and his assistants to set the second enchantment.

"The other spellcasters should be finished by now, too," said Kathir, "We need to get out of here."

They hurried out of the cave and went to join the others in the spellcasters' chambers. Everyone was already waiting for them inside.

"Everything went all right?" Tallin asked.

"Everything went fine," Komu replied, a satisfied smile on his face. "We ran into a bit of trouble with a few greenskins, but we took care of it."

Bolrakei looked desperate. Her face was tear-stained, and her hair was a mess. "Are you *sure* we need to do this?" she cried, wringing her hands. "We could wait—let's talk it over a little more first."

"We've talked it over long enough," said Tallin.

Bolrakei started to cry. Tears rolled down her chubby cheeks.

"There's just one more thing to do," said Sela. "We'll give Druknor, Delthen, Komu and his assistants all some time to escape the mountain. Follow Bolrakei outside; let her guide you to safety. Mugla and Skemtun will stay with us, since they are the most familiar with the interior caverns. As soon as you are outside the mountain, send us a telepathic message. You must hurry."

"Don't worry about us," Councilor Delthen said. "We'll be fine."

Bolrakei was strangely silent throughout the conversation, and she did not object when they started to leave the spellcasters' chambers.

"I'm surprised that Bolrakei stopped fighting us," Kathir said once she was out of earshot.

"Me too," Skemtun said. "Maybe she's just accepted it—like I have. That was definitely not what I expected. I actually feel a little sorry for her."

Skemtun headed over to Bolrakei, and just as he approached, he saw her take something from inside her dress. Skemtun knew what it was as soon as he saw it. A section of rock, burning red with a web of magical runes.

"Ye stole one of the runestones?" Skemtun said with shock.

Bolrakei gasped and spun around. "I don't know what you're talking about!" She jerked back and hid the stone behind her back.

Tallin heard the exchange and ran up to Bolrakei; he grabbed her by the arm and wrenched it from her hands. "What have you done?! The spell won't work unless all the runestones are set! You're trying to sabotage us!"

Bolrakei stumbled backward and fell to the ground. She was bawling now, snot and tears running down her face. "You're doing an evil thing! You're going to destroy my home. The only home I've ever known. Don't do it, please! I'll be forced to live in Highport, surrounded by those *awful* Vardmiters and all those dirty pigs and—and!" Her voice cut off with a sudden wail.

Tallin grabbed Bolrakei and lifted her up despite her protests. "Better alive in Highport than dead in

Mount Velik," he growled. Sela and the others came forward and surrounded her.

"She's stolen this," Tallin said, holding up the stone. "She tried to sabotage the spell-web."

"Which location did you take the stone from?" said Sela. "Answer me!"

"A spot near the main hall," Bolrakei said, still sniffling. "Right near the doors."

"The stone must be replaced—and quickly," said Sela. "Someone has to put it back—right now."

Skemtun spoke up. "I know where it is. Kathir and I will go back and replace it. The dragon riders can prepare themselves and get ready for our signal."

"You'll both be killed," said Tallin.

"We'll be fine," said Skemtun firmly. "I know the main caverns like the back of my hand. There are lots of spots to hide along the way. We can make it."

Kathir didn't hesitate. "We need a concealment spell. The best you can manage."

"I can't give you that. It won't last," Tallin said. "Not without the caster present. You need a mageborn to go with you, and we can't spare any of the spellcasters to help you."

Mugla stepped forward. "My concealment spells aren't great, but it's better than nothing. I'll volunteer to go. I'll be able to give them some cover if an emergency arises."

"No," Tallin blurted out. "You can't move fast enough. Plus, you're the last living dwarf spellcaster! We can't risk losing you."

Mugla paused as she let out a heavy sigh. "Now who's not thinking with their head, my dear? Yer thinking with yer heart. I'm an old woman, and if something happens to me... well, it's better than it happenin' to one of ye."

Tallin winced.

"I wish there was another way, but there isn't," she finished. "My mind's a bit foggy, and Skemtun knows the upper caverns better than anyone, so he'll be our guide. Kathir will protect us with his sword, and I'll be there to make sure that the rune-stone is replaced and enchanted properly."

"How will you know when it's time to strike?" asked Druknor.

"I'll send Tallin a message when the runestone has been replaced," said Mugla. "I'm a telepath, too, just not a great one."

"But how will you escape? The fire will devour you," said Tallin.

"Don't worry about that. We'll manage to escape," Mugla said absently.

"Wish us luck," Skemtun said finally. He smiled and waved his hand, but there was a dark brooding in his eyes.

Everyone grew silent for a moment. They all realized that Mugla, Skemtun, and Kathir would almost certainly die.

"I wish that luck would help," Tallin said quietly. "Now, go!"

Kathir, Mugla, and Skemtun jogged for the chamber exit. They went as fast as they could, and Mugla did all she could to keep up. At one point, Kathir picked her up and carried her; he jogged down the corridor with Mugla flung over one shoulder like a sack of potatoes.

Unsure of how to respond, Mugla managed to giggle like a schoolgirl.

The enchanted stone glowed eerily in the dark, and its light grew stronger as the minutes ticked by. Their time was running out.

"You don't really have to be here for this," Kathir told Skemtun. "You probably could have stayed behind."

"Ye need me to find the way! Plus, ye think I'd let ye do this alone?" Skemtun replied. And then, more jokingly, "Ye can't send a human to do a dwarf's job, mate."

"Very funny," Kathir said with a wry smile. Then he froze.

Up ahead, an orc popped out from behind a wall. It spun at the sound of their voices. Kathir sprang into action immediately; he put Mugla down and dispatched the creature. They kept running.

"It's best if we all keep quiet at this point," Mugla whispered. "My concealment spell isn't strong enough to mask your voices. I'm not powerful enough to make it any stronger."

Skemtun and Kathir both nodded. Skemtun turned to Kathir and whispered quietly, "Just in case we don't make it—I wanted ye to know...I'm proud to have ye as a friend."

"I feel the same," said Kathir softly.

Skemtun smiled. "Now, less talking, more running!"

They sprinted through the tunnels toward the main hall. They hid in alcoves whenever they saw orcs nearby. Their progress slowed as they got closer to the center of the mountain. The orcs were everywhere.

"We're very close," Skemtun whispered.

He could hear the fall of the hammers and the roaring of the forges. The hall doors lay ahead, and they were once again guarded by a pair of orcs.

The guards sniffed the air curiously, and a shocked look on their faces revealed that they knew that there were intruders nearby. As one tried to raise the alarm, Kathir stepped out and sent his dagger into the creature's fleshy neck.

Skemtun and Mugla cut down the other with a firebolt and a quick strike of an axe.

"I can't believe we made it," said Kathir, panting.

Mugla carefully placed the runestone into a niche near the doors. "There! That's done."

"We did it," said Skemtun.

"But it's not over," Kathir said, pointing to the doors, which were swinging open ominously.

A sea of shocked orc faces lay beyond—and all of their eyes were staring at them. For a moment, nobody moved. At the back of the hall, King Nar stood, massive and deadpan, in his black armor. Nar stared at them over the crowd for a moment, and then he laughed. The sound was deep and booming, and it rolled through the room like thunder.

Nar gestured to the orcs around him. "Who are these mice inside our new home?" he shouted. "Kill them all! I will wear their bones."

12. DESTRUCTION

Mugla screamed, "Run!" as hundreds of green faces turned toward them. Kathir grabbed her and threw her over his shoulder again, and he and Skemtun sprinted down the passage as fast as their legs would take them.

"Turn here!" huffed Skemtun, "There's a storage alcove nearby. We can hide in there." Kathir darted in after him.

They could hear the orcs shouting and running behind them. The sound of a war horn sliced through the air.

Skemtun threw a hasty glance over his shoulder. "Almost there," he said as he ducked into a hidden passageway and eased himself into a narrow alleyway, not much more than a crevice inside the rock. The space was so small that Kathir had to roll himself into a ball in order to fit inside.

Mugla raised her hands and muttered a quick spell. "Be still!" she whispered frantically as she cast a concealment spell around them. They froze, not even breathing, hoping that the orcs would pass them by. They heard the shouts of the orcs as they ran past.

Eventually, Skemtun whispered, "They've sounded the alarm, and they're lookin' for us, now.

There's no way we're gettin' out of here alive."

"Don't be so hasty. I'll do everything I can to keep you both alive," said Kathir. "We need a diversion. I'll cover your escape."

Skemtun shook his head. "I'm not leaving ye behind. I won't let ye become a martyr... I won't let ye."

Mugla's face was streaming with sweat, and her hands were trembling. "Whatever ye decide, ye need to do it quickly. I'm spent—I can't hold this spell much longer."

"Do ye have enough strength to contact the dragon riders?" asked Skemtun.

Mugla nodded. "Aye... but I can't maintain both spells at once. I'll have to stop the concealment spell." Her breath rasped in her chest.

"I think we're safe for the moment. Can ye contact Tallin and then cover us until we get to the atrium?" asked Skemtun.

"I'm not sure, but I can try," she replied weakly.

"What do you have planned?" asked Kathir.

"The dragon riders will be enterin' the mountain from the caldera; the atrium is right below it, and it's the only place large enough to hold 'em all. If we can make it there, then the riders can pick us up after they activate the runestones. It's our only chance to get out of this mountain alive."

Kathir nodded. "Let's do it, then. Mugla, are you ready to contact the dragon riders?"

Mugla gave him a trembling nod. She stopped the concealment spell and took a deep breath. Then her eyes took on a blank, dazed look. Her lips moved silently as she chanted a new spell. Seconds passed, and then she gasped. Her body went limp as her final measure of strength drained out of her.

"Catch her before she falls!" said Kathir.

Skemtun grabbed Mugla's limp body. Her skin was ashen. He slapped her cheeks gently. "Mugla! Hey, come on, wake up."

Mugla blinked, her eyes dazed and unfocused. "The wall's are spinnin'. Ugh...my achin' head."

The war horn sounded again. They glanced warily at each other.

"We've got to get out of here now," said Kathir, his concern written plainly on his face.

"Were ye able to contact the others?" asked Skemtun.

Mugla nodded. "I wasn't able to reach Tallin, but I did contact the elves. That's why I fainted. Telepathic communication with elves is grueling. Even when they're *not* trying to be jerks."

"Are they coming?" asked Skemtun.

Mugla nodded again. "Aye, everythin' is ready. I asked them to give us five minutes to reach the atrium. No matter what, they'll come in with the dragons when those five minutes are up. If we don't reach them in time, then our goose is cooked."

"We'll make it," Skemtun said with determination. "We have to—I'm not dyin' inside this mountain with a bunch of stinkin' greenskins."

Skemtun poked his head outside the gap, just far enough to see down the passageway. "The passage is clear... for now. Are you ready, Mugla?"

Mugla nodded and muttered the words to the concealment spell once again. The energy seemed to drain from her, and she swayed a little. "We've got to move quickly," she said, "that's the only hope we've got."

They all hopped up and dashed down the narrow passage, Skemtun leading the way. The atrium became visible, and they rushed down the winding stairs into the bottom of the cavern. The minutes ticked by.

They backed themselves against the wall and hid in the darkness, slipping past a group of orcs as their backs were turned. They made it to the atrium with only seconds to spare, and then disaster struck. Kathir tripped, hitting Mugla in the back. Mugla stumbled to the ground.

She hit her head on a rock and landed with a loud crack. She lay there with her eyes closed, blood trickling from her temple. The concealment spell dissipated, and they became visible to the orcs.

"Oh no," Skemtun said, trying to swallow his panic.

"Bad luck," said Kathir as he drew his sword. "We've got to stand and fight now."

Skemtun drew his axe, and they positioned themselves back-to-back so their opponents couldn't jump them from behind. For a few seconds, nothing happened. Then one of the orcs saw them, shouted, and raised his blade. Kathir struck the orc with a dagger through the eye.

"First blood is ours," said Kathir. "It's not much, but in situations like these, one must be thankful for small victories."

Skemtun gave a short bark of laughter. "Victory or not, if the dragon riders don't get here quick, we're all dead."

The orcs were closing in rapidly, and Skemtun and Kathir were soon flanked on all sides. Kathir grunted as an orc managed to slice into his side. Blood flowed from his ribs.

The next blow hit him squarely between the eyes, causing blood to gush from his forehead. Kathir staggered, clutched his head, and collapsed. The room spun, and he couldn't see.

"Kathir!" Skemtun shouted, placing himself in front of Kathir and Mugla. Skemtun was surrounded on all sides by orcs. The orcs paused for a moment and started to laugh.

"Go ahead and laugh, ye blighters!" Skemtun shouted. "Even if I die here, a whole lot of ye'll be followin' me to the grave!"

An orc dashed forward, and Skemtun was struck in the stomach by a mace. Waves of pain shot through him as he felt his skin split open. He stumbled back, warm blood drenching his tunic.

Just then, there was a loud roar from above, and the dragon riders swooped down from the caldera into the atrium. The orcs bellowed and scrambled back in fear.

Skemtun rose to his knees, holding his stomach. He didn't need to look at it to know his wound was bad. He reached down and wiped Kathir's bloody face with his torn sleeve. "Kathir...can ye hear me?"

At first, Kathir didn't move, but then, he blinked his eyes rapidly and shot up into a seated position. "I'm here!" he said, but his expression was dazed.

The dragons were breathing fire in all directions, and the elves were chanting loudly, surrounded by a glowing nimbus of magical energy. The orcs screamed and raised their hands up to cover their eyes from the light.

Tallin shouted down at them. "Kathir! Skemtun! Hurry! We've already activated the runestones. Grab Mugla and give her to me, and then the two of you split up between the other dragons."

Kathir staggered to his feet, picked up Mugla's tiny frame, and carried her over to Duskeye. Mugla groaned but did not wake up. Tallin placed her in front of him on the saddle and tied a rope around her body to keep her from falling.

"Move! We don't have much time!" shouted Tallin.

Skemtun tried to run toward Fëanor and Blacktooth, but he stopped and doubled over with pain.

"Are you alright?" asked Kathir, grabbing his arm.

"I got hit by a mace—my ribs are broken." Skemtun gasped for air and held his gut. Blood oozed between his fingers and spattered onto the floor.

"Let me help you," said Kathir, wrapping one arm around his friend's waist. When they reached Blacktooth, Fëanor looked down at them with a frigid stare. "Put the dwarf behind me on the saddle," he instructed in an unfriendly tone.

"Can you climb up on your own?" asked Kathir.

Skemtun shook his head. "No, I don't think so." His hand pressed over his wound.

Kathir picked up his friend and placed him on the saddle. He wiped his bloody face and said breathlessly, "Chin up, friend! We made it! I'll go ride with Sela and Brinsop."

But before Kathir could move, an orc threw an immense spear at them. Kathir's eyes widened with shock—he had no weapon to deflect it.

Determined to protect Skemtun, he instinctively blocked the weapon with the only thing he had—himself. His black eyes blazed with pain as the spear pierced his body.

"No!" screamed Skemtun, watching his friend fall. He tried to reach down, but Fëanor stopped him.

"Don't get down, or you shall die here, too. You cannot save him, dwarf."

Kathir dropped to his knees, gasping for breath. His dying eyes met Skemtun's. "I promised to save you, and I did."

"No! Let me help him!" cried Skemtun.

"Go, my friend... save yourself. Make sure I do not die in vain." Then Kathir fell, crumpling to the floor. He shuddered once and lay still.

"No!" Skemtun sobbed, shaking his head. "Please. He can't be gone." He tried to reach down, but Fëanor stopped him again, pushing him back onto the saddle.

"It's too late to save him," said the elf, "but we can still defeat the orcs. Hold on."

All the dragons rose up into the air, breathing dragonfire as they flew upward. A brief moment passed, and there was the sound of a tremendous explosion. The air around them was filled with dust.

"The eruption's started!" cried Tallin. "Everyone, move out now!" The mountain rumbled, and the earth started to shake.

The dragons flew up through the caldera, which was now filled with choking black smoke. They scattered in opposite directions, flying as quickly as they could.

From the sky, the riders could see thousands of orcs streaming out of the mountain, shouting and pushing through the front gates as they tried to escape the deadly lava flow. Some were horribly burned, their flesh hanging in blackened strips. Others had entire limbs blown off from the explosions.

There was so much death and destruction. The orcs were their enemies, but it was still a ghastly sight.

Mugla groaned, and Tallin helped her sit upright on the saddle. She had a smear of blood on her temple.

"Are you alright?" he asked.

Mugla nodded. "I'm fine..." She looked down at the chaos below. The orcs scattered in a million directions as they fled the mountain. A huge column of dark smoke trailed upwards into the clouds.

"I can't believe it worked," she said quietly.

"It's a bitter victory," said Tallin. "The orcs have been routed, but Mount Velik has been completely destroyed. The clans will never be able to return."

"That's true," she answered. "But it's still a victory—and a lucky one, at that. We should all be thankful."

Tallin watched the sky fill with smoke. It didn't feel like a triumph.

They'd lost so much. Kathir was dead, and Mount Velik was demolished. The dwarf clans were permanently displaced.

"Let's go, there's nothing else we can do," said Mugla.

The other dragons were already headed back to Highport.

Tallin nodded and spurred Duskeye's saddle. He followed the others north—and away from the destruction.

13. CHOICES

The dragons flew toward Highport, picking up Bolrakei, Komu, and the others along the way. Komu's apprentices were sent ahead on horseback. Nydeired carried most of the others, although with some difficulty. They stopped frequently along the way so the dragons could rest.

Once they reached Highport, the riders delivered their report to Utan, who accepted the news somberly. There was no celebration. The knowledge that Mount Velik had been destroyed eliminated all hopes of merriment.

The elves left soon after that. They were anxious to return to Brighthollow and deliver their news to the queen.

Skemtun was severely injured and was taken to the infirmary to recover. Elias took over his care, but the dwarf's wounds were grave. He had lost so much blood that he was as pale as an egg. The outlook worsened when Elias discovered that the orc's weapon had been tipped with a slow-acting poison.

"His ribs are shattered, and there is much internal damage. One might survive such a wound, but the poison complicates things," Elias said quietly, giving the news Tallin and Sela.

The dwarves slowly resigned themselves to accepting Highport as their new, permanent home. They had nowhere else to go. They would have to make do.

It was decided that an election would take place. New leaders would be chosen for all the dwarf clans, and representatives began secret talks. The talks were contentious, as always. The men hissed insults at one another, but there were no physical altercations as there had been in the past.

Because of his illness, Skemtun voted by proxy, with Tallin acting as his representative. Bolrakei, Utan, and Skemtun remained the leaders of their respective clans. Bimbek was elected the new leader of *Odenskapr*, the warrior clan, which had suffered heavy losses defending Mount Velik against the orcs. Harsk was the new leader of *Strikeforge*, the weaponsmiths' clan. Once all the leaders were chosen, it was time to elect a new ruler.

All the dwarves gathered to watch the final vote. At the main table sat Bolrakei, Utan, Tallin, and the two newly-elected clan leaders. Skemtun was very ill, but for the final vote, he asked to be carried into the main hall on his bed. The clans cheered when they saw him. He raised his pale arm and offered a weak wave.

"Today, we choose our king... ahem...or *queen*," Bolrakei said to a chorus of cheers. "All clan leaders shall be allowed one vote each."

A dwarf ran up to the table and handed Tallin an ornate scroll. "The polls for the clans have been decided. I have the nominees for King and Queen."

Tallin unrolled the scroll, and read aloud: "Bolrakei, leader of Klorra-Kanna, has been nominated for queen by her clan. Utan, leader of the Vardmiters, has been nominated for king by his clan. And lastly, Skemtun, leader of Marretaela, has been nominated for king by his clan. The clans Odenskapr and Strikeforge have decided to refrain from nominating a king."

Cheers filled the hall again, and Tallin sat down.

Skemtun raised his hand. His voice was fragile and weak. "I'm sorry, but I must withdraw my nomination. I won't saddle my people with another sick king. However, I won't abstain from votin'. I cast my vote for Utan."

Utan nodded his thanks, but his face remained expressionless. "I, Utan, leader of the Vardmiters, cast my vote for myself."

"That's two votes for Utan," said Tallin.

Bolrakei seethed and turned to look Skemtun straight in the eye. He returned her glare with a placid expression. She crossed her arms in front of her chest. "I cast my vote for myself, Bolrakei, leader of Klorra-Kanna."

Bimbek spoke. "I, Bimbek, leader of Odenskapr, cast my vote for Bolrakei."

A hush settled over the room. It came down to the last vote, and it went to Harsk, the new leader of Strikeforge. Like his predecessor, Harsk was young and open to new ideas. "I have considered this decision long and hard. Although I believe that Lady Bolrakei would make a good queen," he paused to give her a nod of respect, "I also believe that the clans owe Utan their lives. He saved us and welcomed us into his home. Therefore, I cast my vote for Utan."

Bolrakei's mouth fell open. Her eyes bulged. She began to wheeze. "B-but... that's impossible. Utan is a Vardmiter! A *Vardmiter!* Do you understand what that means?" Her voice rose to a screech. "There's never been a Vardmiter King in dwarf history! Not ever!"

From his bed, Skemtun chuckled softly. "Well, there's a first time for everythin', right?"

Pandemonium broke out at the table. Cheers went up from the Vardmiter clan, while boos and jeers ran through Klorra-Kanna.

Tallin stood up. "The clans have spoken. You must accept this decision and pledge your loyalty to your new King."

Bolrakei slammed her fist on the table. "This is intolerable, intolerable!"

Tallin locked eyes with her. "Deal with it," he whispered, too softly. "Your crusade of bigotry against the Vardmiters is over."

As he finished his words, Bolrakei's face contorted with rage. "You are destroying our way of life!" she cried. "I won't accept this!" Bolrakei spun and stomped out of the hall, followed by her entourage.

"Utan is the new king of the dwarves," declared Tallin, shouting so the entire hall could hear. Then he smiled and looked at Utan. "Congratulations,

Your Grace."

Scattered applause turned into a rousing ovation. Tallin smiled and stepped back as the crowd rushed forward to offer fealty to their new king. The dwarves from Bolrakei's clan stood back, but eventually, they would come around, too. They didn't have any choice.

"So...what happens now?" asked Skemtun, calling Tallin over to him. "Do ye think Bolrakei will cause trouble?"

Tallin laughed. "Undoubtedly, yes. I'm sure she will. But she will also accept the council's decision... with time. She lost the vote, and Utan is the king. Nothing can change that fact."

Skemtun smiled. "I'm so glad to hear that. I was worried for a moment." He fixed his gaze on Tallin's face. "Sela told me to talk to ye privately, but I guess now's as good a time as any. My clan needs new leadership—a strong person—someone who is fair and who will stand up to Bolrakei. I was never cut out to be a clan leader; I was happier being a miner. Leadership was shoved in my lap, and I did the best I could."

Tallin looked at him oddly. "What are you trying to say?"

"I've done many things in the past that I'm ashamed of, but I'm tryin' to do right. I treated the Vardmiters like dirt in the past, and I'm regretful of that. I'm trying to make up for it now. Kathir died tryin' to save me, and he had a dark past too. No matter what he did, in the end, he died a hero, at least in my eyes. I'm hopin' to do the same."

"Hold it," interrupted Tallin.

Skemtun pressed on, pretending that he hadn't heard him. "I'm dyin', and there's nothin' anyone can do about it." His voice broke, and he closed his eyes and took a deep breath. "I'm too old and too tired to explain this twice, so please listen until I'm through. Marretaela needs a new leader—someone who can lead them right. I've chosen ye as my replacement, if you'll accept."

Tallin stared at him, shock written plainly on his rugged features. "I can't be a clan leader—I'm a halfling!"

"That doesn't matter. I've talked to Utan and Sela already, and both of them have given me their blessing.

"I can't do it," said Tallin quietly. "The other clans will never accept me."

"You're wrong. I know my clan will accept you —I've already asked them. Times have changed, and there's no reason why you should be treated any differently."

"But I don't have any experience," Tallin argued.

"Ye're a dragon rider! Ye have plenty of experience. Plus, ye'll have advisors, just like the other leaders. They'll help guide ye—but ye'll be the one people will be followin'. Will ye accept the position?"

A long pause followed, in which Tallin gazed at him. Then a booming voice echoed in his mind.

"*Do it,*" said Duskeye, his gravelly voice echoing

from afar. *"It's about time you were appreciated by your own people."*

"So you were listening in, eh?" responded Tallin. "I'm not keen on this idea. It's too much responsibility."

"More responsibility than being a dragon rider? Come on now, think about it. You'd make a terrific leader —and you'd finally get the respect that you deserve from the clans."

"Please consider it," begged Skemtun. He paused for breath. "I know ye're very independent, and ye have to make your own choices, but your people need ye. You're their best hope for surviving all these changes—ye've lived in the outside world. Ye could be like an ambassador for them. Ye can help them learn how to get along in this new home." Skemtun's voice weakened and faded as he finished. He fell back on his pillow.

His pleading, coupled with his condition, weakened Tallin's resistance. "To be sure, there is much to be done."

Skemtun looked at him with pleading eyes. *"Please,* Tallin. Do this for our people."

Tallin pursed his lips. After a moment of silence, he finally nodded. "Alright. I'll do it—if the clans accept me."

Skemtun's bleary eyes spilled over with grateful tears. "Thank ye," he whispered, reaching out to clasp Tallin's hand. The old man's fingers were ice-cold.

From across the room, Utan watched their quiet

exchange with a knowing smile. He knew. He always knew.

Skemtun wheezed, and then closed his eyes. That was the last time that anyone spoke to him. Later that evening, Skemtun slipped into a coma and never awoke. Three days later, he died, and Tallin was officially nominated as Skemtun's replacement. As expected, the other clans accepted him unanimously—with the sole exception of Bolrakei.

Sela and Elias stayed to congratulate Tallin on his new position, and there were several days of feasting after Skemtun's funeral.

They wanted to stay longer, but Brinsop announced that she had to return to the desert immediately—she was pregnant... and almost ready to nest.

And if anyone remembered that Brinsop and Blacktooth had spent a great deal of time alone in the forest—well, no one mentioned it at all.

14. DRUKNOR

Druknor left Highport the day after the elections, journeying through the snow back to his isolated keep. It had been a long journey from Highport, and there had been little time to gather supplies, but he was tired of all the dwarf politics and anxious to return home.

The journey had been hard so far, especially without help, but he made his way north on his horse. Twice, he had been attacked by robbers on the road. Twice, he'd left their bodies for the crows to eat and had taken what little they had in the way of supplies for himself.

The robbery attempts hadn't bothered him—not really. What had really angered him was the fact that neither of the robbers had recognized him. In Sut-Burr, he was the absolute ruler. He was the most feared man in all of the Frigid Waste, to whom every smuggler owed their cut. His name was respected and feared; it was whispered among the people in the shadows. Yet these men on the road had treated him like he was just some lonely traveler.

"I'm almost home," he muttered to himself. He yanked the reins harder, forcing his horse to move faster. The beast would keep up, or it would die. Druknor had not built his reputation by being compassionate.

It *would* be better once he returned home. Just a few more days—it wasn't far now. He started to plan what he would do when he got back. A warm bath, some quiet time, and a nice bottle of wine sounded terrific. Then he would set about putting his house back in order and would go from there.

His two dogs were foraging for food somewhere near the side of the road. He whistled sharply to call his dogs back. They'd been hunting long enough. They could bring down a deer in seconds and could kill a man even quicker. But they still knew enough to obey *him*. With dogs, as with people, the key was to be the strongest in the pack.

There was no sign of his dogs. He whistled again. He didn't hear any barking. They should have come running. Druknor kept riding and decided to punish the dogs when they finally arrived. Fear only worked when it was well-maintained.

Somewhere in the semi-darkness, a shadow passed. He reined in his horse and squinted off into the distance. Druknor paused and then cursed himself for being so easily frightened. It was likely nothing, and even if it proved to be something, Druknor would just kill it.

He sighed and brought his thoughts back to his mission, which had failed miserably. His journey to Highport had been a complete waste of his time. Oh, sure, Sut-Burr wasn't going to be overrun by orcs anytime soon, and that was *something*, but Druknor had been invited there by the promise of something more. Far more.

There had been the promise of everything that would happen if Bolrakei became ruler of the dwarves—the pickings from whatever unrest that followed, and the chance to run a smuggling route openly through Highport. There had been the promise of greater favor from Miklagard. Being allied with Miklagard would have given Druknor power and immunity on a vast scale. But nothing had gone as planned, and the entire journey was a disaster from start to finish.

Another shadow moved out in the dim light. This time, Druknor drew his sword, but he did not stop. Few things would dare fight him out in the open.

Druknor whistled for his dogs again. No answer. Was it a bear? Only a very large predator would have spooked them.

"Bugger it," he said to himself.

"Talking to yourself again, Druknor?" The voice came out of the shadows.

Druknor recognized it instantly. His mouth went dry. "Skera-Kina?" he whispered.

"I'm so glad you remember me," she called back.

Druknor whirled around but couldn't see her. Druknor called again for his dogs.

Skera-Kina laughed, a dark, throaty echo that resonated in the frigid air. "Your hounds aren't coming, Druknor. Not today. Not ever."

He tried to make his voice calm. "Are you here to frighten me, Skera-Kina?"

"Yes. But I plan to do more than that," she said. "Much more." She stepped out onto the road, directly in front of Druknor.

Druknor looked around frantically for his hounds. "Don't be a fool, Skera-Kina. You can't kill me—I'm the only spy you have on the mainland."

"Ah, yes... that old excuse again. You're referring to the information you give us. So carefully selected. Do you ever tell anyone the whole truth?"

"Stay back!" he shouted.

"You're afraid."

He could hardly deny it. His hands were trembling on the reins. "What—what do you want from me? A bargain? Is this about the slave prices? We can negotiate, you know."

Skera-Kina's smile turned into a threatening sneer. "I don't care about your business, Druknor. I've got an old debt to settle with you. Do you remember a little *dwarfling* girl you sold to the Balborites?"

"I sold many slaves over the years. What's your point?"

"My point?" she hissed, "*My point* is that you sold that little girl, who was then turned into a weapon. You *sold me*, Druknor. You sold me like a piece of meat!"

Druknor gasped despite himself. Then he forced himself to laugh. "You can't kill me, Skera-Kina. The High Priest won't allow it."

Skera-Kina smiled back at him. "Didn't you hear, Druknor? The High Priest is gone. It's High *Priestess*

Skera-Kina now."

Druknor felt the blood drain from his face. If Skera-Kina was telling the truth, then there was nothing stopping her now. Nothing standing between her and his death. But he wasn't going to just stand there and die quietly.

He charged at Skera-Kina with a roar, swinging his sword. Druknor was strong, but Skera-Kina parried the attack easily. As he passed, she reached up, seized his leg, and pulled him from his horse. He fell from the saddle and planted his face on the ground. The horse ran off, kicking its back legs.

He leaped up with his sword in hand and whirled to stare at her defiantly.

"I've been waiting for this moment for a long time," she said, dodging as Druknor swung at her and missed. "I've spent a lot of time thinking about all the ways I might kill you."

He feinted one way and then kicked up dirt in an attempt to blind her. Skera-Kina ducked low, sweeping her blade at Druknor's knees so he was forced to jump back.

He swung again, and this time Skera-Kina raised her arm to parry the blow. The force of the blow pushed her back a few steps.

"Impressive," she said. "You've been training, I see."

"Perhaps you underestimate me," he replied, trying to sound unafraid. There was something in her eyes that made Druknor shudder.

"Perhaps... but it won't make any difference in

the end, will it? You're still no match for me," She said with a gleam in her eye.

She pulled a small knife from her belt, twirling it with her thumb. She sent the dagger flying toward Druknor's neck, but he swatted it from the air with his sword.

Druknor gathered up the strength he had left. Skera-Kina *wasn't* invincible, he told himself. One well-placed strike was all it would take. He charged forward, throwing attack after attack. Skera-Kina shifted and parried, dodged and blocked, never striking back, absorbing everything that Druknor had. She was mocking him, playing with him. Then, finally, Druknor got lucky.

Skera-Kina's foot slipped.

It must have been a patch of ice hidden under the snow. Whatever it was, Skera-Kina slipped and fell to one knee. Druknor didn't hesitate. He threw himself forward, his sword raised for the blow that would finish her. There was no way she could dodge or roll away. Druknor cried out savagely in triumph as he raised his sword for the final blow. By the time he saw the twinkle in Skera-Kina's eyes, it was too late. It was a trap.

She thrust her dagger up into his ribcage from where she knelt. Fire exploded in his chest. In an instant, he collapsed on his back, staring up at the evening sky while a puddle of blood expanded underneath him.

Skera-Kina's face was calm as she leaned over him. Druknor wanted to reach up to choke her, but he couldn't bring his arms to move.

"You're lucky, you know," Skera-Kina said quietly. "For you, this is the end. My life will be much longer and filled with drudgery. When you see the death god, tell him that he will have to wait a long time for me."

Druknor opened his mouth to speak, but the blackness closed in before he could.

Skera-Kina looked down at his body. There was no joy in this kill. She had an island to rule, and Xiil-tharra would not let her dodge her responsibilities. Already, the shadowkey ached inside her chest. It had been prickling steadily since she left the island's borders, and it just got more painful as time passed. She knew that she would never be able to leave Balbor for extended periods. She was trapped like a fly in a spider's web. She now understood that she had traded one prison for another, but at least this *new* prison was one she chose for herself.

Skera-Kina cleaned her family's sword on Druknor's tunic and stood there, letting the crisp cold of the evening seep into her. Then she started to make her way through the snow without looking back.

The return to Balbor would be long.

15. HOPE

The dragon riders returned to Parthos as heroes and as symbols of hope. They all received special recognition from King Rali for their service. There was a grand celebration, and an enormous feast was planned for all the riders and the citizens of Parthos. The people certainly needed such an event; it would help to raise their spirits after months of living in fear.

Although a significant number of orcs perished during the destruction of Mount Velik, many survived to return to their lives at Mount Heldeofol. No one knew for sure if the orc king survived, but the greenskins kept quiet and stayed away from the human cities while they licked the wounds of their defeat. It would be many years before their numbers recovered enough for them to even consider another attack.

A period of quiet followed, and within a few months, things had returned to normal. In fact, they were even a bit *better* than normal.

All of Shesha's eggs hatched on time, and every single one of her hatchlings survived. Shesha found a small cave near the city where she could care for her brood. All of the dragons worked together to ensure that the ravenous hatchlings always had enough to eat. Within a year, the young dragons were learning how to fly.

Brinsop quietly disappeared into the desert in order to prepare her own nest and to lay her eggs in private. Sela kept their contact to a minimum, respecting the dragon's need for seclusion. As they waited for news, the other riders could hardly contain their excitement.

A few weeks later, Brinsop sent an abrupt message to Sela; she had finally found a suitable nesting site and had laid a clutch of six eggs. Two of the eggs were onyx, and the rest were carnelian red. Sela sent a short reply, and then left her alone again.

It was wonderful news. The dragon race was finally recovering.

Soon, Nydeired, Karela, and Orshek would be old enough to mate as well, and everyone was hopeful that they would also help the dragon race to survive.

Tallin split his time between Parthos and Highport, flying back and forth between the two cities as the dwarves rebuilt their lives in their new home. Whenever he returned to the tranquility of the desert, he found himself wondering how he had been chosen to become a clan leader at all. He found his new role incredibly challenging. The job was just as, if not more, demanding than being a dragon rider.

He wondered if his life would ever be calm again, but he also took pleasure in noting that all the changes were for the better.

One evening, Sela met him outside while he was

looking over the city walls from the castle rooftop. The moon was rising, and it cast silvery shadows on the dunes below.

"Are you leaving for Highport tonight?" she asked. Her voice was soft.

"Yes, the stable hands are preparing Duskeye's saddle. I'll leave as soon as they're finished. He's been enjoying the extra travel."

"How is everything going with the clans?"

Tallin shrugged. "As well as can be expected, I suppose. The caverns are cramped and crowded, but they are working hard to expand them. There's a great deal of work to be done. But there's good news, too. Mugla succeeded in finding an apprentice—a distant cousin of hers tested positive for mageborn powers. He's only a third-degree mage, but at least it's something."

"How are you managing your new responsibilities?"

Tallin smiled. "My days are full. It's a lot of work, being a leader. I have a whole new respect for the position." He laughed. "It's much easier to simply follow along with people who enjoy doing this sort of thing. But life is too short to be unhappy over trivial things, so I'm enjoying the adventure as much as I can along the way."

"That's good news. Did you hear about Druknor? I just got word from the capital today. He never made it back to Sut-Burr. He's been missing since he left Highport. His people were too afraid to contact the king, but they finally did. A report has been filed, but no one seems to know where he's gone. There's no trace of him anywhere. It's like he's disappeared. Vanished."

Tallin shook his head. "I'll bet he'll turn up soon. But if he doesn't, I can't say that I'd be that upset about it. Druknor's made a lot of enemies over the years. He's a wicked man, and many people would like to see him dead."

"I suppose that's true." She was silent for a moment. "It's been a difficult year," she murmured, "but things are getting better."

"Yes, they are," he said. "I've never felt so focused on what I'm doing, and my purpose in life has never been clearer to me. I realize now that I am meant to help unite my people—to help them create a new life and kingdom for themselves." He shrugged. "It feels good to have a purpose."

Suddenly, she moved to embrace him, but then she stopped. Tallin saw her hesitation and moved in close, wrapping his arms around her. His warmth and strength seemed to soothe Sela, and she allowed herself to be comforted by Tallin's embrace. She inhaled deeply and blew out a long breath. When she finally pulled away, her lashes were lowered and her cheeks were pink.

Tallin was unused to seeing her so vulnerable. "Do you feel better?"

She nodded, looking a bit ashamed. "You're smiling," she said.

"I guess I am," he admitted. Then he laughed and reached down to kiss her.

They were interrupted by a shout, which was followed by the appearance of the twins, Galti and Holf, bounding up the steps to the rooftop. Sela and Tallin pulled away from each other abruptly.

"Did we interrupt something?" Galti asked loudly, looking at both of them with a rather curious expression.

Sela and Tallin glanced at each other and laughed.

"No... not really. We were having a conversation that can wait," said Tallin. "We needed to take a break anyway. What do you need?"

Holf reached out and handed Tallin a scroll sealed with purple wax. "This just arrived for you by messenger."

Tallin recognized the stamp—it was the official seal of Balbor. "Who left this?" he asked, trying not to sound concerned.

Holf shrugged. "I didn't recognize her—the woman rode off as soon as she left it."

"A female messenger dropped this off?" he asked.

Holf nodded. "It was a woman, I could tell from her voice, but her face and body were completely covered. At first, I thought she was a nomad. She didn't say much—she just dropped it off in the receiving room and left. Why... does it matter?"

"No... it doesn't matter." He broke the seal and scanned the scroll's contents. As he expected, the message was from Skera-Kina.

"Dear brother, I hope this letter finds you alive and in good health. I would have written earlier, but my

schedule had been fairly hectic lately. I'm pleased to inform you that Druknor Theoric has been permanently dispatched—he will no longer trouble either one of us. Now that Druknor is gone, however, I have realized that Balbor has lost an important source of goods and labor. Because of this, I would like to propose a pact of amity and commerce between my people and yours. This agreement would benefit us equally. It would be of great assistance in stemming the famine on Balbor and would strongly encourage me to stop sending assassins to the mainland. Consider my proposal and let me know your answer before the next full moon. Signed on behalf of the High Priestess of Balbor, Her Grace, Skera-Kina."

"What does it say?" asked Sela, growing concerned as Tallin's brows knitted together.

He handed her the scroll. Her eyes widened when she read it. "We cannot accept a treaty of this kind. Not with Balbor."

Tallin raised one eyebrow. "An open refusal would be deemed a horrible insult. Skera-Kina would never forgive the slight."

"That may be true, but we'll just have to deal with the problem when it arises... as we always do," she replied with a sigh. "The war is never over for us. The fighting never stops."

They both looked up into the sky. It was full of stars, and the moon was rising.

Tallin gazed into the desert and added quietly, "When I was in hiding during the Dragon Wars, I didn't know what to think or believe. The future seemed very dark back then. But now, I have hope.

I realize there will always be challenges, but they don't need to be seen as obstacles. We can overcome them all. And one day... we will have peace among all our lands. I'm certain about that."

THE SAGA CONTINUES IN BOOK SEVEN: The Shadow Grid Returns

A Sneak Peek at Book Seven: The Shadow Grid Returns

O utside the desert city of Parthos, Elias Dorgumir looked up into the afternoon sky, watching as three carnelian dragons played hide-and-seek in the darkening clouds. He marveled at the dragons' grace and beauty. They flew higher and higher with each gentle movement of their jewel-colored wings.

Even from a distance, Elias could see that all three were wild, adolescent females, less than a year old, but already old enough to have a dragon stone prominently displayed at the base of their throats.

These three dragons would be added to next year's census. Creating the yearly census of dragons was one of Elias' proudest achievements. The dragon race had made a spectacular recovery from near-extinction during the last decade.

With a trio of roars, the little dragons clustered together and disappeared into the clouds, flying toward the safety of the caves sprawled along the southern borders of Parthinian territory.

It was a perfect spring day and the temperature was still mild. He had almost forgotten the peaceful tranquility and wonderful smell of the desert. Elias inhaled deeply, savoring the clean, dry desert air as he walked along the outer limits of Parthos.

He had been away for years, returning only sporadically while working as a traveling healer throughout the kingdom. His healing skills were always in demand, so constant travel was part of his life.

Although his work ethic never waned, his duties sometimes limited his efforts to track and monitor the numbers of dragons. He had also grown tired of the lack of a community, and the inconstancy of life on the road.

Striding over the rippled dunes soothed and comforted him. Despite the harsh weather of the Death Sands, the desert was his refuge, and he loved the wild peacefulness of it. His homesickness melted away like a candle in the sun. Ten years of almost-constant travel, and now he was finally back home.

Just days ago, he had celebrated his twenty-fifth birthday. His years seemed to dissolve away in all he had seen and done. Deep in his soul, he'd always known that he would return to the desert. He dearly hoped he was home for good.

He walked until he reached the gates of Parthos, where he picked up the faint smell of burning camel dung, evidence of nomads nearby. Elias couldn't see their tents, but he knew that they were near the city, since it was one of the few places in the central desert with a safe water supply. A small herd of camels trotted lazily outside the city, grazing on dry grass and shrubs.

In the distance, coming from the same direction that the young dragons had left, a gigantic pearl-colored dragon appeared. Elias shielded his eyes with his hand and looked up, then smiled broadly. It was

Nydeired, who had undoubtedly spent the day in the desert trying to woo nesting females. Elias had hoped to meet him later in the evening.

He was surprised by Nydeired's early return. Silhouetted against the sun, the dragon's bright scales glinted yellow and orange with every sweep of his broad wings.

As the largest dragon in existence, Nydeired towered above palm trees and houses, his wings stretching outward like two enormous sails.

Elias heard the dragon's gravelly voice echoing inside his mind, *"I am coming back to the city."*

"I see you," he replied, "Meet me on the ramparts."

Elias jogged through the city and up the castle steps to the rooftop, one of the few places in the city with enough space for Nydeired to land. He briefly saluted the guards at the fortress steps, then rushed up the stairs and waited.

The huge white dragon landed with a thud, stumbling a bit before righting himself. He whipped around, and his powerful tail knocked over a stack of bricks in the corner. The bricks spilled down the slope of the roof, piling up against the opposite wall. Elias groaned and shook his head.

"Sorry," said Nydeired guiltily.

"It's okay, don't worry about it." Elias signaled one of the servants at the doorway to come and clean up the mess.

Elias understood Nydeired's difficulty. Everything about him—from his enormous bulk to his thrashing tail—*everything* made being around humans difficult. Nydeired carefully folded his wings into his body and waddled over to where Elias stood.

"How did it go?" he asked gently. Based on the telepathic feelings he had been receiving from Nydeired all day, he already knew the answer.

Nydeired's shoulders slumped. *"The females rejected me. All of them, young and old. I don't understand. I show as much enthusiasm as any other male."*

Elias pursed his lips. Nydeired was still a young dragon, but old enough to mate, nonetheless. He had been having a difficult time attracting the interest of any available females.

"What went wrong this time?" asked Elias.

The dragon blew out a puff of smoke as he spoke. *"There were twelve nesting females at the southern caves. Two other males were there, one emerald and one sapphire. The males fought over the females before the mating dance. Well, I'd expected that. But the females wouldn't even allow me to dance!"*

"Well, did you try to dance anyway? You could have impressed them that way."

"I couldn't. They chased me away before the dances even started. They wouldn't even let me get close. They don't want me, Elias. What's wrong with me?"

"Nothing's *wrong* with you," Elias replied. "Really —there isn't. Female dragons are just very particular. They always have been. And they have more males to choose from now. That's not your fault."

"But what should I do?" he growled, stomping his foot in frustration. *"They won't even give me a chance.*

I always approach them respectfully. Even so, they do not want me as a mate. I've done all I could to catch their eye."

Elias grimaced as he watched the stonework underneath Nydeired's foot crumble to gravel. He knew that the palace steward wasn't going to be happy about that.

Carefully, he replied, "You ought to ask Brinsop what you should do. I know it's hard for a male dragon to approach a high-ranking female for mating advice. But I'm sure she'd give you a sympathetic ear."

"I did ask her for advice. She suggested that I bring a mating gift to one of the females and offer it to her even before I began the mating dance. So I did that—I brought a freshly-killed camel for one of the younger females. She was an onyx dragon, larger than the rest. I thought she might be less... intimidated by my size. But it didn't work. She chased me away like all the others."

Elias bit his lip. "I'm sorry, my friend."

"That's not the worst of it. The onyx female told me that I was ugly and frightening."

"Come now... you know *that's* not true. You're *not* ugly, and you're certainly not any more frightening than any other large dragon."

Nydeired stared off into the horizon with a dejected look on his face. *"Maybe she was right. I'm the only diamond dragon in all of Durn. There are no other dragons like me. Perhaps I am ugly and frightening—at least to them."*

Elias touched Nydeired's wing and squeezed. "I

don't think you're frightening—not at all. Have patience, my friend. The females are bound to be a little skittish, especially the younger ones. Just give them time to get used to you."

"I'm trying." The dragon sighed, resting on its haunches. *"I would never hurt any of them."*

"I know that," Elias said quietly.

He didn't know what to say without sounding trite. He leaned forward and embraced Nydeired's enormous silver-white neck. The dragon whined, then began purring softly. Nydeired shifted his stance and his shoulders relaxed somewhat.

At least he seems calmer now, Elias thought to himself.

"Am I interrupting something?" A chestnut-haired woman appeared in the doorway across the roof. Nydeired pulled away and stepped back, giving her room to pass.

Elias smiled and waved. "Sela! It's good to see you. No, you're not intruding. We were just having a friendly discussion."

They embraced briefly but warmly. "Welcome back," she replied, before looking at Nydeired and giving him a soft smile.

Her warm eyes reflected experience and age, but her skin glowed with a surprising youthfulness. Sela was the leader of the dragon riders, as well as the regent of Parthos. She was also a powerful spellcaster in her own right.

She patted Nydeired's side affectionately. "I heard you were back in the city. It's good to see you again."

The dragon snorted. *"It's good to see you, too,"* he managed. He was still upset and in no mood to be chatty.

"You've been doing great work with your census," Sela told Elias. "There are hundreds of dragons in the desert now, and their numbers are growing."

Elias smiled proudly. "I do what I can. The nomadic tribes are doing their share to help. They help track the hatchlings and help defend the nests from wild predators and poachers."

"Well, now that you're here, you can see the results for yourself."

"That's part of why I came back," said Elias.

Sela gave Elias a long, searching look. "How are you, really? You look thinner." She pinched his forearm. "I thought you'd be in Morholt helping prepare for the Spring Fair."

"I decided to skip it this year."

"Skip it?" she echoed in surprise. "You've always enjoyed the fair before. Why the sudden change of heart?"

Elias shrugged. "It's so crowded and full of people. I missed the desert. Plus, I wanted to help Nydeired with some... private matters."

Nydeired looked away, embarrassed. Sela was also a dragon rider, so Elias knew that she understood Nydeired's current... *difficulties.*

"Oh, very well, then," she said brightly, quickly changing the subject. "Anyway, welcome back to Parthos. Do you need anything while you're in the city?"

"I'm planning to stay awhile. I'd appreciate my old room, please—the one with the view of the gardens."

"That shouldn't be a problem," she said. "Your old suite should be vacant right now. I'll check with the palace steward."

"That would be wonderful. A hot bath would be great, too. The journey from Morholt was long, and my back still aches from that blasted saddle. It's not an easy trip."

She glanced at the darkening sky. "It's getting late, and it's almost dinnertime. Won't you join me for dinner? The chef is preparing a special meal tonight. Cured mutton and stewed pigeon. I've been craving mutton for a few months. I found some last night in the street market."

"Thank you, I accept. Nydeired might be hungry, too."

The dragon swung his black eyes in Sela's direction. *"I am a bit hungry. Some fresh meat would be nice."* Food always made him feel better.

"Marlson slaughtered a camel two days ago. I'll have the kitchen send up some meat for you, or..." She hesitated, a sly look in her eye. "You could join Brinsop. She's taking her dinner in the desert tonight—literally. She's hunting wild goats. I'm sure she wouldn't mind some company."

"A goat hunt?" The dragon brightened considerably. *"I prefer the taste of a fresh kill. Perhaps I will join Brinsop."* He licked his scaly lips. *"Thank you for the*

suggestion."

Sela smiled. "My pleasure entirely, glad to be of help."

As Nydeired flew away, Sela slapped Elias on the back. "Elias, follow me. There is something I want to show you."

She strode back inside the keep, with Elias following closely on her heels. Servants paused briefly to greet them before continuing on with their work.

Freshly-cleaned draperies hung on the windows, and newly-built cupboards covered the southern wall of the dining room. The waning evening light showed through the windows, casting a soft glow on the pale sandstone walls.

"You've made some changes here, I see," Elias said, casting a quick glance around.

Sela smiled and waved her hand expansively. "Yes, I've redecorated a bit since you were here last. Do you like it?"

Elias nodded. "I *do* like it. It feels warmer now, more spacious and homey."

"There's more," she said. "Wait until you see our new wine cellar. I'm quite proud of it."

She led him down a long corridor and a flight of stairs, stopping at a metal door. She took a key from a ring hanging at her belt and turned the lock, swinging the door open.

"Watch your step. It's dark in here," she warned. "The light crystals have gone out." She muttered a quick spell under her breath, and a thin tongue of flame danced at her fingertip. Rosy light brightened their surroundings as the light crystals sputtered to life. "That's much better."

Elias swept his gaze over the room. The cellar was a tidy underground space, with rows of iron-bound barrels lined up along the wall. On the other side of the room, colorful wine bottles filled the shelves.

"This is incredible!" said Elias. "How did you build this so quickly?"

"I've been working on it for years, actually. I've always enjoyed winemaking as a hobby. I used to make small batches to share with the staff. A few years ago our chef convinced me to sell a few bottles in the street market. The wine sold remarkably well, so I hired a vintner and invested in proper equipment. We sold our first 'official' batch last summer." She pulled a dark bottle from one of the dusty shelves. "This wine is made from cactus fruit. Nomads harvest the fruit and sell it to us."

She uncorked the bottle and poured a small measure into a glass. "Here, try some. I haven't tried this vintage yet, but the others have all been delicious. It's a fragrant wine, and it goes perfectly with the spicy foods the nomads love."

She offered the glass to Elias. The wine smelled strongly of sweet fruits and a little bit of spice.

Elias gently swirled the wine. He lifted the glass to his nose, taking in the sweet aroma, and took a sip. "Hm. It tastes a bit like berry juice. Honey, too."

"You're right—it does contain honey. The precise recipe is a secret, but it includes honey, spices, and several types of herbs. Take the rest with you, if you wish."

Elias waved his hand. "No thank you. It's good, but I prefer ale to wine."

Sela chuckled and pushed the cork back into the bottle. "Your tastes have changed with age, my dear." She put the bottle back on the shelf, and the light in the room began to dim. She turned and faced him, her expression suddenly serious. "Elias... The truth is, I brought you down here because I wanted to speak to you privately."

"Pardon?" Elias asked.

"The wine was merely a ruse to speak to you alone," she said with a rueful smile. She shut the door and glanced around to ensure they were alone. "I have some sensitive matters to discuss."

"Are you in some trouble?" Elias asked with genuine concern.

"No, no trouble. But I *am* worried about some things. I recently received an invitation to attend the official opening ceremony for Aonach Tower. I know you've only just arrived, but I hoped you might accompany me. I need a palace escort since it's an official event. I'll be attending as Parthos' representative."

Elias blew out his cheeks. He didn't want to upset her—but the truth was, he didn't want to go. He absolutely *hated* formal events. He didn't see the point in them, and all the pomp and pageantry made him uncomfortable.

"Isn't there anyone else who could go?"

"Oh, there are a few other people I could send,

but there isn't anyone else in Parthos that I trust as much as you. The other dragon riders are scattered across the continent. Tallin is still working with the dwarf clans at Highport, and Galti and Holf are even further away in Redmoor. That leaves just you and Nydeired."

"Sela, I just don't know. Let me think about it just a little."

She nodded, but he could see that she was disappointed. An awkward silence fell.

"So have they finished rebuilding the tower already?" he asked, trying to change the subject. "That place was nothing but rubble the last time I saw it. The grounds were a terrible mess and the construction had been delayed several times. How did they get it finished so quickly?"

She leveled a cynical eye on him. "They did it the old-fashioned way. By using bribes."

"Bribery?" he replied, somewhat taken aback. "Are you sure?"

"Yes. There's plenty of evidence that the High Council of Miklagard bribed the carpenter's guild to abandon all their other projects in favor of completing the tower ahead of schedule. Many people were upset, especially the merchants and shopkeepers who were waiting for their own construction projects to be completed. They were pretty vocal about their displeasure."

"Why is the High Council involved in this?" Elias asked. "Don't they have their own mageborn school?"

"Miklagard ran out of space years ago, and it's become a real problem for them. The High Council has been turning away dozens of mageborns every year. Most of them have marginal powers—level ones and twos, mostly. But some are stronger, especially those with rarer gifts."

Elias sucked in a breath. "Ah. That's the real trouble, isn't it? All these 'weaker' mageborns still have enough power to be dangerous. So what's happening to all the rejected mageborns?"

"Unfortunately, many of them have turned to the Shadow Grid for their training," she said grimly. "And the Grid welcomed them with open arms."

Elias shook his head. "I can't believe I haven't heard news of this until now."

"They've kept it quiet. For the High Council, it's a huge embarrassment."

Elias frowned. The Shadow Grid was a highly secretive group. How could they fight an enemy they couldn't see?

Sela continued. "As a result of the High Council's idiocy, the Shadow Grid's membership has grown exponentially in the last few years. The Grid now has spies in every city, even here in Parthos. I can't even trust the palace servants anymore."

"Ah. So that's why we're talking down here, instead of upstairs in the main hall."

"Exactly. There have been quite a few thefts recently, especially in the kitchens. Several scrolls have disappeared from the library, too. Nothing serious so far, but even so, we have to be careful. Of course, this ultimately leads back to Delthen and the High Council."

Her expression soured. "The council has been trying to increase its influence for some time. Councilmember Delthen was the primary driver behind the rebuilding."

"Delthen..." Elias said slowly. "I've heard bits and pieces about him over the years. He has a great deal of power in the northern provinces."

Sela gazed up at the ceiling. "Master Komu, the council's former leader, passed away last winter. He was a kindhearted man, if a little misguided sometimes. His replacement might not be so good-natured. The High Council will elect Komu's successor after the official mourning period has ended. Delthen is almost certain to be chosen."

Elias leaned heavily against one of the barrels. "But why is Delthen so interested in controlling Aonach Tower? I don't see how it benefits him at all."

"It's probably an indirect way of keeping the Shadow Grid from gaining more members. The Council's indifference towards low-level mages is partially to blame for the Shadow Grid's exploding membership."

Elias sat down on the corner of a barrel, his shoulders hunched. "So what are we going to do about this?"

"I'm going to attend the opening of Aonach Tower," she replied. "I'm planning to bring up the issue with Delthen in person. He can't avoid me if

I'm right in his face." She gently patted his shoulder. "Look, enough of this unhappy talk. Would you join me for dinner? I could definitely use a glass of wine right now."

That brightened him up. "That sounds like a great idea. I'd appreciate a tankard of ale, myself."

They ascended the stairs and returned to the main hall. They agreed to chat about innocuous topics as they walked. After Sela's warning about possible spies, they had to be cautious about what they discussed around the palace staff.

"I'm glad you enjoyed the wine," Sela said, carrying off the pretense effortlessly. "It's become quite popular, you know."

"It was good," Elias said stiffly, nowhere near as good at playing along. They shared a quick meal in the dining room, and he retired to his quarters.

A warm bath was waiting for him, but Elias didn't quite feel up to it. Instead, he turned to the iron furnace in the corner.

The small, pear-shaped furnace stood on four clawed legs, fire blazing in its wide mouth. He crouched before it to warm his hands. The fire painted shadows across the walls of his room, and the kindling popped and hissed, spewing minute sparks into the air.

Strong, high flames... perfect for foretelling.

Should I do it?

After some thought, he decided to try. "*Hniga!*" he cried out. His bedroom door slammed shut. The bolt lock slid into place, giving him the privacy he needed.

He grabbed the poker and fed the flames with more kindling. Once the blaze was burning brightly, Elias bent his knees in front of the little furnace and focused his eyes on the flames. He reached out, palm facing outward, until the heat was almost painful. His vision grew dim and hazy.

Squeezing his eyes shut, he whispered the spell. "*Oviss-Syna-draumr.*"

The flames sputtered and then flared, weaving into serpentine shapes. A strange sensation came over him—a feeling of being closed in.

"Show me the future of Miklagard," he said out loud, "and the High Council."

He gestured with one hand, and from within the flames, an image slowly materialized. A dark forest, filled with fog. The fog thinned, revealing a wood filled with evergreens, their thick branches covered with a blanket of snow. Above the trees towered a rose-colored dome—the magical shield that had protected generations of spellcasters from attacks. The image was peaceful and serene.

For a long moment, nothing happened, and Elias thought that his spell had failed.

Perhaps nothing will happen after all, he thought. *And we are making a fuss about nothing.*

But he had judged too soon. In the vision, shadowy figures began to converge near the dome, surrounding the city. The black-garbed figures formed a dark chain around the city like a corset.

Elias' breath caught in his throat. Hundreds of

hooded men and women, linked hand in hand, circled the city, their bodies creating a living ribbon around the dome.

He narrowed his eyes and focused his attention on their hands. He could clearly see guild tattoos on their wrists and arms. These were all Shadow Grid mages. The spellcasters raised their arms and rotated around the perimeter of Miklagard. They began to utter a monotonous, droning chant.

Dark sorcery.

He had heard the spell before. The words chilled his blood. It was a demolition spell, but stronger, darker, and more devastating.

As the spellcasters chanted, inky blotches began to appear on the crystal shield. The taint spread upon the dome like a deadly miasma. A shockwave pulsed, then another, shaking the ground underneath the crystal city.

Now a chorus of screams filled the air. Inside the city, young and old fell to their knees, writhing in agony. The hooded chanters raised their voices, and the screaming from inside the city grew louder. People pounded on the inside of the dome with their fists, only for their hands to sink into the shield as if it were soft pudding. The people inside Miklagard were trapped and suffocating in a fog of dark magic.

The chanting outside the city grew louder. A few of the Shadow Grid mages collapsed from the strain. When that happened, another hooded mage stepped forward to take his place and protect the integrity of the chain.

Elias watched in horror as another shockwave tore through Miklagard, opening up the ground in several places. The city was in chaos.

The chanting ceased abruptly, followed by a terrible silence. The crystal shield trembled, and a web of cracks began to spread upon its surface, radiating from the ground to the top of the dome.

With a final thunderous explosion, the shield burst outward in a shower of jagged crystal and smoke. The people inside the city collapsed, their bodies convulsing in their final death throes. Elias screamed and raised his hands, instinctively trying to protect his face from the phantom explosion.

The horrific vision overwhelmed his senses. He collapsed backward. Bursting stars filled his vision for a moment. He groaned and turned on his side, covering his head with his arms.

Seconds later, the fire inside the little furnace collapsed and died, as if someone had thrown water on the flames, reducing them to plumes of smoke and feeble embers.

The vision faded. He lay still, staring at the wall. He felt completely drained of power, and was in so much pain he could barely move. His right hand throbbed. Without looking at it, he knew that it was badly burned. He didn't even have the energy to cast a simple healing spell.

He heard Nydeired's worried voice calling out to him. *"Elias?"* The dragon touched his mind with a gentle psychic probe. *"Elias, are you alright?"*

He felt the dragon's reassuring presence nearby—
he was either on the roof or on the plateau directly
behind the city, but Elias didn't have enough energy
to reply. His mind felt numb.

"*Elias, speak to me! I felt your distress through the
dragon stone.*"

He could barely think. He didn't want to worry
Nydeired, so he tried to project a confident, reassuring tone. "I'm fine, just overly tired from everything
that's happened today."

"*You're lying to me,*" he replied sharply. "*What happened? Tell me the truth.*"

Elias sighed and rolled his eyes. Using his elbows,
he dragged himself to a seated position. His body
felt like it weighed a thousand pounds. "Something I
shouldn't have done."

"*What did you do?*" Nydeired asked insistently.

"We'll talk about it later. After I've had a chance
to rest."

"*But—but...*"

"We'll talk about it tomorrow, alright? I'm going
to bed now."

His legs wobbled when he tried to stand, but he
managed to limp over to the bed, where he collapsed. It wasn't as if he had any choice in the matter
—he doubted that he had the energy to do anything
besides sleep.

Even in his exhausted state, Elias sensed the
dragon's worry. The soft touch of Nydeired's mind
continued to prod at him, searching for assurance
that he was unharmed.

Elias shielded his memory of the vision from Nydeired's mind. He didn't want to reimagine the sight, let alone share it with anyone else. He knew that Nydeired didn't believe his excuse. But he hoped that the dragon was at least reassured of his safety. At last, he felt Nydeired's probing stop.

Just before he drifted off, Elias heard Nydeired's gravelly voice in his mind. *"Sleep, my friend. I shall stay awake and watch over you tonight."*

Somehow, that reassurance wasn't enough.

The next morning, Elias woke to a pounding headache. He was physically and mentally exhausted. His sleep had not been restful. Dark dreams plagued him, visions of destruction and death. He wanted to stay in bed with a pillow thrown over his head and forget what he'd seen the night before.

But he couldn't.

He forced his eyes open and looked around. He was alone in his bedchamber. The door was still bolted shut from the night before. Beams of morning sunlight streamed through the half-closed curtains, casting a kaleidoscope of color on the tiled floor.

He managed to sit up, wincing as pain shot up his arm. He glanced ruefully at his burned hand. The skin of his palm was badly blistered. His memory of the injury was foggy, and that unnerved him more than the pain.

He tried to gather his thoughts, forcing himself to recollect as much detail of his vision as he could. Was it merely a warning, or a promise of things to come? He couldn't be certain. He felt empty, detached from the whole experience.

Then he heard Sela's soft, telepathic prodding. "Elias? Are you still sleeping?"

"I'm awake," he answered just as softly. It was unusual for Sela to communicate this way, and the gentle contact took him by surprise.

"Nydeired asked me to wake you. I think something might be troubling him. It's late morning already, but we let you sleep in. I've been holding breakfast for you."

"Ah. Give me a moment. I'll be right there."

He stumbled out of bed and pulled on his boots. So Nydeired had asked someone else to wake him, instead of doing it himself. After what happened last night, Elias couldn't blame him.

His injured hand throbbed and made dressing difficult. His belt accidentally brushed his burned palm, scraping a line of fire across his flesh. He yelped in pain.

Biting back curses, he paused to smear some ointment on the burn before wrapping it clumsily with a ribbon of gauzy cloth. It was the best he could do for now. He still felt completely drained from the night before. His head was throbbing even worse, which he hadn't imagined possible. But he straightened his spine, opened the door, and walked to the dining room.

Sela sat alone at the dining table, sipping a cup of coffee and reading a letter. Elias could tell by the yellow wax seal that it was an official message from the king.

She smiled and lowered the scroll as Elias entered the room, but she looked worried as he came near. "You look terrible, my friend." She stared at his gauze-wrapped hand. "What in Baghra's name happened to *you* last night?"

He pulled out a chair and sat down. "I assure you, I feel much worse than I look."

A servant poured coffee into his mug. He took a sip of the scalding liquid and winced as it seared a trail down his throat. It was a chilly morning, and the coffee tasted good. So did the warmth of the fireplace in the corner.

He gestured towards the letter. "Any news from King Rali?"

She sighed. "Yes, bad news. There have been recent raids in the southern provinces, mostly theft of livestock. One of the border tribes reported similar thefts a few weeks back. The thefts were minor, just one or two heads of cattle, sometimes a few horses. I believed they were tribal skirmishes and nothing more."

"Now you believe otherwise."

Sela nodded grimly. "These are not little tribal skirmishes. These thefts are too careful—too well-organized. The thieves take what they want and leave without a trace. They're trying not to attract attention to themselves."

"You believe it's the Shadow Grid."

"Yes," she answered. "These raids are almost certainly the work of the Shadow Grid. The Grid steals the livestock, then smuggles the animals north, selling them in Ironport or Syrd. It's only a matter of time before raids start happening in larger cities."

"The guilds won't be happy with a few heads of cattle for long. They'll want larger stakes."

Sela sighed. "I know. The rumors have trickled down to me slowly. It's mainly merchant gossip, which I usually ignore. But people are complaining about smugglers along the trade routes again. It's worrisome."

"That's troubling news," Elias said, reaching for his mug. He took a sip and winced.

Sela stared at his bandaged hand, arching one quizzical eyebrow. "Do you want to tell me what happened last night?"

"I cast a pyromantic spell," he admitted. "That's how I injured my hand. I wanted to know what would happen in the future. As for what I saw, well... it was awful." He described what he had witnessed. Sela's eyes widened in shock.

"Are you certain of this?" she whispered, her hand clasped over her dragon stone. "Could it have been a dream, rather than a vision?"

Elias shook his head. "I wish it were. I'm not a powerful seer, but my Sight is every bit as accurate as my father's was, and that's what frightens me. My visions tend to be accurate when I *do* have them. I know what I saw, and it was horrible." His mind and his injured hand bore witness to the truth.

"Miklagard will be destroyed? All those people will die?"

Elias nodded slowly. "That's what I saw. Either this is certain to come to pass, or it's a very serious warning. We can't ignore it."

"On that, we're agreed. We must do something, even if it's just to offer a warning to the residents of the city." She glanced down at his bandaged fingers. "Let me see how bad it is."

He tucked his hand into his lap. "Don't worry about it."

"Let me see your hand," she repeated. "I know you're a healer, but I have some healing skills myself. Don't be stubborn."

With a defeated sigh, he held his hand out to her. She unraveled the crude bandage and cradled his burnt palm, *tsking* in sympathy. Huge blisters glistened across his skin.

"This burn is serious, Elias. Why would you let it fester like this?"

"Divination spells are exhausting for me. I could barely drag myself into bed last night. I didn't have the strength to cast any healing spells yesterday. Or today, either." He pointed to the almost-empty mug. "I feel as drained as this cup."

"You are a silly, stubborn, pig-headed young man," she huffed. She ordered one of the servants to bring bandages and healing salve. "I'm not as talented a healer as *you,* but I can certainly make you more comfortable."

The servant returned shortly with a small wooden box in his hands. She opened the box to reveal a selection of first-aid materials, including antiseptic and wound dressings. She pulled out a small pot of salve. As she unscrewed the pot, a sharp herbal fragrance filled the air.

"This is my special recipe," she said. "It's going to sting a little."

Elias gave her a lopsided smile. "I've managed worse."

She murmured a simple pain-relieving spell and applied a thick layer of salve to his palm. "The spell will relieve your pain, and the ointment will reduce swelling and block infection."

Elias exhaled as the throbbing slowly subsided.

"Feel better?" she asked.

"Yes, much," he replied with a smile.

"It's comfrey ointment. I made it myself."

Sela was good at potions and other alchemical creations that come from natural ingredients. She knew by instinct what worked and what didn't.

He flexed his fingers. "That's good stuff, my hand feels almost normal already." There was still some stiffness, but the pain was almost completely gone and he could use the hand with almost no restriction.

They finished breakfast, then headed toward the palace rooftop, where they expected to meet Brinsop and Nydeired.

"I'm on patrol today," Sela said as they walked up the stairs. "So Brinsop and I will be gone for most of the afternoon." She paused at the end of the stairwell and put her hand on his shoulder. "You never gave me an answer yesterday."

His forehead creased. "An answer to what?"

"About accompanying me to the opening ceremony at Aonach. It's next week, so we'd have to leave tomorrow morning to arrive in time for the ceremony."

"Oh," Elias replied. He'd forgotten all about it. Probably because he wanted to subconsciously block it from his memory. He *hated* parties.

The two emerged on the rooftop. It was a bright, clear-skied morning, rooftop flags snapping in the warm wind. Nydeired lumbered over to Elias. He greeted Nydeired with a pat on the snout. He didn't fail to notice the dark, disapproving huff the dragon gave him when he spotted his bandaged hand.

"I'll go with you," he said finally. "I know you don't really need my help, but after what I saw during the vision last night, I can't stay here and do nothing. I feel like maybe I'm *supposed* to go."

"Great," she said with a smile. "I'll have the staff pack your saddlebags for you. We'll be gone for at least two weeks."

She seemed pleased and even a bit excited about the trip, but Elias felt the opposite. Worry had already settled in the pit of his gut. He wanted to believe that his visions were faulty somehow, despite everything he knew. He wanted to believe it was a figment of an overactive imagination. But he knew that was a lie.

Suddenly, the future seemed incredibly bleak.

The next day, Sela and Brinsop sat waiting on the palace rooftop, saddled and ready to start their journey. But Elias and Nydeired had already hit a snag. The dragon's ceremonial saddle no longer fit him comfortably. Elias adjusted and readjusted the straps, but to no avail. They were too short.

Ceremonial saddles were cumbersome but beautiful, with intricate metalwork and engraving all along the skirt and fender. Unfortunately, Nydeired's saddle had been sitting neglected inside the palace stables for years, and now it was too small for his back.

Elias yanked the straps again, but no matter how he positioned them, they wouldn't reach all the way around Nydeired's massive belly.

"It's no good—there's no way I can ride like this. The saddle is slipping all over the place."

Sela went over and peered up at Nydeired's underbelly. "The saddle is too small, but the straps are the real problem. If only they were a bit longer."

"I'm sorry I didn't check it earlier," Elias mumbled. "It fit him fine a few years ago."

"*I can't help it that I've grown,*" Nydeired whined.

Elias chuckled. "You didn't have to grow so *big.*"

Nydeired snorted a plume of smoke at him. "*You're making fun of me.*"

Elias smiled. "I'm just surprised, that's all. I wonder when you'll stop growing."

The dragon looked away. Elias felt a twinge of guilt for bringing up what was obviously a touchy subject. Namely, Nydeired's unusually large size.

Sela picked up on the dragon's hurt feelings. "I'm sure Elias didn't mean to embarrass you," she assured him. "You're a fine-looking dragon."

Nydeired looked away, pouting as much as a dragon could pout. *"You're just saying that to me to make me feel better."*

"I'm saying it because it's true," said Sela firmly. "You're as handsome as you ever were. Even *handsomer*, if that's any comfort to you."

Nydeired preened a little at that. Like all male dragons, he was acutely conscious of his looks. Females preferred healthy, unblemished males as partners, although their preferences were influenced by many factors. Basically, female dragons were notoriously picky.

Sela tugged at the saddle, fiddling with straps. "I'll call the palace saddler and have the straps extended. He should be able to fix it. We should be on our way shortly."

The saddler soon arrived, looking rushed and grumpy. He was a burly, middle-aged man with a short beard and a shock of gray hair at each temple. He examined the saddle, running his hand across the expensive metalwork. He tugged on one of the fastenings. "This strap doesn't fit right. It's too short."

"We know that, Ulric," said Sela. "Can you fix it?"

Ulric nodded. "Aye, I can fix it. It'll take about an hour, I'd reckon. I'll expand the main strap and adjust it under his belly. That should solve the problem. "

Rushing through the repair, the saddler modified the leather straps, stitching on an extra length of leather to make them reach.

"That should do for now," he said, straightening up. "Just bring the saddle back to me when you return, and I'll give it a more permanent fix."

"Thank you," said Elias, looking up into the afternoon sky. The sun was already well over the horizon. "At least we managed to get out of here before nightfall."

With that, they were on their way. Brinsop and Nydeired flew in close formation, their wing tips occasionally brushing against each other. As a high-ranking female dragon, Brinsop usually ignored younger males. However, she seemed uncharacteristically friendly towards Nydeired, at times even affectionate, albeit in a motherly way. Brinsop seemed oddly protective of the younger male, despite the fact that Nydeired was easily more than three times her size.

The older dragon's kindness was appreciated. Nydeired was visibly relaxed around her. There was still a customary formality, but with warmth.

The afternoon turned into early evening. Lines of golden dunes passed them in a sandy blur below.

The first few days passed as easily as hours. They flew onward towards the desert border, stopping only briefly to rest when the sun was at its highest.

Disaster struck three days into their journey. The hasty stitching on Elias' saddle suddenly snapped, and the straps fell loose. His world tipped sideways and he grabbed onto Nydeired's neck, crying out for help as the saddle slid down the dragon's back. It hung uselessly from the dragon's tail, caught on a sharp spike.

Nydeired howled and flew into a panic, flailing wildly as he tried to stabilize himself.

Elias circled his arms tightly around Nydeired's neck, trying to hold on. He could feel Nydeired's hard scales scratching at his arms and ripping his clothing. Nydeired's head twisted downward at an odd angle from the additional weight.

"Hold on, Elias!" Sela shouted. "Don't let go!"

"I'm trying!"

Sela snapped her reins and whipped Brinsop around, trying to maneuver herself underneath the other dragon's huge body.

Nydeired began hyperventilating, his massive bulk thrashing in panic.

"What do I do? We're too far up—I don't want Elias to die!"

In distress, he kicked his leg straight back. Elias lurched downward, almost losing his grip. The heavy saddle, which had been hanging on by a thread already, finally broke away from Nydeired's tail and plummeted to the ground. A shockwave rippled across the sand when it hit. The terri-fied dragon bucked again, throwing Elias backward.

Elias felt a sudden, sharp pain in his ribs.

"Stop it!" shouted Elias, "You're going to hurt both of us!"

The dragon whimpered.

"Nydeired! Stop thrashing about!" barked Brinsop. *"Straighten your spine, or Elias will fall!"*

The older dragon's sharp command halted the frightened dragon enough that he paused—his jerking movements stopped.

Elias tried to draw a calming breath, but a stabbing pain cut it short. He felt hot blood flow down his sweaty skin. He held on even tighter, screwing his eyes shut.

Brinsop's firm voice sounded again. *"Nydeired, open your wings and glide down slowly! Watch and follow me. I'll maneuver below you. If Elias falls, I shall catch him. Now move!"*

Nydeired began his slow descent, holding his body as steady as he could. They had almost reached the ground when Elias lost his grip and fell to the sand. He landed on his back with a thud, knocking the wind out of his lungs. His body buckled as he struggled for air.

Sela landed and rushed over to him, kneeling by his side. "Are you injured?"

He felt a terrible pressure on his side. He reached up to touch his ribs, then saw that his hand was smeared with blood. "Yes," he grunted breathlessly. "I'm bleeding, and I've broken some ribs. It hurts to breathe."

Nydeired paced back and forth, gnashing his jaws.

"Help him, help him!"

"I'm trying!" Sela pulled up Elias' torn shirt. She took a sharp intake of breath as she touched the wet skin. A stream of blood flowed down his side and onto the hot sand. "Your torso must have scraped against the... uh..." She paused and glanced at Nydeired, who looked ready to break down from guilt and fear. "...*metalwork* on the saddle. You scraped against the metalwork."

But she and Elias knew the true cause of the wound. They could clearly see a large streak of blood on one of Nydeired's massive back spikes.

"It's not so bad," Elias said with a wince. "It's not good, but it won't kill me. I can sense that much."

"No... you'll live, but..." she lowered her voice. "Aside from your broken ribs, your flesh is slashed down to the bone. I can stabilize you and stop the bleeding, but we're not going anywhere tonight."

Elias looked off into the distance. The expensive saddle lay in a crumpled heap halfway down a nearby ridge. It was a jumble of twisted metalwork and frayed leather. "I think that saddle is *really* beyond repair now. What a crappy repair job! Ulric probably needs to rethink his career choices."

His small attempt at humor fell flat.

Sela shook her fist angrily. "I'm going to *throttle* that saddler when I get back to Parthos. He'll be lucky to get a job shoveling latrines once I'm done with him."

Elias smiled weakly. "It could have been worse."

She sighed. "Yes, of course, it could have been

worse. I'm thankful that it wasn't."

Elias tried to sit up, but pain shot down his side when he moved.

Sela pressed down on his shoulder. "Don't try to sit up yet. Let me heal you as best I can."

"I don't think a pain-relief spell will help much this time," said Elias dryly.

Sela shot him an affronted look. "I might not be the healer *you* are, but I can certainly cast a simple spell to stop blood loss."

She cast the spell while pressing against the wound, using pressure to help stop the bleeding. A few minutes passed, and the flow of blood stopped. She sat back on her heels, pleased that her healing spell worked.

"Thank you," said Elias, exhaling deeply. "I can breathe much easier now."

The wound had scabbed over but was still oozing a little blood. The bruising was already darkening into a spectacularly bright purple.

Sela looked at the wound again. "It still looks pretty terrible. Do you want me to try again? I might be able to heal your ribs. It's unfortunate that we're not close to a village. If I had access to my herb pantry and a cauldron, I could create a potion that would heal your wounds in less than a few hours."

He could tell that Sela was slightly offended by his earlier comment. Sela was right—there was more to healing than just enchantments, and she would know. Her comment wasn't a boast; she was a respected potion master. Her knowledge was second only to Mugla Hoorlik, the famous dwarf witch of the Highport Caverns.

"Thank you, Sela," he replied earnestly. "But I can finish the rest of the healing now, thanks to you. I feel strong enough."

Elias started chanting softly. His body gave off a slight blue glow as a more advanced healing spell knitted his broken ribs. As his chanting grew deeper, a delicate web of fragile skin materialized over his wound. He cast the same spell on his minor injuries, which healed quickly. After several long moments, Elias exhaled deeply. Breathing freely felt like a luxury after what he'd just been through.

"Are you finished?" Sela asked, touching his side. Underneath all the crusted blood, the skin already looked a lot better.

"Yes," he said wearily. "My healing spell has done its work, but I'll have to rest for at least a day. I probably won't be able to ride tomorrow, either."

Nydeired finally had the courage to approach him. *"How do you feel?"* he asked, his gravelly voice tinged with worry.

Elias smiled and reached out to touch him, placing his hand on Nydeired's snout. "I feel better."

Elias dragged himself to a sitting position, and Nydeired rushed over to prop up his back.

"I'm so sorry," said Nydeired.

Elias coughed slightly and winced. "Don't feel guilty, it was an accident. It wasn't your fault. *You* didn't break that saddle. The saddler did a shoddy job."

"*Do you think I can't smell your blood on my scales?*" Nydeired snapped—sullen, fretful, and remorseful all at once. His clawed feet shuffled restlessly in the sand. "*My own spikes nearly gutted you like a fish!*"

"*Enough of this talk, Nydeired!*" Brinsop said abruptly, flaring her wings. "*Don't start brooding over how you might have prevented this. It's already done. This isn't the first time he's been hurt, and it won't be the last. Be grateful he is mending, and focus your thoughts on helping him, instead of worrying over something you can't fix.*"

Cowed by Brinsop's sharp reprimand, Nydeired nodded, somewhat mortified, but calm at last.

Sela shaded her eyes with her hand and looked into the horizon, contemplating their next step. The afternoon sun beat down on them now, but it would be dark in a few hours, and the freezing night temperatures worried her more than the heat.

"We're too vulnerable out here. We have to find a place to sleep that's not exposed to the elements. The temperature after sundown will be too cold for sleeping outside, even with our cloaks."

Elias shook his head. "I know this area of the desert well. The closest village is several leagues to the south. I can't ride, or I'll risk splitting my side open again."

"Let's rest awhile. We'll figure out something," said Sela.

A few minutes later, a small silhouette appeared on the horizon, walking toward them across the sand. As the figure drew closer, they recognized the man as one of the nomads. His curly black hair was cropped short, and his body was painted with white runes, a sign that he was not only a desert-dweller, but also a shaman.

He drew nearer, only to pass right by Elias and Sela, approaching Brinsop instead. He bowed and spoke to her in perfect *dragon-tongue*.

"Greetings, Great Matriarch. Peace be upon you, and your kin. I am Haluk, elder shaman of the northern tribes. I'm honored to make your acquaintance."

Striding closer, Brinsop sniffed him slowly, starting at the top of his head and down to his feet. She tilted her head curiously, then reciprocated his oddly formal greeting. *"Well met, man of the sands. My fleshling companions are called Sela and Elias. The younger male dragon is called Nydeired. We encountered a problem during our journey."*

Haluk nodded politely in Sela's direction, then returned his attention to Brinsop. "Dragon-sister, I heard your call of distress. How may I help you and your kin?"

"I appreciate your concern, flesh-friend," Brinsop replied in her deep, powerful voice. *"We are no longer in immediate danger, but one of our party was gravely injured."*

She pointed at Elias with one clawed digit. *"This male fleshling needs shelter for the evening. He must rest in order to heal his injuries."*

Haluk bowed again. "Then please allow me to be of service. My tent is nearby. My home is humble, but you are welcome to spend the night. I have soft mats for sleeping and clean drinking water. Your fleshling friend may rest and tend to his injuries there."

"You are honorable and generous, man of the sands," said Brinsop, with a slight nod of her head. *"We accept your offer of hospitality."* Brinsop's formal tone never wavered; it was as though she knew what Haluk expected her to say.

"Please follow me." Haluk turned and walked back in the direction that he had come.

"I guess that solves our shelter problem," Elias said as he struggled to stand.

Sela reached down to help him, and he struggled to his feet, leaning on her for support.

"Do you want me to carry you?" asked Nydeired.

Elias shook his head and waved him off. "No offense, but I'd rather walk—I've had more than enough riding for today."

Nydeired snorted but did not argue further.

Elias limped along slowly with Sela's help.

Rather than scrabble along uncomfortably in the sand, Brinsop and Nydeired took flight. They stayed close to Elias and Sela, circling in the air directly above them as they walked. Nydeired kept a close watch on Elias and whined anxiously every time his rider stumbled even slightly.

"You seemed to recognize this man," Sela said as they walked. "Have you met Haluk before?"

Elias nodded. "Yes, although I didn't remember him at first. I met Haluk many years ago, when I was exploring the Death Sands on my own. He was staying with a tribe, setting protective charms on their tents. We only spoke briefly, but I watched him perform several spells while I was there. I've never met anyone else who knows so much about object enchantments. He could enchant anything —statues, stones, even children's toys. I remember him enchanting a little doll so that it would cry when the child laid it down, and laugh when it was tickled. The enchantment only lasted a few hours, but the little girl was absolutely delighted. He's a gifted spellcaster."

"Did you notice he went straight over to Brinsop? He seemed to almost ignore us. I certainly appreciate his offer of help, but he seems rather... aloof. Did he refuse to speak to you when you met?"

"No, but he spoke very little. He doesn't speak the common language—his tribe considers the language unclean. If you want to ask him a question, speak to him in *dragon-tongue.* That's the only way he'll answer."

They followed Haluk for a while, then stopped at a seemingly empty place. The shaman reached into a small pouch hanging from his belt and produced a polished stone about the size of his thumb. He twirled the stone in his hand while muttering an enchantment. The air shimmered, and a large canvas tent appeared out of nowhere. Behind the tent, several palm trees also appeared, offering much-welcome shade.

Elias opened his mouth to speak, then remembered to use *dragon-tongue*. Unaccustomed to speaking it aloud, Elias faltered over the guttural sounds of the unique dialect. "Haluk, please tell me, what kind of spell is this?"

Haluk gazed at Elias, as if acknowledging him for the first time. "It is an illusion that hides my tent from human eyes. It is a simple spell, only meant to fool the eye at a distance. The illusion does not block sound or smells, so anyone who is close enough to the tent would be able to sense that someone is here. But in the vastness of the Death Sands, a simple spell works well enough."

Haluk lifted the tent flap for them. "Please, come inside. My apprentice is preparing my evening meal. You are welcome to join us."

Elias and Sela walked into the tent. Brinsop and Nydeired stayed outside, preening their scales in the waning afternoon sun.

Inside the tent, a warm fire blazed brightly, the floor rugs were clean and swept, and a clay teakettle filled the air with the delicious scent of cinnamon tea. A teenage boy sat near the hearth, preparing flatcakes on a heated stone.

The boy jumped to his feet and bowed when they entered. He had dark brown skin and a heart-shaped birthmark below his lower lip.

Haluk rattled off a quick command to the boy in his native language, then turned again to Sela and Elias and addressed them again in *dragon-tongue*.

"This is my apprentice. His name is Tinlaap. He shall help you with anything you need. I'll sit outside with the dragons. It is not often that I have the pleasure to speak with a dragon, especially an elder female. If there is any other way I can be of service, feel free to ask."

Then he turned around and abruptly exited.

There was plenty of room inside the tent, and Elias lay down on the sleeping-rug in the center of the floor. His body felt sore all over, but the severe pain had settled into a dull ache. Sela sat down beside him with her legs tucked underneath her. Although it was late afternoon, the inside of the tent was surprisingly comfortable. The trees blocked out much of the sun, and the firelight cast light shadows along the tent walls.

Muffled voices drifted in from outside. Nydeired said something, and Haluk laughed as if he were talking to an old friend.

"Something tells me that Haluk won't be joining us," murmured Sela. "He's a lot more interested in spending time with Nydeired and Brinsop than either of us."

Elias quietly agreed. "I've never heard anyone who wasn't a dragon rider speak such perfect *dragon-tongue*. His intonation is flawless. Even his mannerisms are perfect. If he didn't have human skin, I'd think he was a dragon himself!"

Somewhat forgotten in their idle chatter, Haluk's apprentice gathered a few warm flatcakes and butter onto wooden plates and served Sela and Elias. Then he filled two clay cups with *shubat*, fermented camel's milk, and placed them in front of the guests on a little wooden table.

"Thank you," Sela said automatically.

"You're welcome," the boy replied.

Sela paused through a mouthful of *shubat*. "You speak the common language?"

"Yes, fluently," he answered shyly, looking down at his hands. "As does much of my family. My father is a camel breeder—he used to take me along on his trade routes. Because of his work, he spoke many languages. My brothers and I learned how to speak the common language from him."

As he spoke, Tinlaap fetched a small glass lamp with a crystal wick. He said a few words, and the lamp lit up with a magical light. Its soft glow spread through the entire tent, chasing off the shadows.

"That's a neat little trick," said Elias. "Is that a light crystal inside?"

The boy smiled and nodded, pleased by the dragon rider's interest. "It's a crystal lamp—I designed it and embedded the enchantment on the crystal myself. The lamp doesn't use any oil, and the brightness of the flame can be adjusted by touching the crystal. A single spell will charge the crystal for an entire day, if needed."

"You know basic spellcraft fairly well," said Sela. "How long have you been an apprentice?"

"Almost a year," said Tinlaap. His voice turned sad. "I'm not much of an apprentice. My powers aren't strong. This crystal magic you see is one of the few spells I can do well."

"It's enough to impress me," said Elias. "Don't you

enjoy learning to use your gift?"

"Enjoy?" he repeated quietly. Tinlaap glanced nervously in the direction of the closed tent flap. "Magic has many uses, but it is not something to be *enjoyed*. It's *work*."

"Work can be fun, too," said Elias, "and even rewarding, sometimes."

Tinlaap shook his head. "The life of a shaman is solitary. The tribes may honor me and know who I am, but I will be alone, just like Haluk. I don't want to live like that."

Sela and Elias exchanged a concerned glance. Tinlaap was getting upset.

"My father's work brought him many friends. Before my gifts were discovered, I had expected to become a merchant like him. He was teaching me everything he knew about the camel trade. I would have been an excellent merchant! Then one day, we were weighing some crystals that my father planned to trade for camel hides. The crystals lit up in the palm of my hand, like tiny stars. After that, my father stopped teaching me his trade and started teaching my brother. When Haluk came to our village, my family sent me to him to become his apprentice. Haluk agreed to train me—but only out of duty, I think. It is lonely here with him. He's cold, for one thing, and he doesn't seem to like me. I miss learning under my father."

"Learning how to use your powers is important," said Elias quietly. "Perhaps you could still become a merchant in the future, after you've completed your training."

Tinlaap crossed his arms over his chest. "That's not our way. Our spellcasters are duty-bound to help all the desert tribes. My father says I *owe* it to my people. I wanted so much to be a merchant like my father, and now I won't even be allowed to live with my own family. All the tribes are my family now. That's what Haluk tells me. But I don't want that. I want a normal life, and a family of my own. If I become a shaman, I cannot even take a wife! I ask you—what kind of a life is that?"

Sela and Elias both looked at the boy with concern and sympathy.

"Worst of all," Tinlaap continued, "my powers are weak. I'll never be a *great* shaman, only a mediocre one. Haluk can't teach me *most* of the spells he knows, because they are beyond my ability. What good am I to the tribes if the only thing that I can do is create light crystals and trinkets?"

Sela gave him a reassuring smile. "I'm sure you're underestimating your talents. You're still learning. Give yourself time. I didn't realize I had a knack for potion-making for several years. You may have an undiscovered gift or another unique talent."

Tinlaap sighed. "Not likely. Even when I do try other sorts of magic, I never get far." Then his voice cracked. "Haluk gets frustrated with me so easily, and over the slightest things."

Sela's expression grew serious. "Frustrated? Does he strike you?"

He shook his head abruptly. "No, no, he's never

hurt me. He's not a cruel master, but he loses his patience when I can't get a spell right. His silence... tells me a lot."

"What do you mean?" asked Elias.

"He disapproves of me," Tinlaap replied glumly. "That's why he barely speaks to me. When he *does* speak to me, he won't allow me to speak the common language, even though I *know* he understands it. He only speaks the language of his tribe—that is, unless he's talking to animals. He'll speak with the birds for hours and not say a single word to me all day. He even talks with yellow vultures! Can you believe that? *Vultures!* He prefers the company of those dimwitted birds to me."

"Perhaps he prefers the company of animals to people," Elias explained. "Some people are like that—they grow uncomfortable if they're around people very much. Many dragons are the same way. Some dragons won't tolerate the company of humans."

"I guess," Tinlaap conceded. "It wouldn't be so bad if I could understand animal-speech. Haluk can talk to *any* animal. That's one of his gifts. Snakes, bats, rats, it's all the same to him. He can talk to them all. But I can't! I can't speak to animals *at all,* not even birds. So I can't understand him when he does it. That seems to bother him. Haluk says it's basic magic and I *should* be able to do it. It makes me feel even worse."

Sela reached out and patted Tinlaap's hand. "Don't be discouraged, young man. While it's true that most spellcasters can speak to lower animals, like birds and mice, your powers aren't useless just because you can't. Every spellcaster's gift is unique. As for Haluk, he does seem a bit stiff and formal, but that's probably his nature. He's used to living the life of a hermit. Having an apprentice around him all the time may unnerve him."

Tinlaap sighed, folding his fists in his lap. "I don't think Haluk wants me here. My training must be such a waste of time to him."

"Your magical training *isn't* a waste of time," Sela said firmly. "You must learn how to use your powers correctly, or you'll wake up one day and hurt yourself—or someone you love."

The boy tucked his head down, chastised. "Maybe you're right, but it doesn't matter much anyway. Haluk told me that my training is almost finished. He said that I've reached the *'natural limit'* of my powers—whatever that means. He said there was nothing more he could teach me." Tinlaap paused for a moment. "I miss being around others. All my life, I've lived among my family and friends. I can't imagine living completely alone, as Haluk does. I don't *want* to be a hermit."

The boy turned a startled eye at the sound of Haluk's laughter outside the tent. He waited until his master's voice grew quiet again. "I shouldn't burden you with my troubles," he said. "You are my master's guests. Never mind the things I've told you. Please, eat."

The boy turned his full attention back to tending the hearth. Elias wasn't sure whether he had stopped speaking out of fear of being overheard, or whether it was to cover what he deemed a breach of etiquette.

Elias glanced at Sela, who seemed to share his concern. They ate their flatcakes in silence, listening while Haluk and the dragons continued their lively conversation outside.

Then Elias began to feel a strange sensation, like tiny insects buzzing around in his head. He shut his eyes tightly. He'd felt a similar feeling before, when charm spells were being used around him.

Elves! He thought in alarm. *Are there elves here?*

It wouldn't be the first time they managed to take him by surprise, appearing seemingly out of nowhere. But as he searched the area with his mind, he felt none of the usual nausea or disorientation that came with their arrival. Elias opened his eyes. Sela was looking at him with a puzzled expression.

"You look pale. Does your head hurt?" she asked. "You didn't hit it in the fall, did you?"

"No, I... I'm alright. Just thirsty, I think. Pass me a cup?"

She handed him a drink and he closed his eyes, slowly downing half of it. The buzzing in his head was softer now, but he could still sense something odd. In his mind, he saw little motes of dust gathering in a swarm, darkening, forming a picture of... of...

A picture of what? Was he having another vision? He couldn't possibly be having one again so soon—

and unbidden. He briefly considered casting a divination spell to enhance it, make it clearer, but decided against it. He didn't have the energy for anything like that right now.

He kept his eyes closed and let his mind wander
on its own. After what happened last time, he didn't
want to use a divination spell in such close quarters
with somebody else. It was too risky. The aftermath
might accidentally hurt Sela or Tinlaap.

Tinlaap. As he thought that name, the buzzing
grew more insistent. Something about this boy was
resonating with his sense of Sight. What it was
exactly, he didn't know. But more and more, he had
a growing feeling that somehow, this young apprentice mage was... *important.*

THE SAGA CONTINUES IN BOOK SEVEN:
The Shadow Grid Returns

A SPECIAL THANK YOU

Thank you for reading. If you enjoyed this book, please help spread the word by leaving a review on Amazon. Your reviews help other people discover this series.

You can learn more about me and get information about new releases by joining my official mailing list here: www.KristianAlva.com.